Peter
SQUARED

A Novel by
Ken Goldberg

MacAdam/Cage Publishing
San Francisco

All characters in this book are fictitious. Any resemblance to real persons, living or dead, is strictly coincidental.

MacAdam/Cage Publishing
155 Sansome Street, Suite 520
San Francisco, CA 94104
www.macadamcage.com

Copyright © 2000 by Ken Goldberg (1947–)

ALL RIGHTS RESERVED.

Publisher's Cataloging-in-Publication
(Provided by Quality Books, Inc.)
Goldberg, Ken, 1947-
Peter squared: a novel / by Ken Goldberg. –
1st ed.
p. cm.
LCCN: 00-103679
ISBN: 0-9673701-1-6

1. Mentally ill – Fiction.
2. Obsessive-compulsive disorder – Fiction.
I. Title
PS3557.O348P4 2000   813.6
QB100-467

Manufactured in the United States of America.

10 9 8 7 6 5 4 3 2 1

Book design by Dorothy Carico Smith

Peter
SQUARED
A Novel by
Ken Goldberg

Acknowledgments

I want to acknowledge the Reverend Rudolph Nemser. A man of humor and wisdom, he inspired me to write PETER SQUARED with his November 26, 1995 sermon. I deeply appreciate Lehea Kuphal and John Freeman. As free-lance editors, they helped me craft a publishable work from my first drafts. Pat Walsh, MacAdam Cage editor, deserves great recognition. Available on demand through Instant Messaging, he tolerated my anxiety, often answering the same questions over and over again, while always focused on the steps we needed to take to make PETER SQUARED happen. I appreciate his editorial work and his editorial restraint, making necessary changes while mostly respecting my work as written. There were others, family and friends, who muddled through the early drafts, helpful in ways large and small, contributing feedback and support. They are Maryka Goldberg, Jeanne Goldberg, Claire Kerr, Beth Forhman, Pierre Tribaudi, Cindy Arthurs, Lucy Kuder, Lou Naylor, Lisa Tracy, and Eric Miller. Thanks goes to Charles Clark, 11th-hour copy editor. Finally, there are my children: Matt for his keen insight, Sasha for her love of the far side, and BB for his joyful exuberance.

For Maryka, who always believed in me.

1

Thursday Morning

43 years x 365 days is approximately 40 years x 400 days or 16,000 days.

Peter Branstill imagined himself in third grade, looking at the number, 16,000. On top of a test, red ink read:
INCORRECT. DON'T ESTIMATE. DO IT AGAIN, YOU IDIOT.

Peter reached over to the nightstand, where his calculator, notepad, blue pen, and No. 2 pencil lay precisely where they should. (Long ago, he studied the best placement of these items, calculating a 2-inch gap from the front of the nightstand, placing his tools halfway between the edges of the table. His bed was positioned to ensure that the 34-inch extension of his arm, while lying in the exact middle of the bed, perfectly met the calculator, notepad, blue pen, and pencil – no waste of time and motion groping around.)

Peter turned on the light and began to calculate.

Born June 19, 1952, a leap year, his forty-three years included thirty-three 365-day years and ten 366-day years. Today was July 13, 1995. Eleven days in June plus thirteen days in July, a total of twenty-four days past his birthday. He wrote in the pad in pencil:

12,045 + 3,660 + 24 = 15,729

15,729 days alive before finally going mad.

He repeated the calculations twice just to be sure. Satisfied, he recorded the number in blue ink and went to bed. As always, he lay on his right side, with his right hand under the pillow, his left forearm parallel to his body, elbow bent at a 135° angle, and palm face down on the mattress. After assuming the position, he slept.

At 6:00 a.m., the alarm rang. He looked at the night table, and saw a sheet of paper with last night's work: 12,045 + 3,660 + 24 = 15,729. Peter saw the number, 24, reminding him that his birthday was last month. Like decades past, Peter threw a party for himself alone in his room. This year, however, was special. He had received a birthday card from an octogenarian in his office. Shortly, he pictured Mary, his boss' secretary, elderly and approaching retirement, with him, celebrating his birthday.

Unwittingly, Peter reached for his crotch, took his penis in his hand, and began to stroke it as he pictured himself with her in the nursing home, giving her medication, wheeling her down the white halls to her hospital bed. In her last gasps of life, she proclaims her love for him. The doctor watches patiently before pronouncing Mary dead. Peter climaxes.

■ ■ ■

Peter got out of bed, went to the bathroom, and put on a blindfold to shield his own view of himself. He bent his knees partway down so he could urinate at an exact 45° angle. After flushing the toilet and waiting for the tank to refill, so as not to disturb the settings for his shower, he turned the hot and cold water handles to the exact places he marked, with waterproof tape, for a constant shower temperature of 110° F. Afterward, he stepped on a floor mat and dried the four quadrants of his torso, starting at his belly and moving around in a clockwise fashion, drying each part for exactly twenty seconds, the amount of time needed to be perfectly dry without chafing his skin or reapplying moisture from the towel. He removed a piece of soap from the left side of a balance scale he kept in the bathroom, placed the Ivory soap he had used for his shower on the right side of the scale, and with his hands felt the scale for good balance. By opening a new bar of soap every Sunday, and starting with seven pieces of soap cut from another bar, he was able to ensure reasonably uniform depreciation of soap through the week. He then walked back to his bedroom, where he had laid out his clothes the previous night.

Once dressed, he took off the blindfold.

Peter always wore the same clothing: three-button black suit, oxford shoes, black cotton socks, white button-down shirt, and a solid navy blue tie, always ready according to a methodical plan of cleaning and uniform wear. His five suits were purchased exactly six months apart. He rotated the suits on a five-day schedule, and replaced each suit two and one half years after it was purchased. In the same way, he had four pairs of shoes, seven pairs of socks, three ties, and eleven shirts, also rotated daily, and replaced according to an exact schedule for uniform wear. Although he felt decadent having so many shirts, he held to these numbers knowing that by using numbers without common divisors, he could ensure that every combination of shoes, socks, shirt, tie, and suit would be worn together throughout the rotation.

Peter had installed a dehumidifier in the bathroom so that he could return, fully dressed, to a bathroom free of the dampening effects of his shower. He looked at himself while shaving with a Schick electric razor, fixing his glance at the skin to be shaved without actually seeing the rest of his face. He combed his hair holding the comb at a 13° angle, parted to ensure that one third of his hair lay to the left of the part, the other two thirds to the right. Each year during the third week of November, he took pictures of his scalp so that he could plot a revised part line ensuring the same proportions, allowing for hair loss.

He fixed a breakfast of an individual package of Shredded Wheat, 2 percent milk from a pint container purchased the night before, to be used within twenty-four hours of purchase, one sliced, recently bought banana, or six grapes, or three strawberries, depending on which fruit was in season, and an 8-ounce glass of orange juice, which, like the milk, had to be purchased and used in one day.

Peter looked at the clock: 6:50 a.m. *What should I do,* he thought, *now that I'm mad? Should I wait and rock? That's what Mom did when she went mad.*

I could dial 911. Maybe they'll take me away, Peter thought. *But why call the police? I can take a cab, or a bus, or even walk to the emergency room. What would I say?*

"Hello, I'm Peter Branstill." *No, they won't know why I'm there.*

"Hello, I'm Peter Branstill, and I just went mad." *They'll want to know more.*

"Hello, I'm Peter Branstill. Here's my ID. I've come to report that I just went mad. Do you need me for anything else?"

Pacing back and forth, wondering what to do, Peter caught his reflection in the mirror across the room. He glanced at his watch, 7:00 a.m., the time he usually left for work.

With no better plan, and at a loss for anything else to do, Peter left for work.

2

That Girl

Walking out the front door, Peter reached into his pocket, fished out a small appointment book, and opened it to July. He circled the number 13 and put a small dot in the lower left-hand corner of the box for July 13: the circled number indicating he thought he had gone mad this morning, the dot for masturbating once today.

Peter walked two and one-half blocks to catch the 7:20 a.m. bus. The ride usually took forty minutes, getting Peter to work one hour before his workday began at 9:00 a.m. Many years ago, terrified of being late, Peter spent hours after work studying the bus route – the published schedule, and his own detailed records of the actual block-by-block progress of the bus – to learn that even with ordinary delays, he could always get to work on time by taking the 7:20 a.m. bus. He was only truly late when his bus was delayed by a major event, such as a severe snowstorm, a blackout, or a street closing. When the bus drivers went on strike, Peter walked to work, though he was sure the strike was merely a hoax directed at him, imagining all the way that he was being passed by a bus full of laughing and jeering passengers. He began to wonder if he still existed, and it seemed as if the extremities of his body were floating away as his cells dispersed into air.

Today, Peter's bus arrived at 7:20 and proceeded toward work according to schedule. Before the bus reached his stop, a plain-looking, thirtyish woman said "Excuse me" as she squeezed past Peter to exit the bus. From the time he exited the bus until he went to work, Peter wandered aimlessly near his office building, thinking only about this woman. *She smiled. She likes me.*

Walking to work, the woman's image took many forms in his mind. The plain-looking woman turned into a tigress, a go-go girl, a shy flower, a loving partner. Peter spent hours with her: at the movies, over meals, on vacation, taking trips, sitting by the fireplace, making love. At times, the images soured. Peter pictured her angry or insulted, slapping him across the face. HOW DARE YOU TALK TO ME! WHO THE HELL DO YOU THINK YOU ARE? I WANT WHOLE MILK! GET OUT OF MY BED. She became a girl from his childhood in Miss Weintraub's third grade class: PETER BRANSTILL, YOU JERK. I HATE YOU, GET AWAY, YOU CAN'T PLAY WITH ME. Then she returned to womanhood and loved him. Peter pictured himself sitting with her at a fine restaurant. She looks in his eyes expectantly as Peter graciously lights her cigarette before lighting his, and orders for two, Shredded Wheat with fruit and milk, a glass of orange juice on the side. He checks the expiration dates on the milk and juice before kissing her.

Aroused and wanting to masturbate, he checked his appointment book to look up the last time he masturbated twice before work. Finding two dots in the lower left-hand corner of the box for February 10, and a capital G in the right-hand corner for having felt very guilty that day, he walked past a peep show without going inside. Instead, he went straight to the third floor of an unremarkable building on 44th Street, west of Fifth Avenue, to his job of twenty-five years at Lerner and Schwartz, Public Accountants.

Peter's work performance was indistinguishable from one day to another. Whether the bus was precisely on time or later than usual, whether he was blessed by good thoughts or tormented by fear, whether he woke up thinking he had gone mad or feeling sane, each day Peter sat at his desk, face pointed diligently toward the ledger, and produced the exact same amount of work.

All day, while mail was not dropped in his hopper, and his phone did not ring, and he was not asked to lunch, Peter remained sitting at his desk, where including two five-minute water breaks and a one-hour lunch break, he never once altered the routine he had followed in twenty-five years of working for Lerner and Schwartz.

■ ■ ■

When Peter first started at the firm, he was occasionally invited out to lunch with other employees. Dreading their invitations, he'd hide in a bathroom stall, the supply room, or the stairwell. Since the others often left quite late, they'd catch him off guard from time to time, just when he thought he was safe. Once Mary saw him coming out of the men's room as she and four others were leaving for lunch. "Hey, Peter! We were just looking for you. We're going to Callahan's. Want to come?" Looking sheepishly away, Peter muttered, "OK." As the group walked to Callahan's, talking on the way, Peter lagged three steps behind.

PETER BRANSTILL, WHAT WERE YOU DOING IN THE BATHROOM? *Uh, I was getting some files for Mr. Lerner.* FILES? HA, HA, HA. YOU WERE TOUCHING YOURSELF. PETER TOUCHED HIS PEE-PEE. PETER TOUCHED HIS PEE-PEE. *No I wasn't. I don't do that here. I never use the bathroom at school. I wait 'til I get home.* Despite his pleas, Mary and the others seemed to chant: PETER TOUCHED HIS PEE-PEE. PETER TOUCHED HIS PEE-PEE.

At Callahan's, the group was led to a large table for eight in the center of the room. With the others sitting five in a row, Peter went to take the middle, vacant seat, leaving a seat between him and the others. But Mary intervened, with an embarrassed laugh, rising from her seat, reaching for Peter's hand, and pulling him next to her. Throughout the meal, Peter sat thinking about Mary, picturing them in bed together while inadvertently pushing his food around. Toward the end of lunch, Phil, another young man working for the firm, looked at Peter's plate and asked if something was wrong. Trying to think of an excuse, Peter sat there, staring blankly, until Phil offered an explanation, "Maybe a stomach virus. They're going around, you know." Mary added, "Wish I could control myself the way you do." Walking back to the office, Peter kept thinking, *lost control, Peter lost control,* picturing stains on the front of his pants.

Over time, the invitations ceased and Peter was on his own for lunch. He preferred to leave the office, and unless the weather was extremely severe, he always went to a local park.

The park attracted a diverse crowd. In one area, elderly people sat on benches. Several Jamaican women chattered rapidly with clipped accents across from a gathering of old Russian Jewish couples sitting quietly, without uttering a word. Most days, a man played the accordion nearby among his Polish compatriots. There was an open area where a younger, working crowd gathered, the more active ones playing volleyball and Frisbee. There was also a newly built wooden playground where young mothers and nannies brought their children and charges to play. Another section was set aside for chess players, and one final section was controlled by drug dealers. After much study, Peter identified the park bench that was most distant from each of these groupings, and that is where he ate lunch each day.

Arriving at his bench, lost in thoughts about the woman from the morning, he quickly, carefully inspected it for any signs of use by others between his visits and for possible bird droppings. He made a mental note of the state of the bench, which he would later record in a notebook he kept back at the office. In his mind, the bench was divided into three segments. He would choose a spot from among the three so that every three days he will have had lunch on each of the three different places. If there was no contamination on the bench, he would choose a seat based on the scheduled rotation. If there were signs of contamination, he would note the date and choose an uncontaminated part. Since he viewed his buttocks as a source of contamination, he would only take the same seat two days in a row if the remaining choices were clearly contaminated.

Sometimes the bench was occupied when Peter arrived. When that happened, he considered two factors – contamination and proximity to the other person – in choosing a seat. It took great pains to inspect the bench without arousing attention. From a distance of 30 meters, he would divide the bench in his mind to see if one of the three designated seating areas was fully unoccupied. If there was an available seat, Peter would alter his route to approach the bench from the left side, so he could inspect it out of the corner of his left eye while walking slowly past. He knew he had better peripheral vision from this side, having many years ago studied the issue with a self-made field-of-vision test. Each year, he retested his peripheral vision on May 19 and threw a small party for himself to celebrate Field of Vision Day. Howdy Doody, Buffalo Bob, and Clarabelle Clown – his childhood puppets – joined the party sitting respectively at the 90°, 180°, and 270° positions of his circular dining room table.

In order to approach the bench from the left, he'd turn toward the drug dealers, walking straight until he was about 25 feet away, when he'd turn right toward the volleyball and Frisbee games. He cautiously walked past these players, considerably more frightened by them than by the drug dealers, expecting that they'd taunt him for wanting to be part of their games. He'd then walk past the bench, and assuming it passed the first inspection, he would walk past the next four benches before turning around and coming back for a final inspection.

On the days all three seats were occupied or the available seats failed inspection, Peter skipped lunch. Instead, he would wander aimlessly for the remainder of the hour. Even though he ate at his desk during inclement weather, he was too embarrassed to simply return and have lunch there. Whenever this happened, it would be a particularly painful day.

Once, a woman with a baby stroller sat next to him while he was eating lunch. Peter continued thinking about that woman for months, wondering why she chose his bench when the children's section was nearby. *Maybe she wants me.* NO ONE WANTS YOU! Peter looked at the baby and thought: *That's me.* He looked at the woman again. *Are you my mother?* Peter pictured her holding him, feeding him, diapering him, putting him to sleep, Howdy Doody by his side.

For months, Peter scanned the park often, hoping to see her again, changing his route to and from his bench to pass the children's playground, until he saw them playing on the swings. Thrilled, he watched them play, his gaze fixed, his mouth open, until he realized that this woman was black whereas the woman on the bench had been white.

Last week, an elderly woman sat next to him and started talking. Lonely and with many stories to tell, she babbled while Peter half-listened. Instead, he tried to concentrate on his sandwich. She told him about her life as a nurse and a missionary. She had won many awards, spoke several foreign languages, had been married to a wonderful man, and had three children – all with successful careers. After demonstrating her skill with foreign dialects, she brought out pictures of children and grandchildren, seeming unaware or unconcerned that Peter listened very little to her story. Through the entire lunch he thought about a torrid affair with this senior citizen. That night the dancer behind the glass partition at the peep show spoke to him with an accent, reminding him of his multilingual acquaintance. As he masturbated, the dancer's image changed to the old woman and then to that of Sally Branstill, his own mother.

On this day, Peter's bench was unoccupied and in good shape. He approached it, chose the next seat on his rotation, and sat down to eat his sandwich. He took great pains to bite off the perfect squares, rectangles, and trapezoids he had etched into its surface that morning. As he ate, he again thought about the woman on the bus.

He repeated her words many times in his head, "Excuse me… Excuse me… Excuse me… Excuse me." In a Mae West *why-don't-you-come-up-and-see-me-sometime?* voice, Peter imagined her saying, "Excuse me," followed immediately with a disgusted EXCUSE ME, MISS WEINTRAUB. PETER BRANSTILL PEED IN HIS PANTS.

Hearing two people talking loudly walking by, Peter broke from his reflections. Looking down, he saw that his sandwich only had one triangle remaining. Chewing his last bite and watching the couple pass, arm in arm, the woman on the bus returned to his thoughts. *She must be thirty years old.*

30 x 2 = 60, he thought.

■ ■ ■

At 5:00 p.m., Peter left work highly aroused, anticipating a night with the girl whose face he could now hardly recall. He planned to go home, make dinner – five ounces of grilled chicken cooked on a skillet in exactly one tablespoon of oil, canned string beans, canned small potatoes, and a fresh kaiser roll with a ³⁄₈-inch pat of sweet butter spread on it, the dinner he'd been having since reviewing his diet plan on the first Saturday of November last year. When it came time for bed, he would settle down with the girl of this day's dreams. He walked toward the bus and could not stop thinking deliciously about the intimate evening, but the closer he got the more he realized he could not wait. He wanted to go home, but while waiting for the bus near Times Square, the neon warble of the nearby peep shows was too enticing. He checked his wallet – three tens and a twenty – more than enough.

Peter waited for the bus, acting as if he planned to board. The bus was crowded. He feigned an attempt to board, graciously passing his turn with a muffled ahem to another passenger. He felt proud while waiting for the next bus. He must seem patient to anyone who might be watching. Waiting while three more buses came and went, he carefully scanned the crowd, afraid that someone might notice his ruse. The crowd looked faceless, like a two-dimensional cut-out black-and-white cardboard display. Peter began walking briskly toward his favorite peep show, a plain storefront with a sign advertising *Private Booths, Sexy Girls*. Turning the corner, he passed a man who resembled Andrew Lerner, his boss.

PETER BRANSTILL! YOU PERVERT. IN THIS SLEAZY PLACE! ME? I ONLY GAWK AT GIRLS ON SPECIAL OCCASIONS AND HOLIDAYS. RIGHT! YOU DO IT ALL THE TIME. WAIT TILL EVERYONE KNOWS.

Peter pictured an Inter-Office Memo.

To: All Employees
From: Andrew Lerner, President
Re: Peter Branstill's Sexual Habits
Date: July 14, 1995

Last night I saw Peter Branstill at *Private Booths, Sexy Girls*. I was there celebrating my wife's birthday. It is company policy for all employees to refrain from patronizing peep shows except on Holidays and Special Occasions. Frequenting these places more often is grounds for dismissal.

Peter broke his train of thought just as he caught a glimpse of himself, pale, open-mouthed, grasping for the door of the building.

There was a fat man behind the counter, a jagged scar beneath the stubble of his unshaven face. He tapped his long, dirty, unclipped nails on the MasterCard/Visa sticker pasted to the top of the formica counter. Peter stood alongside four shifty men, thinking he was the only one in the world who came here for illicit gratification.

He longed to enter a private booth but acted as if he might be there for some other purpose. He walked to the table of pornographic books. *Just act like you're shopping for a close friend.* He spied a locked cabinet of sexually useful objects. *This is even better: Buy something for your girlfriend. She'll love the vibrator and beg for more.* Peter then sauntered over to the private booths trying to look curious but naive: *I wonder what they have here,* he thought as he opened the door.

Entering the booth, Peter shuddered, seeing the peeling paint, the dirty walls, and semen on the floor approximately 1½ feet away at a 39° angle from the exact center of the room. Taking out his tape measure, careful not to step in the semen, Peter saw that the booth was 3½ feet wide, 3¾ feet deep. To ensure maximum distance between himself and the walls of the booth, Peter faced the right wall, his body perpendicular to the screen separating him from the girl. With his head turned 80° left, Peter watched the screen rise, staying up for ten seconds. The girl crooned though a microphone in a husky voice as the screen descended: "If you want more, ten bucks."

Peter could not believe his eyes. It was her, the girl he had met on the bus. He knew it was her. She wanted him. She rode the bus all the time and now she had to meet him, had to have him. Many times she had crossed his path, too shy to speak. She must have followed him to 42nd Street and got herself a job at *Private Booths, Sexy Girls,* just to meet him. *What a fool I've been,* thought Peter. *She wants me. She's here, and she's dancing only for me.* IDIOT! NO ONE WANTS YOU.

Peter quickly stuffed $10 in the slot and added another $10 and another $10 to let her know how much he loved her. She lifted the screen. Peter reached for his crotch. It was her, dancing with desire. Peter felt aroused. She turned around and pressed her ass against the glass partition. Peter came. The screen went down. Peter was in love.

Peter left the booth filled with excitement. When he hit the street, he suddenly felt plagued by the fear that she wasn't really the girl on the bus. He wanted so much to think it was her, but a nagging doubt prevailed. He could not remember what the girl behind the glass partition looked like, but he had to know if it was her.

Without any pretense, he ran back and rushed to the booth. The red light above the door blinked: OCCUPIED. His dream girl was dancing for another man. Peter left defeated. Was it her? His spirits sagged: Was she a common whore? Then a more disturbing thought crossed Peter's mind: The dancer was a horse. Maybe this place featured horses, dancing horses for horny men to jerk off to. Peter was now sure he had gone mad making passionate, masturbatory love, climaxing at the vision of a horse's ass a few feet away through a glass partition.

■ ■ ■

At Times Square Peter boarded the 47 bus and went home, replaying over-and-over the image of the horse. Recently, Peter found himself picturing horses often at the point of climax. Just last week, he thought he was enjoying himself, riding horseback with a woman through a field of wild flowers. Arriving at their special place, they shared a picnic lunch, knowing that thoughts of passion were racing wildly through each others' minds. They made passionate love again and again until the horse replaced the woman, augmenting his arousal and disgust at the same time. As soon as he entered the horse from behind, it changed from a live animal to a cartoon character, the type that can mimic human movement, personality, and characteristics. Peter and his cartoon horse copulated for hours in his bedroom, which left Peter feeling horribly ashamed of himself.

Peter got off the bus and briskly walked the four blocks to his apartment. The thought of the horse began to subside. By the time he finished dinner, he had successfully convinced himself that the dancer was the woman from the bus. Calmed by this thought, he masturbated four times to an image he conjured up that vaguely incorporated the two women he had met that day. He stopped before masturbating a fifth time, knowing he must masturbate in powers of two:

$2^2 = 4$.
$2^3 = 8$.

Overcome with desire, he jerked off four more times to the point of physical exhaustion. A wan smile crossed his face. He slept.

3

Rating Orgasms, Rating Dirt

Highly aroused Friday morning, Peter woke up in terror, realizing he could no longer conjure up the image of the girl he had met on the bus. He reached for a pornographic magazine and masturbated to the image of a stranger. Before returning it to the shelf, he picked up his pencil and wrote the number −10 under the number 15 already on the magazine cover, and calculated:

15−10 = 5.

He carefully filed it back in his collection of pornographic magazines according to its new rating, 5.

Many years ago, Peter studied and developed the Orgasm Index (OI) to help him choose magazines that were most likely to produce pleasing orgasms. The OI rated two qualities: valence and intensity. When Peter felt good after having an orgasm, he gave it a positive rating, valence equals +1. If he felt guilty afterwards, valence was −1. Intensity was rated on a scale from 1 to 10. By multiplying the orgasm's valence by its intensity, and adding the result to the sum of scores, the rating would continuously adjust upward or downward according to the quality of the last orgasm he'd achieved by using positive and negative numbers in the scale. Peter's only regret was that he used the number 1 rather than 0 as the low point on his scale, a decision made out of fear that he would vanish if he ever had an orgasm devoid of intensity.

On the 19th of each month, Peter bought a new magazine and masturbated to its images for each of the next five days, then filing it according to its five-day cumulative score. Since his bookshelf held exactly one hundred magazines, he would discard the magazine with the lowest rating, placing it in the brown paper bag his new magazine came in and placing that in the incinerator, waiting for hours to ensure it was completely destroyed. Each night from the 24th of the month on, he then masturbated to the magazine at the head of his collection.

∎ ∎ ∎

Peter got out of bed, followed his morning routine, and was shortly on his way to work. On the bus, he realized that today was July 14. With July 19, 1995, only five days away, he thought about his next magazine, deciding to buy *American Horseman* rather than a typical X-rated selection. He then recalled Dr. Richard Kline, his child psychologist, and wondered if Dr. Kline knew he would someday become a horse-a-philiac.

A robust man who seemed more kindly to Peter than most people he knew, Dr. Richard Kline met with him for two years, until shortly after the start of fifth grade. Usually wearing a checkered jacket, blue shirt and bowtie, cardigan, tasseled loafers, and argyle socks, Dr. Kline would open the door to welcome Peter into the treatment room from the waiting room each Wednesday at exactly 4:00 p.m. Peter valued his promptness, recognizing that the doctor was the only person he knew as consistent as he. Each week, Peter checked his watch with the doctor's entrance, resetting it if necessary. Once in the office, Peter sat down on the couch as Dr. Kline took his seat in a large reclining chair, patted his bald pate twice, and asked Peter how he was doing. Peter always answered "OK." Dr. Kline would wait for a deeper answer and after a few moments of sitting quietly, his attention fully focused on Peter, he would lean forward and heartily say, "Great, Peter. That's just great. I'm really glad to hear you're doing ... OK." Dr. Kline always paused before saying OK to emphasize Peter's progress.

Dr. Kline would then ask Peter if he wanted to follow up on what they had said last week. Peter never knew what to say, since they had never talked about anything the week before. Dr. Kline would then plunge in with a probing question: "Did you want to talk about school? ... How are things going with your friends? ... Is your mom doing OK? Having a lot of fun with her? ... What's it like now that your dad's not around?" Finally, after a prolonged silence, Dr. Kline would say, "Well, Peter, how about a game of checkers?"

Peter did not like checkers but not wanting to hurt Dr. Kline's feelings, he always said, "Yes." For two years every week, Peter played checkers with Dr. Kline.

Throughout the games, Peter would glance longingly into the adjoining playroom, past the dollhouse, across from the crayons and art supplies, between the board games and a play kitchen set, where in the middle of a pile of stuffed animals was a toy horse. Each week, Peter quietly practiced the question he would never ask Dr. Kline: *Can I play with the horse?* Each week, he shuddered, picturing Dr. Kline filled with rage, pulling his belt from his trousers, cracking it against Peter's exposed back.

Sometimes Dr. Kline met with Sally while Peter sat in the waiting room. *I bet Mom's winning,* Peter would think. *Why don't you play with me?* he wanted to ask his mother. NO ONE WANTS TO PLAY WITH YOU. Peter pictured Dr. Kline speaking with Sally, "Mrs. Branstill, I have very encouraging news for you today. Peter earned four kings and jumped three of my men in one move." Sally beamed with pride, knowing Peter was getting helped. NO ONE CAN HELP YOU! Peter pictured his mother listening to Dr. Kline, a somber look on his face as he said, "Mrs. Branstill, I'm extremely worried about Peter. Today I noticed him gazing at the toy horse while we were playing checkers. We may need to increase our sessions to see if I can redirect his interests away from that horse and onto the checkerboard. You know, I'm deeply concerned that Peter might become one of those men who frequent erotic peep shows and masturbate to dancing horses."

■ ■ ■

At noon, Peter left his desk for the park, arriving slightly late, at 12:10, because he had been delayed about thirty seconds by a woman from the second floor who had entered the elevator on its way down and then held the door while a friend gave her a lunch order to pick up. He stood at the back of the elevator, hiding his annoyance while the others in front were more visibly upset.

When he arrived, he saw a woman sitting on his bench. He

circled the bench before selecting his place. Peter noticed that she was at one end and that the middle and opposite end of the bench were unoccupied. He observed that while the middle was clean – similar to the way he had left it the day before – the far end had some new dirt on it.

Obviously, Peter preferred the cleaner middle seat, but the seat on the unoccupied end seemed more appropriate. With his left hand trembling and sweat beading on his brow, Peter walked closely past the bench and inspected the dirt out of the corner of his eye, using the Graduated Dirt Rating Scale (GDRS) to decide where to sit.

Peter had developed the GDRS to alleviate his discomfort in handling ambiguous situations like this one. He had identified six variables – size, color, discoloration, texture, symmetry, and odor – to evaluate the degree of aversion associated with a particular piece of dirt. He then weighted the variables:

    Size 3
    Color 2
    Discoloration 4
    Texture 4
    Symmetry 1
    Odor 6

With each variable, the dirt was rated on a scale of 1 to 5. By multiplying the ratings and the weighting factors and adding the results, Peter arrived at a total GDRS score between 20 and 100:

    20-40 Minor dirt
    41-60 Average dirt
    61-80 Major dirt
    81-90 Dangerous dirt
    91-100 Lethal dirt

Peter decided that he would sit on the dirt on the far end of the bench if it rated 60 or below, minor or average dirt, but sit in the middle near the woman, at the risk of appearing forward, if the dirt was major, dangerous, or lethal.

Since odor and texture were more difficult to measure than size, color, discoloration, and symmetry, Peter decided to do only the four simpler ratings on his first pass by the bench. Size was 4. Brown was a reasonably acceptable color as long as it was light brown, which it was, so color scored 2. With almost no difference in the color throughout the specimen, discoloration was 1.5 – Peter could not decide between 1 and 2 and since discoloration was weighted 4, an even number, he could use a decimal without complicating his calculation. The dirt was fairly symmetrical, garnering a 2, so in his mind, Peter calculated:

    Size .... 3 x 4 = 12
    Color .... 2 x 2 = 4
    Discoloration   4 x 1.5 = 6
    Symmetry .... 1 x 2 = 2
    Total 24

So far, fifty percent of the weighted score added up to 24. As long as texture and odor were no more than 36 combined, Peter could sit on the far end of the bench, away from the woman already seated there. Since Peter generally rated odor before texture, he worked out the acceptable combinations in his head as he began his second approach to the bench. If odor is 5, texture must be 1; if odor is 4, texture can be 3 or less; if odor is 3, texture can be 4 or less; and if odor is 1 or 2, he can sit on the dirt regardless of how poor the texture may be.

To rate odor, Peter needed to circle the bench and take a deep whiff to register any background smells before his descent. Then, after leaning midway toward the dirt, he would take a second reading of background odors, in case a stray smell confounded his measure. The final reading came when he was close enough to smell the dirt without accidentally contaminating himself by actually touching it with his nose. He would measure texture by brushing the seat with a handkerchief held in his hand, which was now covered by a surgical glove he had surreptitiously slipped on after passing the bench the first time.

With this plan in mind, Peter slowly approached the bench as he rated the background odors. Handkerchief in his right hand, lunch bag in his left hand, eyes focused on the dirt, Peter bent down toward the dirt. At that moment, the woman got up and said to Peter, "It's all yours," and walked away.

Obviously, the middle of the bench was now the best choice. It had no dirt like the seat on one end, and had not been recently occupied like the seat on the other end. The most rational decision was to sit in the middle of the bench. But Peter was not thinking clearly. Obsessed with the idea that he had been exposed, he impulsively sat down on the dirt, without measuring the odor or texture.

There he was: It was lunchtime and he was sitting on dirt. Panicked, Peter immediately began calculating and recalculating the dirt possibilities. *OK. Calm down. Size – 12, color – 4, discoloration – 6, symmetry – 2. 12 plus 4 plus 6 plus 2. 24. Deep breath. Worst comes to worst, texture is five and odor is five. 5 x 4 is 20. 5 x 6 is 30. 20 and 30, 50. 24 and 50, 74. Major dirt.* Peter shuddered. *OK. Could be major, but it can't be dangerous or lethal.*

Peter kept repeating these calculations to himself as he patted the sides of his hip, assuring himself that he was protected, feeling the heavy padding of his emergency security system beneath his pants: two pairs of underwear with a piece of air conditioning filter in between.

4

Smoking

As Peter sat through lunch, calculating and recalculating the dirt possibilities and trying to reassure himself that he would survive, he was approached by yet another stranger.

"Hey man! Mind if I sit down?" Peter did not answer.

"Got a light?" he continued. Consumed with the dirt on which he sat, Peter did not respond. After a few seconds the stranger asked again, "Got a light, man?"

"Yo. Earth to man sitting on the bench. Got a light?"

Peter finally looked up. Standing in front of him was a gangly man with a one-inch asymmetrical smudge on his left cheek. He wore a short-sleeved Izod shirt with the alligator torn off, exposing a swatch of hairless white skin, Western belt, khaki pants, and work boots, one missing a lace.

"No."

"Oh, don't smoke. Wait here a minute." The man took off, asking three more people until someone took out a lighter. Peter's visitor quickly patted his pockets.

"Oops! Outta cigarettes. Gotta smoke?" The passerby snarled but reluctantly took out his pack, giving the stranger a cigarette and a light.

"Mind if I borrow a couple more? Ya know, my money's tied up in stocks and bonds. Gotta get to my broker later this afternoon. Need a couple more to tide me over." The passerby gave him two more and quickly left.

"Thanks, buddy. I'll pay ya back tomorrow."

Peter was shocked. *They're friends?* he asked himself. They didn't seem to know each other when they first talked. MAYBE THAT'S HOW PEOPLE MEET. Peter imagined the rest of the conversation:

Sure, have all the cigarettes you want. Say, you seem like a nice fellow. Whatdayasay we get together this evening? Have a drink? Your treat in return for the smokes.

No, I can't tonight. I've got plans, but...

The stranger returned and sat up on the back of the bench with his feet on the seat. Knowing this would add new dirt to the bench, Peter disgustedly registered the exact place for when he returned tomorrow. The stranger had one foot on each of the two unoccupied thirds of the bench, with his right foot marking the spot the woman had previously occupied. The left foot marked the center of the bench, spoiling the seat Peter wished he had sat on. Now he would have to take the same seat tomorrow.

"Ya know. It's a crock of shit, this shit 'bout smokin'. Bad for your health. I tell ya. Goddamn doctors. Make ya think you're gonna get cancer, heart disease, warts. Who knows what the hell they think? I smoke to stay young. Hell, smokin's good for ya. Ya think I like to bum cigarettes offa strangers? Hell no. But ya gotta, gotta stay healthy. Gotta stay strong. Ya know, the thing 'bout smokin' is that smokin' ain't bad for you if ya know how to do it. Most people smoke the wrong way. Here. I'll show ya." Inhaling deeply, the stranger took a long drag on his cigarette.

"Ya see what I mean. That's how most people smoke. Fuckin' fill your lungs with all that nasty shit. I tell ya, you'll get sick. Now let me show ya how I smoke."

The stranger took a drag on his cigarette by curling up the right side of his lip and sucking air in through a nickel-sized hole formed at the right corner of his mouth.

"Ya see, all the smoke goes into my right lung. Here, I'll show ya again." He demonstrated another inhalation of smoke through the right side of his mouth.

"Ya see? All the smoke goes in the right lung. I'm tellin' ya, people don't give their lungs the proper rest. One week, I only smoke with my right lung. Next week, ya got it, I smoke with my left lung and let my right lung rest. I'd show ya left-lung smokin' right now... it's a little tricky since I'm right-handed. But it can be done. Hey

I may be right-handed, but I'm... *ambi-lung-uous.*" The stranger laughed heartily at his joke.

"Really, man, it ain't hard. Anyone can do it. Maybe I'll go on Opry and show everyone how it's done. Listen. If you're here next week, I'll come by and show ya how I smoke with my left lung. Anyway, gotta go. Group's gonna start now. I just came out for a smoke break."

Peter watched him limp away, stopping to talk with several people on his way. For the rest of the day, Peter pictured himself smoking cigarettes with his left lung, no longer concerned about the dirt on his pants.

5

Visitation Rites

Although Peter never smoked, he was fascinated by cigarette commercials. Smoking had been one of those teenage rites of passage that bypassed Peter Branstill. Still, Peter pictured himself as the Marlboro man. There he was on top of a horse, boldly smoking in front of the children from his old school, the kids gasping with amazement and admiration, LOOK AT HIM SMOKE. THAT'S PETER BRANSTILL. WOW! HE'S ONLY USING ONE LUNG.

Suddenly, the sky darkens as the mood shifts. From the playground, Peter hears: LOOK AT HIM, GUYS. PETER BRANSTILL. TRYING TO LOOK COOL. GET OFF THAT MANGY OLD HORSE, YOU GEEK. WHO THE HELL DO YOU THINK YOU ARE? YOU'LL NEVER BE COOL, PETER. YOU'RE A JERK.

But there he was. Peter Branstill – cowboy, rancher, lover, stud – sitting on top of a horse. The scene changed again. Peter pictured himself having sex with the horse and a wave of guilt filled his head.

Peter struggled with the horse thoughts for the rest of the day. The pain seemed to pass after he left work, and by evening he was peaceful again. The next morning, though, Peter woke up in a sweat from a horrible nightmare. He dreamt he was on the bench listening to the stranger as they shared a smoke. Peter suavely lights two cigarettes at once, seductively handing one over to the stranger as they glance into each others' eyes.

The scene shifts. He is lying with the stranger on a large waterbed with waves and fish, as if they are in the ocean. The stranger entices Peter to undress, and as he lies there naked in the bed, his erect penis looking like a cigarette, the stranger takes Peter's penis into his mouth. The penis separates from his body as the stranger lights it and, with the same sucking motion he displayed that afternoon, smokes Peter's penis. As he does this, one testicle grows large and dark: It's cancerous. The other stays small and normal and tries to pump out semen. A struggle ensues between these two testicles as they try to maintain control of Peter's sexual energy.

Now, a shark emerges from the water. Frightened, Peter woke up in a sweat, his hand on his penis and semen on his body. Looking down at himself in the dark shadows of his room, he thought he saw smoldering ash where his genitalia used to be.

Now certain this was the day he had finally gone mad, Peter reached for his bedside materials to calculate the exact number of days he had been sane.

■ ■ ■

On Saturdays, Peter started out like he did during the week, getting out of bed, urinating, showering, shaving, dressing, eating breakfast, and putting on his suit and tie. He picked up his two laundry bags, one for whites, one for dark-colored clothes, and headed out for the laundromat. He went straight to washing machines Nos. 7 and 8, 7 for the whites, 8 for the dark-colored clothes. If the machines had been in use, he would have mentally grouped the other machines by their assigned numbers in combinations adding to fifteen while waiting for his machines to become free. They were free, so he carefully cleaned the inside of each machine with a Lysol-soaked Handi-wipe and placed his laundry inside, emptying a plastic bag of Tide detergent in each machine, and pouring bleach in the whites from a Tupperware container. He inserted four quarters in each machine, starting them at exactly the same time. Before leaving for the dry cleaner, he placed a three-inch piece of Scotch tape on each door to test if anyone tampered with his laundry while he was gone. Both times this happened, he discarded the contaminated clothes, purchasing new ones.

■ ■ ■

Peter used Tupperware because his mother extolled its virtues every day she was alive. After she passed away, Peter threw out all food, utensils, tableware, and containers, purchasing exact replacements, surprised when he learned that Tupperware was not sold in common stores. He wrote Tupperware headquarters, only to receive calls nearly every day inviting him to Tupperware parties. Finally, a particularly aggressive Tupperware representative knocked on his door. Peter negotiated the sale while looking through the peephole. As the saleslady prepared his order, and Peter counted his money, he reached for his crotch and became erect. She left his containers on the doorstep after he passed the money under the door. For months, Peter masturbated nightly to thoughts of a woman he peeped at in his own home.

■ ■ ■

Peter walked to the dry cleaner carrying a suit identical to the one he wore and the one he would pick up. He looked inside and saw the Korean owner behind the counter. Pleased that he would not be served by an English-speaking student who worked there, he waited for the customer now at the counter to leave. Recognizing the familiar chemical smell of a dry cleaning establishment, Peter looked at his watch knowing he could stay no longer than four minutes inside without jeopardizing his health. He entered quickly, placing his suit on the counter while handing the owner the ticket for the suit he was picking up. The owner entered the number 623 on a control box near the counter, causing the rack of clothes behind him to move.

During the thirty-seven seconds it took for his suit to arrive, Peter thought:

Six hundred twenty-three is an odd number. It's not divisible by two. Its digits 6 + 2 + 3 = 11. 1 + 1 = 2. It's not divisible by three. It can't be divided by four since it's odd. It ends in three, so it's not divisible by five. Can't be divided by six since two and three don't divide it. Separate the first two digits, sixty two, from the last digit, three. Double three: six. Subtract six from sixty-two: fifty-six. Seven goes into fifty-six eight times. Seven goes into six hundred twenty-three eighty-nine times; it's divisible by seven.

Looking up, Peter saw the owner holding his clean suit. He paid him with exact change as they quickly exchanged suits. Peter left looking at his watch, pleased that the transaction took less than three minutes.

When he returned, the washing machines had stopped, and the Scotch tape was still in place. Opening the door to washer No. 7, he pulled out half the clothes and moved them to the dryer across the aisle. He opened the door to washer No. 8 and moved half of those clothes to the next dryer. After moving the rest of the clothes from washer No. 8 to its dryer and the rest of the clothes from washer No. 7 to its dryer, he took out his notebook and recorded the order he used to empty the dryer. Next week, he would empty half the contents of washer No. 8 before taking clothes out of washer No. 7.

From a sealed bag, Peter placed one strip of fabric softener in each machine, placed coins in the slot, and started the dryers exactly at the same time. After inspecting the bench between the washers and the dryers for dirt, he sat down and watched the dryers go round and round. Mesmerized by the steady motion of the rotating dryer drums, he pictured the wheels on a car and drifted into thought about the time Uncle Charlie took him to upstate New York, to stay with Aunt Maureen.

■ ■ ■

Peter was eleven when his mother, Sally, suddenly stopped talking. She wouldn't eat, didn't shop, and stopped serving meals. The carpets not vacuumed, the floors unmopped, without dusting the furniture or disinfecting the bathroom, Peter shuddered as the apartment's dirt density soared to dangerous levels. Sally kept Peter home from school while she sat in her pajamas by the window, rocking back and forth, staring at a nail on the wall where Dad's picture had been. For several days, the phone rang each morning. Sally answered, "No. Peter's sick. He cannot go to school today." She pushed the furniture up against the double-locked doors, hung sheets over the closed blinds and drawn curtains on the windows, turned off all the lights, and waited until the next call, "He's staying home. He's sick."

The next week, there was a knock on the door. Sally turned to Peter and held her finger to her lips, whispering, "Shhh." The door knocked again, "Truant Officer!" After a long pause and a much louder knock on the door, "I know you're there, Mrs. Branstill. Peter's got to go to school. If he doesn't, I'll be back with the police." Peter listened carefully to the steps of four feet walk away from the door.

Sally immediately went to the phone. "Maureen, it's Sally Branstill." After a pause, "I know, I'm sorry. Cindy wouldn't let me. But please, help. I've got to go somewhere. I can't send him back to her and you don't want to know what happened to him the last time. Please help me."

After hanging up, Sally went to the closet and took out cleaning supplies. For the first time in weeks, she quickly and thoroughly cleaned the apartment. She moved all the furniture away from the door, back where it belonged. She packed a large suitcase for Peter and placed it in the center of the living room. After unlocking the front door, she returned to her seat by the window, staring blankly at the nail on the wall.

At 2:30 p.m., there was another knock on the door. Sally stayed stone quiet in the corner, knowing the person outside would open the unlocked door. Peter stood frozen by his mom, watching the door slowly move. A smiling man of average build, dressed in a red flannel shirt and dungarees, walked in and said, "Hi, Sally. How you been?"

With no response from Sally, the smile gave way to a more somber expression as he looked at Peter and said, "Hi, George." The silence continued for several minutes. Then, after making several other attempts to engage Sally, he glanced at the suitcase in the middle of the room, picked it up, looked again at Peter, and said, "George, we'd better just go."

■ ■ ■

Peter sat quietly in the front seat of the Buick next to Uncle Charlie, who in respect for his feelings said nothing. Peter did not know where they were going and he did not know that, by now, his mother was in the hospital. He had stopped asking questions a long time ago.

Finally, Charlie spoke up. "It's been a long time, George. I didn't think I'd ever see you again."

Peter continued riding with Charlie in silence, wondering where they were going, when he would come back home – later that night, in a few days? *I hope soon, before I need to go.* He thought about his father, wondered what Dad was really like, and turned his head slightly toward Charlie, trying to take in his face without being noticed. Smiling imperceptibly, Peter repeated inaudibly, in his head, the words, *Uncle Charlie.*

Looking for something to say, Peter said, "I have to go."

Charlie smiled, "There's a gas station three miles up the road. Can you wait that long?"

"Sure," Peter replied, not really having to go but just trying to make conversation. Well versed in holding his elimination functions, waiting was no problem for Peter. He never used the facilities at school, waiting through the entire school day to use his own bathroom. And even there, if anything was out of order, a hair on the floor or a smudge on the seat, Peter waited until the next day. His biggest concern was that he did not know how long this trip would be, and he began wondering if he would be back home before he absolutely had to go to the bathroom.

Uncle Charlie pulled off the road and filled the car with gas while Peter went into the men's room. It was dirty and disgusting and Peter felt like leaving immediately. But afraid that Charlie would know that he didn't have to go, he made himself stay inside. Peter noticed a condom machine on the wall and put in three quarters and purchased one; he knew men wore these and decided to try it on. Nervous and in a slight sweat – *I shouldn't do this* – Peter unraveled the condom from the package. It was too large for his prepubescent penis so he took it off and put it in his pocket.

When he came out, Charlie asked Peter if he wanted something to eat or drink. Although Peter was hungry, he turned down the offer. Peter hoped the ride would end soon so he could return home to his own uncontaminated food supply. His uncertainty abruptly ended when Uncle Charlie spoke up again to say, "You'll like staying with Aunt Maureen. She's excited to see you and so are the cousins." Peter could vaguely recall what Aunt Maureen looked like but didn't know who these cousins were. He quickly looked out the window and began estimating the angles formed from the apex to the base of the trees they passed.

Periodically, Charlie tried to strike up a conversation. "George, what grade are you in now?... Do you play baseball? You look like a good athlete... How's Mom been?"

And as Uncle Charlie talked, Peter sat quietly, his thoughts almost exclusively focused on basic functions: eating, elimination, and his own survival.

They didn't arrive at Aunt Maureen's house until after dark. Peter was welcomed by his aunt and three cousins, who, after quickly showing him to his room, rushed him down to the dinner that had been delayed until his arrival. Everyone sat down, held hands, and prayed. Throughout dinner, people talked, laughed, and reminisced. They spoke fondly about Peter's father.

Even though by now he was ravenous, Peter ate cautiously. After dinner, the cousins played with Peter while Charlie, Maureen, and Hal – Maureen's husband – huddled in the living room. The cousins were particularly happy that they could stay up late.

The adults finally came into the playroom and announced that it was bedtime. Charlie said he would be driving back home that night. Before he left, he hugged Peter and said, "I love you, George." Peter could not remember his last hug but, with a warm, tingling sensation traveling down his back, he started to smile and decided that while he was here at Aunt Maureen's, he would be George.

In the morning, Maureen woke the other children up and then sat by George for a while rubbing his back. Afterwards she told him to wash, dress, and come to the breakfast table. His job was to set the table.

George felt welcomed but did not know what she meant: They had never set the table at his home. Because he and Sally had separate food containers and utensils, there was no such job as setting the table. They always used different dishes, cups, and silverware, each arranging their own settings differently. Quickly responding to George's lack of skill, Maureen gently showed him what to do.

Maureen and Hal were teachers and Christians and by nature very patient people who wanted to help George. They were certainly not like anyone he had ever known before. George finished the school year in Maureen and Hal's community, adjusting well to his new life until it was summer and the nightmare of Beaver Christian Camp.

■ ■ ■

Peter looked up when a buzzer rang. His whites were dry. A minute later, a second buzzer rang: the dark-colored clothes were done. *What's wrong?* he thought, knowing that in the past these two machines' cycles ran no more than ten seconds apart. He spotted a sticker on the top of the machine, with a number to call if it did not work. He wrote down the number, thinking he should call when he got home.

As he folded the laundry, placing it carefully in the newly cleaned laundry bags, Peter felt more and more anxious, afraid to call yet knowing he should. *It's my responsibility. I'm going to call.* Then he looked at the clothes. They were clean and perfectly dry. He pictured himself talking on the phone,

"Hello, this is Peter Branstill."

"Yes, sir. How can I help you."

"I just came from your laundromat on Broadway. There's a terrible problem. Dryer No. 7 ran a minute too long." Peter hears a gasp. The man's breath sounds heavy. *"We're on it,"* he says, hanging up as sirens sound, the laundromat team on its way. All the way home, Peter replayed this scene until finally they took him, not the dryer, away.

■ ■ ■

Short of breath with chills down his spine, his face flushed and his left hand shaking, Peter entered his apartment and went straight to his pornography collection, picked out the magazine at the front, OI rating 14, and masturbated quickly. Not very intense but satisfactorily reducing his tension, Peter scored this orgasm, 1 x 1 = 1, increasing the cumulative OI to 15. He returned the magazine to the head of his collection before picking up his suitcase and leaving his apartment for the IRT subway line. Back on Broadway, Peter glanced at the laundromat before descending into the New York City subway system: The emergency dryer repair team was not there. He took the No. 1 train to Times Square, transferred to the No. 7, and rode out to Queens.

■ ■ ■

At the Woodcrest subway stop, Peter exited the train, and walked up the stairs and out to the street. By then, the wind had died down, the sun was out, the air warm. Peter walked five blocks to Woodcrest Cemetery. He walked slowly through the cemetery, noticing names and dates of birth and death on the tombstones. As he went, he calculated the exact life spans of the deceased, in years, months, and days, until he reached his mother's grave, a plot bearing the marker Aunt Cindy ordered, with her maiden name, Sally Jane O'Brien. Peter opened his suitcase and pulled out a portable folding chair. He lined up the chair parallel to the tombstone, 6.5 feet away, so that an imaginary line from the center of the chair perpendicular to the stone bisected it perfectly. He sat down to spend the rest of the day with his mom.

Peter pulled from the suitcase a portfolio with pictures of his five suits. Each Saturday, Peter sat by his mother's grave to review one of the schedules he lived by. Today was the third Saturday in July, the day reserved to examine his wardrobe depreciation system. In the suitcase, Peter had pictures of his ties, shirts, socks, shoes, underwear, belts, and air conditioning filters, as well as the suits. Peter was pleased that most of his clothing was depreciating uniformly according to schedule. The one exception was socks. Noting some unusual wear on the right heel of pair No. 1, Peter decided to wear pair No. 2 an additional two days and pair No. 3 one extra day. Peter jotted down his decision in a small black notebook in which he'd recorded the results of his previous annual clothes depreciation reviews.

After returning the notebook and pictures to the suitcase, Peter picked up the chair and moved it 5 feet to the left and 26 feet back, creating a right triangle between the chair, Mom's tombstone, and his father's grave 84 feet away. The triangle was proportional to their seating arrangement each Sunday at Aunt Cindy's house while Dad was alive. Peter and the cousins sat at the children's table in the living room. Sally sat with the other adults in the dining room. Dad had to eat in the kitchen, alone. Throughout dinner, Peter imagined a right triangle connecting him to his parents in the same proportions as the one he created at Woodcrest Cemetery. Peter tried to recall the times he spent with his family.

■ ■ ■

"Goddammit, Sally. When the hell are you going to get rid of that oaf of a husband of yours," Aunt Cindy screamed while Peter sat with his cousins, looking at a lampshade in the corner of the room, 3° off a level axis. "He's a goddamn pig, a dark stain on this family. Look at him, sitting there, licking his bowl like a dog. He's bad for business and shames the family. And worst of all, look at that idiot boy he gave you. God, I wish I never helped you get pregnant." Cindy got up from her seat and walked to the children's table. "Come here, boy," she said, pointing to Peter. Leading him to the bedroom, she whispered, "Don't worry. You'll have a decent name soon. I'm working on a plan. Until then, don't say anything when they call you George. Now, don't feel bad. You'll always be a loser, but it's not your fault. Your parents are incompetent and they gave you bad genes." Then she gave him a hug, a wicked smile stretching and thinning her otherwise broad lips, a face with the sharp features of a classic beauty marred by the rage in her eyes. She added, "That's your hug for the week. Don't touch your parents. Don't ever let them hug you. Don't listen to what they say. They're idiots. Remember, your Aunt Cindy will always take care of you."

Back at the table, Peter felt the triangle fade between his parents and him and, turning to his food, carefully began carving perfectly shaped triangles.

6

Church and State

The next morning, Peter woke at his usual time, proceeding through his morning routines. As if in church, he sat quietly on a chair from 10:00 until noon. At 12:45, he left for Aunt Cindy O'Brien's apartment. Mom's younger sister and the only surviving sibling, Aunt Cindy controlled the family business and the family conversation. Although Sally and Uncles Peter and Mike were gone, and the cousins no longer came, Peter faithfully observed the family tradition of Sunday dinner at Aunt Cindy's apartment. As Peter walked the twelve blocks, he calculated the number of dinners he had had there, forty-three years times fifty-two weeks is 2,236 dinners; thirty-three extra days for each of the 365-day years, twenty extra days for each of the 366-day years leaves fifty-three extra days or seven Sundays – 2,243 dinners. Another four dinners for four weeks past his birthday totals 2,247 dinners. Peter then subtracted twelve Sundays for the time he stayed with Aunt Maureen, thirteen at Beaver Christian Camp, and another twenty-two at Ma Burns' foster home. Twelve plus thirteen plus twenty-two equals forty-seven, subtracted from 2,247 leaves a total of 2,200 dinners. Excited at the result, an even twenty-two hundred, Peter climbed the fifteen steps to Aunt Cindy's brownstone and rang the bell.

Aunt Cindy opened the door and said in a crackling voice, "What the hell's wrong with you, you pathetic imbecile. You make me wait in the dark for hours, an old lady, can't hardly see. Come on, change these goddamn light bulbs. God, you're no better than that worthless oaf, your father. You're lucky I changed your name. Imagine another George Branstill. There should never even have been one of them. Then you come along. It's my own fault, too: teaching Sally how to fuck. Should never have done it. Well, you're finally here, late as always, and dinner's getting cold. I can't see nothing. My eyes are gone. So, put the goddamn bulb in the lamp and eat your dinner. Hurry up. Get up on this chair. WATCH YOURSELF! You're gonna tip it over. Oh, you're doing it all wrong. Don't break the chair, and don't smudge your rotten hands all over my lamp. God! This is how you treat an old lady. You're a worthless... Hey! Where the hell you think you're going? That's not the only bulb to change. Oh Christ, look what you did. The globe's all dirty. Now take this towel and clean the damn thing up. Come on, I don't have all day and dinner's getting cold, not that it matters to you. You never ate, always playing with your food. I told Sally to beat some sense into you. You think she'd do it. Goddamn wimp. Didn't deserve to have kids. And that asshole of a father of yours: George Branstill. Glad he died the way he did."

Peter changed the light bulbs and completed two other chores Aunt Cindy ordered him to do: tighten a loose screw on a chair, untangle the cord to one of her blinds. He then carved the roast, taking care to create slices with uniform thickness. As they started to eat and he cut his own meat further into trapezoids, Aunt Cindy asked, "Did I ever tell you how your mom got pregnant?"

Peter shivered, knowing a simple *yes* was not good enough, needing to know exactly how many times he had heard this story. For the first twenty-seven years, Peter sat at the children's table. Assuming he did not hear the story at all when he was very young, he started his calculations from the age of three. Since his attention to the story steadily increased from that point until he was twenty-seven and allowed to sit at the adults' table, he hypothesized a logarithmic curve representing the growth in his attention from age three, zero attention, to age twenty seven, 60 percent attention. Using calculus, Peter figured that he heard Sally's stories an equivalent of 430 attention-days during those years. There were another 819 real days after he turned twenty-seven. With 1,249 total days, 819 real days plus 430 attention-days, Peter then adjusted the number by 73 percent – the frequency with which Aunt Cindy actually told this story since he first kept records on her story-telling five years ago – leaving a total of 911.77 or an estimated 912 days having heard this story. WHAT THE HELL'S AN ATTENTION-DAY? he pictured Miss Weintraub screaming. NOW DO IT RIGHT. In bright red she marks Peter's paper 72 percent.

"You know, if it weren't for me, you wouldn't have been born. I figured it was OK when Sally first married the jerk 'cause at least she could stay home with Mama and keep her off my fucking back. We thought the jerk could do something useful in the business. That was a big mistake. Dad tried him in sales, but who'd buy anything from a slob like him. Dad put him in the office, but he messed up the typewriter eating a sticky bun while he worked. Dad put him in the warehouse, but all the orders went out wrong. Finally, he became the night watchman. For years, Sally stayed home with Mama while the jerk slept all day. Then he'd go to work, where he'd sleep all night, too." As Sally broke into a hearty laugh, Peter imagined his father sitting at the table with them, a symmetrical gravy stain on his shirt.

"This shit went on for ten years until Mama died. Dad had already been gone for years. All of a sudden, I realize there ain't no little Branstills. I ask Sally about it. She tells me she's been waiting for years, hoping one would come. Well, I don't know what the hell got into me, but I take her to Dr. Kelly, who tells me she's a fucking virgin. God, ten years and he never fucked her once. I tell you, teaching them what to do was like breeding horses." With that Aunt Cindy neighed loudly and broke into uncontrollable laughter. When the laughter became a cough, she put her cigarette out in her tea, got up, and went into the bathroom. Peter listened to her loud, irregular cough, disturbed by its lack of rhythm. After she closed the bathroom door, the cough changed to a pleasing 4-2-3 pattern before it finally stopped.

Sitting at the table, Peter remembered that his mother often told the same tale in softer terms. Soon, he becomes Dr. Kelly, the OB-GYN, a fat man with heavy black plastic glasses, a bushy mustache, and short hair, wearing a checkered tie that hung from the collar of his stained white dress shirt. Peter pictures himself picking up the chart prepared by his nurse, Mary from the office. Peter smiles, seeing it's a fertility case. Spitting as he talks, he shouts at Sally, "Spread 'em out." Reaching deep into her vagina, he feels around and says to

Mary, "5cm, rhombus." Mary records the measurement, a worried expression on her face. "She's asymmetrical and the texture's bad." Peter brings the examination to a halt and sends Sally to his consultation room. Sally waits while he has sex with Mary.

Breaking from the fantasy, realizing he's fully erect, Peter looked around. Aunt Cindy had not yet returned. Peter took several deep breaths, hoping to lose his erection. As he started to relax, he drifted back to his consultation with Sally Branstill.

"Mom," the suave Dr. Peter says, "You want to have a baby?"

"Yes, doctor," Sally says, "George and I met when he was a delivery boy. He brought packages to the firm where I worked before we got married, and I left to stay home to take care of Mother when he went to work. Cindy tells me George is a jerk but he's the nicest guy I ever met. He's sloppy and often eats with his hands and she doesn't like that he's always got gravy on his shirt but I don't care because he's the only one in the family who listens to me. We've been waiting a long time to have a baby. We've wanted one ever since the wedding. It was a big wedding. There were lots of people there, Cindy hired a big band, and we served everyone a meal. The main dish was roast beef with small potatoes, carrots, and a salad. The roast beef was rare, the potatoes were cooked perfectly, and I would've preferred a different vegetable but Cindy thought carrots were best. The caterers wore tuxedos and the whole thing happened in a big hall on 86th Street. I always wanted red flowers at my wedding but Cindy got a mixed bouquet with different types of flowers. But I took the red ones home with me. Cindy got to keep the others. George didn't really want any of the flowers but he had extra roast beef. That was the first time he spilled his food on his shirt, and Cindy got real mad because it was a rented tuxedo. I don't think it fit him too well, but the shoes were the right color, and it was certainly a lot better that he wore a tuxedo instead of his work clothes or even khakis."

Dr. Peter Branstill Kelly leans forward. In a deep voice he tells Sally, "You're a virgin."

Sally responds, "Oh, I'm so happy you found the problem. I don't think it runs in our family. You know, George and I can't have a dog. They won't allow them in our apartment. I have cousins in

New Jersey. They have a house and a yard, and two dogs of their own. I like the small one best. It's a brown and white cocker spaniel with big, sad eyes. I don't get to see it much since we hardly ever go there. I've asked them to bring the dog with them when they come to the city, but they don't. George likes the bigger dog better, but I'd rather have a small dog. Do you think we'll have a big child or a little one?"

Dr. Branstill leans forward again and says, "We'll start treatments next week. Bring Dad with you."

The scene shifts to a consultation with George, Sally, Aunt Cindy, and Dr. Peter Branstill. Peter inserts a banana into a donut. "Here's how you do it," the doctor says. While Dad eats the banana, Peter leads Mom to the stable. Dad starts on the donut as Sally's stomach opens up. Out comes a litter of cocker spaniels, one with Peter's face.

His erection large, Peter looked across the table. Cindy was not there. He climaxed quickly, noting his orgasm in his appointment book in the lower left-hand corner of the box for Sunday, July 16, and walked out the door.

That night Peter dreamt that he was in bed with his parents, Dad on top of Mom while Mom said, "There's a sale at Macy's this week. I may go there to buy Little George's school clothing, and I need hose anyway. Maybe we'll stop at Nedicks and get an orange drink. It's always hot this time of year, but if you take the subway after rush hour, it's not too bad."

Peter asks Dad what he's doing. "We're trying to make you a brother."

"Can I help?" asks Peter. George answers, "Of course, son." As Peter falls asleep, George beams, the scene shifting to Sunday dinner, Sally and George holding a newborn baby, Peter by their side. "It's a girl," he says. "Little George helped us make it." A gleeful Aunt Cindy invites Big George to dine with the rest of the family.

■ ■ ■

On Monday, Peter returned to work, and as usual, at lunchtime, he headed for his bench. Shortly after he sat down, the tobacco philosopher came by, again asking Peter for a light. Just as before, he ran off to the next passerby in search of smokes and got lucky on his first try. The new supplier was generous and doled out four cigarettes, teasing him about the approach. "You've got a great four-cigarette line. A little more polish, you might have gotten a fifth one from me. You gotta keep practicing if you want to make it in the big city."

Peter's visitor had no response to the man's quip. Again, he settled in the same pose, feet on the seat and butt on the back of the bench. The stranger made no reference to his promise to teach left-lung smoking. He did not even smoke in his peculiar way. Rather, he turned to Peter and said, "Don't I know ya from State?"

Peter did not respond.

"Don't I know ya from State? Sure, you were there, I'm sure I saw ya at State."

"No."

"Yeah, you were that guy. I remember. Bunked with Willie Jones. I remember ya. Real quiet, Joe-no-trouble type."

Peter replied, "No, you've got the wrong person, I didn't go to State."

■ ■ ■

As the man continued insisting that Peter went to State, Peter pictured himself at a large university. There he was, Peter Branstill, president of Phi Delta Beta, campus leader, valedictorian, head of SDS, ROTC, star football player. *"You gotta be a football hero to get along with the beautiful girls."* He pictured himself running to catch the touchdown pass. *Peter Branstill: wonder boy, quarterback, placekicker, attempting a 55-yard field goal, a 75-yard field goal, a 90-yard field goal, the crowd on its feet. With three seconds to go, Peter Branstill, the fair-haired star of the Green Bay Packers, makes a 90-yard field goal, running down the field to the 20-yard line, the 40-yard line, crossing the 50, the 40, the 30, they're trying to get him, but here goes Peter...*

"Pilgrim State. I know you were in Pilgrim State Hospital. We were together on G Ward."

The secret is out and they've come back to get me. Was I really there? Shock treatments, ice packs, lobotomy, straitjacket, strapped down. It feels so real. Peter pictured himself curled up in the corner of a dark, damp room, alone. He looked up at the clock. Having no recall of the last five hours, Peter saw that it was 5:00 o'clock and time to go home. He glanced at his IN/OUT box and saw that all his work was done.

7

Psychoanalysis

Peter left work knowing it would be a very difficult evening. He went directly to the porn district, quickly entered a peep show, and went straight to a private viewing booth. Not waiting to be asked, he stuffed $20 in the slot and quickly masturbated to the exposed dancer. He then went home and straight to bed.

But Peter's mind raced endlessly throughout a night of fitful sleep: *He came back, he knows.* Peter was not sure what he actually felt as the long night went on, but he knew things were different from the other times he had been this distressed. It wasn't so much the man's comment about the state hospital that had hit him so hard as the fact that he had come back. *Wow, no one ever comes back,* Peter thought before he remembered the drug dealer.

■ ■ ■

When first approached by the drug dealer, several years ago, Peter turned him down. But he was persistent. For days, he'd go straight to Peter as he entered the park. Rebuffed, he'd then spend the rest of the hour staring at Peter accusingly, raising his eyebrows, scowling, and clenching his fists. Peter finally agreed to buy a joint. When the man returned the next day, Peter declined, pointing out that he still had the same joint. Over the next month the dealer came up to Peter again and again. But each time, Peter produced the original unused joint that he never intended to smoke. Finally the man gave up, saying, "You're strange, dude." The words, "You're strange, dude," haunted Peter. He left the park shaking with fear, knowing this man now knew how bizarre he was.

■ ■ ■

On Tuesday, Peter again ate lunch at his usual bench. And once again, the smoker appeared, going through his usual routine of asking for a light before getting a cigarette from another person. Today, he got only one. Assuming his typical pose he says, "Man, you're cool. Thought about ya last night. Ya didn't even budge. Tried that old State routine, and ya didn't even budge. I like ya, man. You're cool. Ya know, most people get uptight, squirm around, want to get the hell away as fast as they can. Not you.

"It's not that I ain't been to State," he continues. "Hell, I've been there lotsa times. Know the nuthouse inside out. And not just State. Been in and outta so many nuthouses, I guess I'm a genuine nut-case. But you're OK. Ya got style. No, I ain't never seen ya at State.

"Ya work 'round here? Ya one of them big executives? A banker? A lawyer? Own a business?" Peter looked across the park, noticing three people standing together about 20 feet away from a couple. Three plus two equals five, he thought, and began looking for different groups of people – a person by himself walking past a bench with four people sitting on it, a fivesome in lively conversation at least 15 feet from anybody else – whose numbers added up to five.

"Yep, been in State many times. Been in county hospitals, private hospitals, rehab centers. Go to AA and OA, and GA and Say-Hey A: ya know, for recoverin' Willie Mays fans." The stranger laughs loudly at his own joke. After a while, his laughter subsides and he goes on.

"Just kiddin', ain't no Say-Hey A. But Willie was the best. Man, I remember when Willie, Mick, and the Duke roamed the outfields of New York. They were somethin'; I was just a kid. Fucked up then too. Mantle was more like me; ya know, drinkin' and fuckin' himself up. But Willie, hey, I loved that guy.

"Hell, been through all kinds of treatment, therapy. They say I'm schizophrenic, or manic; some say I'm depressed or nervous. Ask me, I'm just plain fucked up. But ya know, what if I wasn't fucked up? Could ya imagine a guy like me? Think 'bout it. Ya work in an office with lotsa folks in fancy suits and silk ties, gorgeous chicks, boss chasin' the secretary 'round the desk. Man, sometimes I think I'd like a life like yours. But ya know, can't sit still long 'nough. I gotta be here and there, back and forth. I get too antsy sittin' 'round. Eight hours a day on my ass, no sir, that ain't for me. But I bet ya like it. Gotta nice house, pretty wife, lotsa money, big car. I can dig it, not bad at all. But ya know, I'm free. Do what I want and go where I want." He takes a cigarette out of a pack he has rolled under the left sleeve of his shirt, puts it in his mouth, strikes a match, lights it, and inhales deeply through the right corner of his mouth. It occurred to Peter he was still ignoring his promise last week to show left-lunged smoking. Peter began looking at other smokers to see who placed their cigarettes in the left sides of their mouths.

"Now, it ain't that I don't want a piece of ass from time to time. Don't get me wrong. It's not like havin' a wife who can cook ya meals, get ya a beer, all the rest of that good stuff. But I get it sometimes. Like right now. There's this strange chick that's got her eye on me. Shit, I don't even know her name. Hanna or Anna. Maybe it's Banana," he says, laughing slightly. "Really, I think she wants to suck my banana. It's strange. She says nothin' to nobody, but I just gotta feelin'." As the man stops to think, Peter pictured himself slicing a banana, carefully placing the pieces in a perfect hexagon on top of his cereal.

"Hey, I gotta get back to my program over at the day treatment center. Ya know, that's where they treat us psychos these days. Used to send us far away, put us in big shitholes. Now we just go ev'ry day to little shitholes."

After laughing for a moment, the stranger goes on, "Really, it ain't that bad. Ya have fun, see people – like Hanna Banana – get to see your headshrinker whenever ya want to. I guess you ain't never seen a psychiatrist yourself. Well, it's a good place, just a block away, right over there. We have lunch at noon. Everyone gobbles down chow fast as they can so they can grab a smoke. They don't let us smoke inside no more. Most of 'em just hang outside the building but I like to walk around. I get here to the park by 12:15 or so, get a smoke, meet interestin' folks like you. I gotta get back, but listen, we need to stay in touch. I'm usually here in the park so if I see ya we'll talk again.

"By the way, my name is John. What's yours?" John says, inviting a handshake.

Peter hesitated, not knowing what to do. John seemed less than completely clean.

"Peter," Peter said without taking John's hand. John boldly grabs Peter's hand, pumping it heartily, saying, "Great, Petey. Glad to meet ya. See ya soon."

■ ■ ■

Peter continued to sit on the bench, thinking about John's words, "I guess you ain't never seen a psychiatrist yourself." Actually, he saw a psychiatrist, Dr. Robert Johnson, after his mother's death.

Afraid that mental illness ran in families, Peter had called a psychoanalytic institute he found through the Yellow Pages and made an appointment with Dr. Johnson. Much like his previous therapy with Dr. Kline, Peter said nothing at all in the first session and added very little over the next three years of analysis.

Dr. Johnson diagnosed Peter as suffering from a schizoid personality disorder, and formed many theories about the origins of Peter's illness: an alcoholic mother, a sexually abusive father, rejection by his more successful brother and sister, and some yet-to-be-uncovered traumatic event. Since there was nothing else to do while he sat in silence with Peter, Dr. Johnson had a lot of time to formulate his theories.

Dr. Johnson once explained to his students: "The schizoid patient must know you are comfortable waiting out the long silences, no matter how long it takes. Eventually, they will trust you and begin to reveal their most private and painful inner thoughts."

But Peter actually felt quite comfortable and enjoyed his relationship with Dr. Johnson. He had always felt safe with his mother, whose ramblings had a soothing, musical effect on him. Likewise, he felt safe with Dr. Johnson, who suffered from asthma and produced a soothing wheeze during their sessions. Peter did not mind that Dr. Johnson had no insights to offer; the wheeze met his needs. But Peter also understood that Dr. Johnson was not as satisfied with the therapy as he was, because Dr. Johnson kept asking questions like: "I wonder what's going on." Or, "You're being very quiet today." Or, "I wonder what you are blocking today." Sometimes, Peter felt like explaining he was the quarterback or placekicker, not a blocker, in his football fantasies.

Generally, Dr. Johnson asked these questions when he was feeling angry or bored with Peter, or when he was drowsy and trying to keep himself from falling asleep. In fact, his gentle wheeze sometimes turned into a jarring snore, which Peter actually liked since it reminded him of the time he sat by his mother toward the end of her life, awaiting her death.

While Dr. Johnson jotted down notes, formulated concepts, and fought fatigue, Peter thought about riding horseback into a field of wildflowers for a romantic and erotic picnic lunch. The nuances in posture that Dr. Johnson observed reflected Peter's struggle to hide an embarrassing erection as he dreamt about sexual interludes with either the girl or the horse.

Because he cared about Dr. Johnson, Peter one day tried to help him out. Recalling his therapy as a child, he asked, "Would you like to play a game of checkers?"

Dr. Johnson pounced on this question as if it was the long-awaited breakthrough he knew would come.

"I wonder why you want to play checkers with me?... What might you be trying to say by asking to play checkers?... I wonder what you are really feeling that you asked to play checkers instead? ... "

Frankly, Peter had no interest at all in playing checkers with Dr. Johnson. He never liked checkers when he played it with Dr. Kline, and only played because Dr. Kline liked to play checkers so much. Peter assumed that checkers was a therapy technique and wondered if Dr. Johnson's school didn't teach it. When he snored in the session, Peter would wonder if Dr. Johnson had slept through the class on playing checkers. Regardless, Peter's attempt to help Dr. Johnson had failed, and he was now met with a barrage of questions he did not understand. Finally, Dr. Johnson said, "Perhaps you want to play with me the checkers game you never got to play with your father," which Dr. Johnson thought was his best interpretation ever.

When Peter failed to respond, Dr. Johnson angrily tossed his notepad to the side and added, "Perhaps you thought your daddy would cut off your penis if you played checkers with your mommy.

Perhaps that is why you now want to play checkers with me."

Feeling sad and rejected, Peter began thinking about computers, picturing himself as an outdated model that was unable to read the files generated by other computers. He imagined himself sitting alone in a large office complex, the only computer with a monochrome monitor, unable to access text files available to the other terminals, which were all happily networked to one another. Peter's CPU sadly downloaded his own files, which could no more be read by the larger integrated system than Dr. Johnson could understand his thoughts.

Peter continued seeing Dr. Johnson, five times a week, for three years, only stopping for the doctor's August vacations and major holidays. Once, not wanting to interrupt the therapeutic process, Dr. Johnson came to work with a high fever and severe flu symptoms, thus unwittingly validating one of Peter's own lifelong beliefs: He must never alter his routines, regardless of how he feels.

Two weeks before the therapy stopped, Dr. Johnson took a rare day off to make the keynote speech at a major psychoanalytic conference. His speech, "Identifying and Intervening with Resistances in the Schizoid Patient," was based on a well-received paper describing his work with Peter. It described many things Dr. Johnson thought had occurred between him and Peter, like the time Peter wanted a hug when he actually was squirming to conceal his erection, lusting for a horse.

He brought the audience to laughter when he described the checkers incident. There was universal agreement that Peter was struggling with guilt over having been molested by his father, a sin he needed to confess but was afraid to speak of, fearing Dr. Johnson's wrath. Another prominent analyst shared a similar reaction one of his patients had, an obvious negative transference in which that patient also failed to see how supportive, sensitive, and empathic his doctor was.

Two weeks after Dr. Johnson's career-crowning moment, Peter abruptly stopped therapy: He simply failed to show up for his session and never came back. Initially, Dr. Johnson felt sad, but unconsciously, he was more relieved than distressed. By terminating treatment, he could never write the sequel to his paper, "Therapeutic Triumph with the Schizoid Patient." Dr. Johnson believed that Peter was angry with him for cancelling the session to present his paper, but Peter was actually responding to a subtle and covert message from Dr. Johnson that they had completed their work. He had helped Dr. Johnson write his best paper ever while enjoying a safe haven following his mother's death. Their work was done.

8

Indianapolis

When Peter returned to work, there was a note on his desk:

From the Office of Andrew Lerner
Peter, Please see me.
Andrew

Peter shuddered, picturing himself at the peep show last night, certain he had been seen. Expecting to be fired, knowing he would miss the firm, he looked longingly at his desk, two pencils and two pens in a container that also kept twenty-five paper clips, twenty-four rubber bands, eight each of assorted sizes, his name stamp and date stamp, touching each other, three quarters of an inch to the right of his calculator placed exactly parallel to the ends of the desk. Peter slowly walked down the hall to Andrew's office, gave his standard business knock – three knocks in perfect sequence unlike his 2-1-2 informal door knock. After Andrew said, "Come in," Peter opened the door.

"Peter, it's that time of year: the Sterling and Warner audit. I'm going to Indianapolis tomorrow, to their main office. Jeff Billingsworth was going to help me, but we just learned that his son was in an accident this morning. I need your help. Here's your plane tickets and hotel reservations. I know you don't usually like to do this, but we're in a bind. Say you'll do it."

Andrew tapped his fingers on his desk nervously, waiting for Peter's response. Knowing this was the first time anyone asked him to work beyond his standard 9-to-5, Monday-through-Friday hours, he hoped Peter would agree, regretting giving him any choice at all.

For years, Andrew's brother-in-law, Carl Schwartz, the vice president of Lerner and Schwartz, Public Accountants, wanted to fire Peter. Despite his many barbed comments – "The guy's useless... he's just floating by... what other accountant works this little in tax season?" – Max Lerner, Andrew's father and founder of the firm, always defended Peter, the sad, directionless boy he saved from obscurity in high school. With Max gone for years, Andrew president in name only, and Carl truly in charge, Andrew stuck his neck out, claiming with certainty that Peter would go if asked.

While Andrew waited, Peter tried to think of a way out. *I can't go. What if they give my apartment to someone else while I'm gone? What will I eat? Who'll take care of Howdy? What if I wake up mad? Why can't Jeff Billingsworth go? Oh yes, his son was in an accident. That's it. I'll tell Andrew my son was in an accident, too.* Finally, Andrew asked, "So what'll it be, Peter. You'll go?" Jarred by Andrew's voice, having forgotten where he was, Peter looked up and asked, "Yes?"

"Great!" Andrew beamed. "I knew you'd do it. Take your tickets and reservations. Go home and pack. You'll fly out tonight. Here's some materials to review on your way. And don't forget, a big meal on the firm. I'll meet you in the hotel lobby at 8:30 tomorrow morning."

Peter stayed in front of Andrew's desk still thinking of how to tell Andrew about his son. "Anything else, Peter?" Andrew asked. "No," Peter replied. After leaving Andrew's office, he packed up his things and left the office building. Once on the street, he walked to *Private Booths, Sexy Girls,* where he bought three new pornographic magazines for the trip. While there, he masturbated to a girl in a private booth, knowing it would be two days before he came back. He then exited the show and walked to a newstand where he bought a copy of *Horse and Saddle.*

On the bus home, Peter paid particular attention to each of the passing sights: *There's Joe's Newsstand. There's the Midtown Coffee Shop. Okay, Joe's Newsstand, Midtown Coffee Shop. Now, there's the corner of 47th and Broadway, the sign's bent. Joe's Newsstand, Midtown Coffee Shop, bent street sign.*

When Peter got home, he opened the drawer in his file cabinet and pulled out the folder labeled New York City Maps, where he had filed three maps of the city: his first-place map and the first and second runner-up maps. After a few moments' thought, he decided that this was a critical situation and removed the first-place map from the folder. After relabeling the first runner-up map to first-place map, and the second runner-up map to first runner-up map, he returned the two maps to the folder, the folder to the file, and closed the drawer. He opened his appointment book and wrote in the box for Thursday, July 20, the day he'd return to the city, *Buy a new second runner-up New York City map*. He then recorded the locations of Joe's Newsstand, the Midtown Coffee Shop, and the bent street sign on this map along with all the other landmarks he could remember.

Peter read his itinerary, learning that he was to fly out in the evening, work at Sterling and Warner all day Wednesday, work there again on Thursday morning, then fly back home. He packed the clothing he had already scheduled to wear Wednesday and Thursday, his toiletries, and the four new magazines in a brown tweed suitcase he got from his mother, the one she took to the hospital when she give birth to him. After leaving the apartment, he walked to Broadway and flagged a cab.

■ ■ ■

After exiting his cab at LaGuardia, Peter walked up to the ticket counter and checked in. A young woman stood behind the counter wearing the same crisp navy blue uniform the other counter personnel wore. She stamped his ticket and asked him for his bag. Reluctant to relinquish the suitcase, but knowing he had no other choice, he complied. She stapled a luggage ticket to his plane ticket.

Peter watched the conveyor belt take his suitcase, by the counter, past the other ticket agents, into an opening in the wall. For another minute, he stood there, watching the belt, hoping his suitcase would reappear. Convinced it was gone, and hopefully on the plane, he turned away and walked toward the gate. Feeling anxious at the security checkpoint, watching his briefcase pass under an X-ray machine, thankful that his pornographic magazines were in the suitcase, not the briefcase, he passed through the metal detector, picked up his briefcase, and walked toward the boarding gate.

Peter counted fifteen people lined up to board the plane, forty-three others in the nearby waiting area. He took his place in line and waited, until a voice loudly announced, "Boarding Flight 147 to Indianapolis, Gate 27." Peter saw people get up from their seats and join the line, now already forty-six people long. After the voice made a second announcement, the line began moving toward a walkway that led from the building to the plane. Peter followed the line, briefcase in hand, until he reached the plane where two women and a man – the flight attendants – stood by. The man looked at Peter's ticket and directed him to Seat D, Row 25, his assigned seat, toward the middle of the plane. Peter vigilantly eyed the numbers on the seats until he reached Row 25. He looked down at Seat D, a center seat, and saw a large, irregular, mottled red stain. Before even calculating its value on the Graduated Dirt Rating Scale, Peter knew he was in trouble. Quickly, he made a partial assessment of the stain's GDRS, based on its color, discoloration, size, and symmetry, resulting in an astonishingly high value of forty-nine.

Dirt, thought Peter. He looked around. None of the other seats were stained. He thought he could quickly take another seat but then looked at his ticket; the assignment was clear.

Passenger: Peter Branstill
Flight#: 147
Destination: Indianapolis
Date: July 18, 1995
Row: 25
Seat: D

Even with perfect odor and texture, this stain would rate as at least major dirt. With serious odor and texture problems, Peter might have to sit on dangerous or lethal dirt.

I've got to get out of here, he thought. He turned around to flee, looking straight at a crowded line of passengers waiting to sit down. Afraid of the mob, he knew he had to sit. So, with his feet planted on the floor, Peter continued to turn, taking a deep whiff when he was directly facing the woman in the line behind him, noticing the pungent scent of the perfume she wore. Then, continuing around, he lost his balance, tripping over his own feet, began to fall, and took a second, deep whiff about halfway down, just as the man sitting in the seat across the aisle from him reached out to brace Peter's fall. Peter detected no odors now. Continuing the fall, the upper part of Peter's body turned toward his seat, his face descending quickly, his nose settling approximately 3 inches from the stain.

■ ■ ■

Peter felt pleased. The boy who was laughed at in gymnastics and failed phys. ed. just made a perfect free-fall from a standing position straight to the stain. Peter pictured the fall again, this time spinning three times in his mind, as the announcer shouts:

"He NAILED the landing. For the first time in Olympic competition, Peter Branstill just nailed a perfect triple Lutz. Here come the judges' ratings. 9.9, 9.9, 9.9, 9.6 – the Russian judge – 9.9, 9.9, 9.9, 9.9."

Peter took a deep whiff. Unsure if he was smelling the fabric or the stain, Peter assigned the stain a high odor score of four, increasing the total score so far by twenty-four, to seventy-three. Peter shuddered, realizing the score would be at least in the high range of major dirt, or possibly even dangerous or lethal dirt. Peter glanced forward and saw the flight attendant push hastily through the crowd. He looked back at the stain, knowing he could not accurately test its texture, his surgical glove in his pocket, not on his hand. But eyeballing the stain, he saw it was smooth. With texture inversely related to danger, the stain garnered a five for texture, catapulting the full GDRS rating to 93, *lethal dirt*. He could not sit on the seat, but he was helpless now that the two flight attendants were by his side. They lifted him up from the place he landed, and set him directly on the seat.

"Are you OK, sir? Can we help you? What happened? We can take you off the plane and call an ambulance."

Peter cried to himself, knowing he would have welcomed their offer while he was still on the floor. But now firmly seated, the damage was done: There was lethal dirt on his pants.

■ ■ ■

Sirens rang as the ambulance rushes Peter to the emergency room of Metropolitan Hospital. With worried expressions, the medics quickly pull Peter's stretcher from the back. *"WE'VE GOT DIRT!*

LETHAL DIRT!"

As they move Peter to the bed, the medic goes on, *"It's bad, doc. Large, irregular, smooth, mottled, red."*

"My God!" the doctor exclaims. *"Does it smell?"*

"Four."

∎ ∎ ∎

Peter convinced the flight attendant he was OK and settled in his seat. Reflecting on the texture score, Peter began to question his long-held assumption that texture was inversely related to the dirt's danger, an idea he developed at Beaver Christian Camp. Peter realized that then he studied dirt in a warm, outdoor setting, dirt that was generally smooth when moist, drying out and forming minute ridges with time. The smooth dirt transferred readily to pants and carried more live bacteria than the drier, textured dirt. But indoor dirt, in a climate-controlled environment, adhering to a cloth seat, would generally wear down and become smooth. Peter began to wonder if texture should be broken into two factors, texture and moisture, with both coarse and moist dirt associated with dirt danger. With this adjustment, the dirt on which he sat would come in as dangerous, not lethal dirt.

Peter fished out his notebook, turned to the third Saturday in September – the day he annually reviewed the GDRS at his mother's grave – and wrote: *Divide texture into texture and moisture.* He returned the book and began thinking about Albert Einstein's theories as they applied to the relationship between dirt danger and time. *If the dirt is lethal today, but would not be lethal in September after I correct the scale, am I dead today?* Peter drifted into a light sleep repeating this question to himself.

∎ ∎ ∎

Peter left the plane to be met by two tall, well-built men in black suits. *"Mr. Branstill. Please come with us."* They led him to a room off to the side where there were a dozen similarly built and dressed men standing around Peter's open suitcase, his four magazines spread at the top.

"Mr. Branstill. It's a federal crime, and a public hazard, to transport

pornographic materials on a commercial airline. You are under arrest."

Peter suavely reaches in his pocket, pulls out his wallet, and shows his identification. *"I have diplomatic immunity,"* Peter says. *"I'm with Lerner and Schwartz, Public Accountants. I've been called to audit the books at Sterling and Warner in Indianapolis."*

One of the men shakes with fear and quickly apologizes. *"We didn't know, sir."* He offers his hand for an apology. Peter scoffs at the handshake, noticing dirt on his hand. *"Don't let it happen again."*

As Peter starts to leave, one of the agents, watching him from behind, points in horror and screams, *"Red dirt! There's red dirt on his butt!"*

Sirens ring. The hazardous waste materials team, in protective gear, rush in and wrap Peter's butt in air conditioning filtration material. The door automatically locks, a sign flashing: QUARANTINE!

■ ■ ■

Peter woke up to see a flashing sign over his seat. PLEASE FASTEN YOUR SEAT BELTS.

"Ladies and gentlemen," a voice announced over the intercom, "we are beginning our descent to Indianapolis, Indiana. The temperature is 76°. The skies are clear. The captain has asked that you fasten your seat belt. We hope you've had a good flight."

Peter deboarded after the plane descended. He entered the men's room, looked at himself in the mirror, and saw a featureless oval where his face belonged. Several hairs were out of order, disrupting the 1/3 / 2/3 split he required around his part. On his rumpled shirt was a large sweat stain. Peter left the airport for the Sheraton Hoosier Hotel and checked into his room.

Once there, Peter took out his measuring tape to locate the exact middle of his bed. He then measured the standard distance from the middle of the bed to the night table, finding the proper location to place his calculator, notepad, blue pen, and pencil. He walked to the shower, thermometer in hand, and tested the dial until he located the proper place for a 110° shower. Walking back to his bed, he counted the number of steps needed to reach his clothes the next morning when leaving the bathroom blindfolded. He hung his shirts, suits, and ties in the closet, lined the dresser drawers with waxed paper before unpacking his underwear and socks, and measured the exact midpoint of the left wall of the closet, placing his shoes there. He set out his Shredded Wheat and plastic bowl, plastic silverware, canned orange juice, and packaged 2 percent milk – the type that did not need to be refrigerated. Before going to bed, he set a template on the center of the top of the dresser with Howdy's, Clarabelle's, and Buffalo Bob's places marked. After carefully removing the puppets from their protective wraps, he placed each where it belonged. Once in bed, he tested each of his four new magazines, carefully rating a single-case Orgasm Index for each magazine. Then Peter fell asleep.

9

The Audit

Peter met Andrew in the hotel lobby at 8:30 a.m. Wednesday morning. He had been pacing nervously, in his room, for the last hour and a half, fully dressed and ready to leave at the usual time, 7:00 a.m. Andrew greeted him warmly, escorting him to his rented car. Instinctively, as he did in taxis and as a child, he went to the back seat of the car. Andrew laughed loudly: "You're such a card, Peter. I love that deadpan humor you have. Now, come on, get in the front and we'll drive to Sterling and Warner."

Peter closed the back door, opened the front door, glanced at the seat, which was free of dirt, and got in. As they drove, Andrew talked on about the planned audit while Peter looked out the window, hoping to find a park for his lunch. He found three, the last Dawkins Park, only two blocks from the offices of Sterling and Warner.

■ ■ ■

At Sterling and Warner, Andrew introduced Peter to Harold Sterling, who boldly took Peter's hand. "Welcome to Indianapolis. We'll get you fellas set up right away so you can begin to work." As he led them down the hall, he turned to Andrew and asked, "Whatever happened to that pretty secretary Max used to bring when he came here?"

"Oh, Mary. She's still with us. She'll be retiring at the end of the year."

"She was some looker. Did she ever get married?"

"No, not sure what happened. She had a boyfriend, Danny. I think they broke up. I don't think she had any others. We don't ask, but we'd sure have known if she got married. Hard to believe someone didn't get her. She was a fox."

"Well, your dad was lucky. She was a damn good secretary, too," he added as a knowing smile crossed his lips.

Andrew laughed and said, "I know what you're thinking, but it didn't happen. Mary's Irish and Dad was Orthodox. Believe me, it was strictly business. And talking about business, let's get started. We've got a lot of work to do."

The talk ended and the three men settled down to work. Peter punched out numbers at his usual slow, steady pace, picturing himself eating lunch at Dawkins Park.

■ ■ ■

The trumpets announce that Prince Peter the Brave, Explorer, Conqueror, has arrived to claim his throne. Entering Dawkins Park, Peter waves to his subjects, motions his entourage back. Watching from the playground, the children cheer Peter standing by the bench, his valet announcing, "It's clean, Sire." As he takes his seat, the guards point to the feast. Peter opens his lunch bag, a medley of sumptuous treats in splendid geometric shapes. The musicians play jolly tunes as the strippers and horses dance for his pleasure.

Suddenly, Peter's all alone. Five men in leather jackets appear with whips and chains. They taunt him, demand money, and threaten his life. Peter keeps on eating, hoping to finish his sandwich before he returns to the audit. He carelessly severs the corner of a triangle but keeps his cool. The slip goes unnoticed by his assailants. Angered by his poise, dishonored in their defeat, the five men depart, spitting at him as they leave.

"Mayday," cries the medic. "It's spit." *I'll rate it,* says Peter. YOU FOOL, snicker the children. IT'S NOT DIRT, IT'S SPIT. In a lab coat, with clipboard in hand, a bespectacled scientist leads Peter to the isolation room. "We've got to de-spit you," he says. "It could be lethal." *What are my chances,* asks Peter. "Fifty-fifty," the scientist replies. OH FOR GOD'S SAKE, cries Miss Weintraub. GET IT RIGHT. She marks his paper 72 percent in red. With Peter strapped to a chair in the cylindrical glass experiment room, the scientist says, "This is powerful stuff. If it fails, you're dead. If it works, you'll never get dirty again."

The scientist pushes the button. Peter hears a tone, BEEP, BEEP, BEEP. He looked at his watch. Noon. Peter turned off the alarm, got up from the desk, picked up his brown bag, and began to leave for lunch. Andrew, who was working in the same room with Peter and Harold, looked at him as he was about to walk out the door and asked, "Where you going, Peter?"

"Lunch."

"Lunch," Andrew laughed, surprised and embarrassed. He turned to Harold and said, "Lunch." Harold replied, "God, I can't think of the last time I got out to lunch on time. You know, sometimes I think we all get trapped, working long hours, never taking time for ourselves. Peter's right. Let's go to lunch."

Andrew added, "I'll tell you, if it weren't for Peter, I think we all would've gone mad a long time ago. He's the only one who knows how to stay off the treadmill and enjoy his life. Yeah, let's go to lunch."

Peter cringed, feeling this sudden act of solidarity close in on him. He tried to recall the size of the benches in the park he saw as they were driving. They were typical three-seat benches that could easily accommodate the group. Peter needed to take a seat on the cleanest part of the bench. As he struggled to figure out how he could get the seat he wanted without seeming rude, he looked back at Andrew and Harold, noticing that neither had brown lunch bags. *What are they going to eat?* he asked himself, a question quickly answered when Harold directed the threesome to his car and drove to a nearby restaurant.

■ ■ ■

The hostess led the three businessmen to their seats as Peter worried about how he would look opening his lunch in the restaurant. He politely waited for the others to order and be served when Harold said, "Fellas, I don't know what you like, but this place has got the best damned barbecued baby back ribs in town. Trust me, you'll love them." Without looking for approval, he turned to the waitress, saying, "Three orders of your best," as he winked at her.

By the time the food came, Andrew and Harold were deep in

conversation, reviewing the audit. They failed to notice Peter sitting there, unopened lunch bag in hand, staring blankly over his plate of Indianapolis' best barbecued baby back ribs, thinking only about Andrew's words. *"I know what you're thinking, but it didn't happen. Mary's Irish and Dad was Orthodox. Believe me, it was strictly business."*

■ ■ ■

Rabbi Max Lerner tells the young Peter Branstill, "You're a good boy. I remember when I first met you. You were floundering in high school with no direction. You've done good, working for the firm. Now I need a favor from you. Remember Mary, the pretty secretary. She's Irish. I'm not allowed to be with a schikse. The rumors? Yes, we're in love but we've never done it. Please, Peter, do it for me." As Peter takes a drag on his cigarette, inhaling deeply into his left lung, Mary calls to him from the bed, "Happy Birthday".

■ ■ ■

"My God, you didn't eat a thing!" laughed Harold, looking at Peter's plate, the ribs untouched. "You know, I saw the brown bag. Never even thought you might be on a diet. Can't tell why, you're so thin. I know, some fellas have really high cholesterol even if they don't show it. Well, you got class. Didn't say anything to embarrass me."

Andrew laughed and joined in. "That's Peter. You know, we used to ask him out to lunch years ago. But there's only so many times you want to make a pig of yourself, sitting next to someone with such great self-control." The men got up and continued laughing as they walked to Harold's car, Peter silently picturing himself biting off, triangle by triangle, the sandwich inside his brown paper bag.

■ ■ ■

After work, driving Peter back to his hotel, Andrew said, "I'm going to dinner in about an hour. Want to join me?" Peter did not respond. "Unless you just want some time by yourself," Andrew added, grateful he even came to Indianapolis, remembering that Peter stays by himself. YOU'RE ALWAYS BY YOURSELF, the children scream. YOU'LL JUST GO HOME AND JERK OFF. "I'll get you at 8:30 again. Bring your bags and leave them in the car.

We'll go straight to the airport when we finish the audit."

Back in his room, Peter thought about Andrew's words, "Bring your bags and leave them in the car." *The magazines,* he thought, *they'll be in the suitcase, in Andrew's car, out of my control.* At home, he disposed of one magazine each month, putting it in the brown paper bag his new magazine came in, placing that in the incinerator, and waiting hours for it to burn. Unsure what to do, he grabbed the telephone book from the night table and opened it to Waste Disposal. None of the ads there seemed geared for his needs. He looked under Garbage and found a line suggesting he look under Trash Removal. There were several trash removal companies under that heading, all for commercial purposes only. Then, looking for Sanitary Landfills, he came across the heading Stationery Stores, and realized a paper shredder would solve his problem. With an Office Max at Eagle Plaza, Peter quickly left the hotel, grabbed a cab, and went to Eagle Plaza.

The cab took Peter far from the city, into the suburbs to Eagle Plaza, a large, semicircular shopping center with seventeen stores. Across the street there was a shopping mall. Peter saw several large, open parking lots, but no subway station. Peter felt like he was in a different world. He scanned the expanse, hoping to see a peep show: None were there. While gazing at the stores, the driver interrupted Peter's thoughts, "Thirty-five bucks, sir."

"Oh, I'm sorry," Peter said, surprised the ride cost this much. After paying the fare, the cabbie asked, "Hey, listen. It's none of my business, but how are you getting back?"

"I'll take another cab back."

"This ain't the city, bud. It may not be so easy."

"Can you wait?" Peter asks.

"Sure, but it's $15 an hour to wait."

"That's okay," Peter said. "I should be back in a few minutes."

Peter walked away from the cab into the store and bought the cheapest model paper shredder after inquiring if it could shred 246 pages, the total number of pages in the three pornographic magazines. He planned to keep *Horse and Saddle.* "And many more," the salesperson chuckled, as he handed him a box with the shredder inside.

On the ride back, the cabbie, a talkative type, commented, "You know, there's an Office Max thirteen blocks from your hotel." WHAT AN IDIOT! When Peter did not reply, the cabbie asked, "You work for the government?" Still, no reply. "My uncle was in military intelligence in the Navy during World War II. I think they broke codes or some sort of shit like that. But he had all sorts of tales about secret agents, spy versus spy. It ain't as glamorous as everybody thinks. No daggers, and sexy girls, nothing like that at all. It's just a job. Just like any ordinary guy who gets up, goes to the bathroom, wipes his ass, eats breakfast, and goes shopping. You know, them spies are like me and you, could be doing nothing more than going to Office Max and buying some pens, if you know what I mean."

■ ■ ■

Back in the hotel, Peter sat by the desk looking at his paper bag lunch, and the dinner he planned to eat this evening. By now, the sandwich would have spoiled, and it was past the planned time for dinner, hours past the standard margin of error ± 20 minutes. Hungry, but unable to eat either meal, Peter went to sleep.

That night Peter dreamt that he walked into his hotel room to find Max and Mary there, having sex. Peter checks his key: *This is my room.* Max responds: *"This is our room. We've used it for years. I may be dead, but I've still got rights. Your aunt should never have said the bad things she says about me." I'm sorry, Dad,* Peter responds. "I know. You still keep the triangle going." *What are you doing, Dad?* "We're making you a little brother." *Can I help?* "Of course, come in bed." Peter climbs into the bed, falling asleep, as Max and Mary continue relations.

The phone rings. Peter answers, *Peter Bond, 007.* "We need your help, right away. Come to the lobby." Absolutely, Peter says. In the lobby, Peter skillfully hides behind a large potted fern. In the cabbie's voice, a person on the other side of the plant says, "Don't move, just listen. We found a pornographic magazine in the lobby. Your assignment: shred it." The man leaves the magazine in a brown paper bag on a small table nearby. Peter picks up the magazine and opens it to a picture of a beautiful young colt. He looks up. Max and Aunt Cindy are there. Max tells Aunt Cindy, "George made it."

Peter woke up in the morning with a strong urge to masturbate. He reached over for his magazines, but they weren't there. He looked across the room and saw a pile of shreds in the wastebasket. Carefully sifting through the shreds, he placed thirty-five strips on the end table, and masturbated to the image there.

■ ■ ■

The audit ended smoothly. Harold thanked Peter and Andrew for their work, suggesting that Peter come back next year to help out again. "Not as good-looking as Mary but a hell of a lot funnier than Billingsworth," he quipped.

On the plane back, Andrew asked Peter if he could see some of Peter's calculations again. Inside his briefcase, Andrew quickly spotted Peter's copy of *Horse and Saddle*. "Goddamnit, Peter. You are a puzzle. Here you go, quiet as a mouse, nobody knows nothing about you, and you're a goddamn horseman. How long you been riding, buddy?" Following a brief pause, Andrew went on, "No, you're not gonna do that shit to me. You may be shy and quiet, and it's okay to be private at work, but hell, we just spent two days together, you did a helluva job, now we're off the clock so let's talk. How long have you been riding?"

Peter replied, "I don't ride."

"You don't? Why the magazine?" *Oh God,* Peter thought. *What am I going to do. Try to keep your cool.* "I just like the pictures." *Oh no, I shouldn't have said that.* "And the stories, too."

Placing his hand to his chin, scrunching his brow, Andrew sat in deep thought for half a minute looking at Peter before his face broke into a broad grin, "Well, that's even better. You like to read the stories and look at the pictures even though you never rode a horse. Peter, this has been great going away together like this. The more I know you, the better I like you. You take lunch during a big audit and still do a great job. You can get away from the rat race of New York by just buying a country magazine. Sometimes, my mind's just a crazy jumble. I wish I knew how to relax the way you do. Well, I try." Andrew pulled out a book from his briefcase, showing it to Peter: *Yoga for Travelers*. "Well, you just read your magazine, forget the figures until we get back to the office tomorrow, and I'm going to meditate all the way home."

10

Sammy

When Peter arrived home, he checked the door, finding each of the seven pieces of Scotch tape he left connecting the door and the doorframe, two on each side, two on the top, one on the bottom, intact. Opening the door 10°, half his usual 20° opening, taking extra precautions because he'd been away so long, he listened carefully for scurrying noises, a telltale sign of a surprised intruder. With no sounds, he took a deep whiff: no unusual odors. He hummed for a half second: *The echo's not the same. Something's wrong.* Peter hummed again: the same errant echo. Peter thought: *Should I go in? Should I call the police? Should I get a new apartment?* Thinking more, he realized the change in sound might have been caused by the smaller door opening. Increasing the angle to 20° and humming again, he sighed deeply, hearing his expected echo. Peter opened the door to 33°, the angle needed to squeeze through the door without touching it, and went in. Starting to the left, he walked through the apartment, staying exactly 6 inches from the walls. Five minutes later, after reaching the front door again, he walked to the center of his living room and turned slowly 360°. Completing this procedure from the centers of his kitchen, the bathroom, his mother's bedroom, and his own bedroom, convinced no one had been in his apartment and that nothing changed while he was away, he took his hat off, hung it on the rack, and then walked to the living room window to look at the apartment building across the street. Fixing his gaze at the third window to the left on the fourth floor of that building, he saw, while standing 8 inches from the right side of his window, that a straight line connecting the middle of that window and his nose was still perpendicular to his window: *Good, no earthquakes.* Relieved, he went to the kitchen and prepared his standard dinner of chicken, string beans, potatoes, and a buttered kaiser roll. After dinner, he opened his suitcase to unpack. He hung up the suit he was wearing, suit No. 4, on hanger No. 4, hung up the suit in his suitcase, suit No. 3, on hanger No. 3, and took suit No. 1 off its hanger, placing it on the staging hanger near the shelf where he set out his clothes for the next day. He checked that suit No. 2 was still on hanger No. 2 and looked at a picture of suit No. 5, the suit at the dry cleaners, attached to hanger No. 5. Then after hanging up the rest of his clothing, washing his face, and brushing his teeth, Peter went to bed.

In the morning, Peter woke up, completed his usual routines, and left for work. On the way, he paid special attention to the various landmarks he noted and later recorded on his map on the way home from work Tuesday. They were all there: Joe's Newsstand, Midtown Coffee Shop, the bent street sign. He patted his pocket to make sure he had his map with him, planning at lunch to check today's observations with the map.

As Peter entered his office, Andrew rushed up and greeted him warmly, again congratulating him on a successful audit. Andrew called Carl over to tell him about their successful trip. "Accountants *do* audits," Carl mumbled under his breath, walking quickly away. "Don't mind him," Andrew said, congratulating Peter two more times before returning to his office. Peter looked at his watch before sitting down at his desk. The time was 9:20 a.m.; he had lost 1/9 of his work morning. Increasing his pace by 12.5 percent, Peter completed his morning's work on time. Putting on his hat and picking up his lunchbag, Peter left for the park. By 12:10 p.m., he was sitting on the bench expecting to eat by himself and had just separated a parallelogram from the rest of his sandwich when John came jogging toward him. Out of breath he said, "Petey. Where ya been? I missed ya."

With a shocked look on his face, Peter turned to John and said, "Away."

"Oh, of course: business," John said in a knowing way. "I used to be in business. Bet ya couldn't guess, but it's true. John Waller. Yep, that's me. John Waller, President and Chief Executive Officer of Waller Enterprises. That's Waller Enterprises, Inc." emphasizing the

"K" sound at the end for effect.

"We made all sorts of things. Widgets, and gadgets, and wadgets, and whoozits. A *Fortune* 500 company, New York Stock Exchange, *Wall Street Journal*, MBA, DNA, LBJ. We were, like, at the top of the heap. And ya know how I did it, a guy like me? Connections. That's how you do it. Ya meet people, rub elbows, play the game. And man, I played it good. Fred. He's the guy that got me started. I called him Fred. His real name was Frederico. Frederico something or another. Big guy, President of the Bank of Italy. At first, I called him Frederico Pizza Pie. Then we got real close so I started callin' him Fred.

"I was real down and out one day, so I goes right into the bank, figure what the hell, I ask to see the president. I tell him I need a loan. I'm John Waller, President of Waller Enterprises. We got cash flow problems. He takes me real serious. Now, I ain't dressed no better than I am here, and I've tried this before and gotten the royal brushoff. But Fred takes me real serious. So I fill out the whole fuckin' application and he asks me for my credit references. I don't know what the hell to do; I ain't got no credit. But I remember the time Sparky lent me ten bucks; I paid him back most of it. So I tell him Sparky and he writes it down. I think the guy's gonna throw me the fuck outta his office, but he don't. Just tells me to come back tomorrow.

"Hell, I'm no fool. He's just fuckin' with me, or maybe he's gonna call the cops; I can't figure out if I'm comin' back. But I don't know; somethin' inside told me to go back. So the next day I'm in Fred's office again. Tells me I'm approved for a $100 loan to pay back when I can. Has me sign some fancy-lookin' contract and gives me $100 straight outta his wallet.

"Next day I see Fred leaving the bank. He sees me and calls me over. I'm startin' to get it; he's fuckin' gay and thinks he's gonna get me. Well, fuck him, I think, but I go over. Ya know, I used to let fags suck me off for money when I was a kid. So I'm tryin' to decide. Do I roll him? Do I fuck him? But it ain't like that; he really wants to be a friend. Shit, Fred and me got to be best friends. Before ya know it we're hangin' out together, lunch here, a drink there. He even took me out fishin'. Man, this dude's got this big motherfucker of a boat. I tell ya, it's so big ya gotta take a cab to get from one end to the other. So we go out fishin'. Now Fred don't know I know how to fish, so he gives me a pole and asks if I wanna try. I play him on and say 'Guess so.' Shit, I'm pullin' in one fish after another. The guy tells me I'm a helluva fisherman, says he ain't never seen nobody fish so good the first time. So I just break out laughin' and tell him it ain't my first time. No, I fished lotsa times with my dad. My dad was some helluva guy. Used to take me everywhere. Went fishin', huntin', ball games, everywhere. John and Pop. Never seen him without me or me without him. A helluva guy.

"So, did you get to fish while you were away?"

Peter answered, "No."

"I know. You guys just don't know how to relax. It's all business. That's why I left the dog race myself." John takes a drag on his cigarette and stops talking for several minutes before going on with, "Talkin' 'bout dog races, I never told ya 'bout the time I went to Florida...," words Peter hardly heard, now that he was deeply immersed in thoughts about the map in his pocket. *I can't check the map now. Try to think. Joe's Newsstand, Midtown Coffee Shop, bent street sign.* Again, he thought *Joe's Newsstand, Midtown Coffee Shop, bent street sign.* Each time he said *bent street sign,* he shuddered, knowing he should notify the authorities about this problem. He pictured himself on the phone.

"New York City, Department of Public Works."

"Hello, this is Peter Branstill."

"Yes, sir. How can I help you?"

"I ride the Broadway bus between 88th Street and my office at Lerner and Schwartz, Public Accountants, every day."

"Yes, you just got back from Indianapolis: the Sterling and Warner audit. Heard you did a helluva job."

"Before I went, I checked everything out, just to make sure it was still there, the same, when I got back. I noticed your street sign at 47th and Broadway was bent. It still is."

Peter hears a gasp. The man's breath sounds heavy. "We're on it," he says, hanging up. Sirens sound as the SWAT team of the Department of Public Works is on its way.

"Ha, ha, ha!" John laughs loudly. "Did ya get that? Who's the master and who's the dog. Boy, did I get 'em at the track. Ya know what I always say, if ya can't take the heat, then don't put your dishes in the kitchen. Anyway, I'm glad you're back. I gotta go but I'll see ya next week."

■ ■ ■

Back at work, Peter passed Carl in the hall. "Hear you do audits now," he said. "And it only took you twenty-five years." As Carl left, Peter began to think. *I started working for Max part-time in my senior year of high school on February 15. I was eighteen years old then. I'm forty-three now. I left for Indianapolis on July 19 and started the audit the next day, so it actually took me twenty-five years plus twenty-eight minus fifteen, thirteen days, plus sixty days for two thirty-day months, April and June, thirty-one days for May, and nineteen days in July. Thirteen plus sixty plus thirty-one plus nineteen equals one hundred twenty-three: 25 years, 123 days to do my first audit.* For the rest of the afternoon, Peter kept picturing himself auditing the books of Waller Enterprises, Inc., showing John the entry: 25 years, initialed CS. "Fuckin' ambi-lung-uous," says John. "Call him in." From the edge of the boat, Peter casts a line, hooks Carl, and reels him in. It's John and Peter, fishing, hunting, playing baseball, never see one without the other. Peter looks up: It's 5:00 p.m. He puts his work neatly away and walks out.

On the way home from work, Peter kept thinking: *After twenty-five years and one hundred twenty-three days, my first audit. I'm a real accountant.* Preparing to board the bus, he looked at his briefcase, knowing he still had a copy of *Horse and Saddle* inside. *I need something else for the ride home.* Peter walked to Joe's Newsstand, and after scanning the magazines for several minutes, trying to keep his eyes off the girlie magazines, he settled on *Business Week,* a fine selection for an accountant. The bus was less crowded than usual, a clean seat available near the middle. He sat down and opened his magazine. Trying to read an article on tax-deferred investments, Peter noticed an Indian woman across the aisle, three seats ahead. Her long flowered dress reminded him of the manicured cemetery where Mom rests. Throughout the ride, he imagined himself held by this woman until the bus stopped at 57th Street, where she stood up, looked back, and exited the bus. *Red dirt!* Peter saw a red spot of average size, round and evenly colored, on her forehead. He couldn't rate the spot without touching or smelling it, but felt chills down his spine looking at the woman's mark. For the rest of the ride, he hid behind his magazine.

At home, Peter started his normal routines, finally calming down as he spun around 360° in Mom's bedroom, having an ordinary evening until bedtime when he picked up *Business Week* instead of a girlie magazine. Finishing the article on tax-deferred investments, he turned the page to see a picture of a large, strong, handsome, rugged, muscular, sensitive animal, staring at him longingly with the words above: *Merrill Lynch, We're Bullish on America.*

In the morning, Peter proceeded uneventfully through his usual routines, arriving at Mom's grave at 1:30 p.m., sitting down and taking out his records on nonfood, personal items – toothpaste, toothbrushes, shampoo, soap, deodorant – studying and fine-tuning his plans. He made one minor decision: to cut a new test bar of Ivory soap. He had cut the old bar in seven pieces of unequal weight, not considering the effects of the bar's rounded edges. He studied one major issue: which toothpaste to buy in light of new toothpaste technology, the tartar control, whitening pastes, breath-freshening products, baking soda, and multipurpose pastes now on the market. Once finished, Peter moved his chair 5 feet to the left, 26 feet back, forming a right triangle with Mom's and Dad's graves. He looked at Mom's grave and softly asked, "Can John come over to play?"

■ ■ ■

Surprised by his words, Peter thought about Sammy, the only boy who ever came over to play. In July 1961, when Peter was nine, Sammy Pietrowski moved into Apartment 5E, two floors above Peter's apartment, 27 feet, 3 inches down the hall. They met in the garbage area in the basement, Sammy bringing a bag down while Peter was preparing his bag, which had become asymmetrical as he carried it downstairs.

"Hey there! I'm Sammy," Sammy called out seeing Peter. "We just moved in. This is cool. I thought I was the only kid in the building." Satisfied that his bag was ready for disposal, Peter placed it in the center of a garbage can, careful that it didn't touch any of the sides. As Peter looked sheepishly away, Sammy added, "So what's your name?" Still looking away, Peter said, "Peter."

"That's great, Pete. Maybe we can play. I got a great room and a neat bongo drum, and lotsa baseball cards. You collect cards, too?"

"Yes," Peter said, picturing his mint-condition card collection, the cards moved directly from the packs to his album while wearing rubber gloves, left-handed hitters and pitchers on the left sides of the album, right-handed hitters and pitchers on the right sides of the album, switch hitters never placed in the album until he had two identical cards, one for each page.

"Great! Let's get together and trade 'em, or flip 'em, or play baseball with 'em. I like to put together a team. I've got an awesome one with Mickey in center, the Moose at first, and Whitey pitching. I'll put my guys up against yours." Peter shuddered, picturing his cards crumpled and stained. "Anyway, I gotta go. Told Mom I'd be right back."

Not coming out of his room the rest of the summer except each Wednesday to take down the garbage, Peter didn't see Sammy again until school started. When he got to his new class, Sammy quickly spotted Peter, saying, "Hey, cool, man. We got the same teacher," unaware this simple greeting cost him two months in the popular clique. Until he found other friends, Sammy pursued Peter actively.

That afternoon after school, Sammy knocked on Peter's door. With Peter already in his room, Sally answered, saying, "Peter, where's your key? I'll change the lock tomorrow. You want some milk and cookies?" Sammy sat at the kitchen table drinking his milk, eating cookies, while Sally told him about how his father died two years ago, choking on a piece of meat.

The next day, Peter couldn't get in the apartment: His key didn't work. Standing, trying to decide what to do, Sammy came up and said, "Hey, Pete. Wanna play?" When Peter failed to answer, Sammy added, "What's the matter?"

"My key doesn't work," Peter said. "No problem," Sammy said. "If your mom ain't home, we'll go to my house." Sammy knocked loudly, Sally opened the door, and Peter went straight to his room. After finishing his milk and cookies, Sally handed Sammy a new key to the apartment. "I had the locks changed."

From then on, Peter waited for Sammy to let him into his apartment after school each day. Sammy and Sally would share a snack, Sammy often showing Sally his homework or telling a story about his day at school, while Peter watched from his bedroom door, holding Howdy in his right hand perfectly perpendicular to the ground, thinking that the real Peter was sitting with Sally at the kitchen table. At school, Peter followed Sammy, pleased with his success, feeling accepted by peers for the first time.

One day, Peter overheard Sammy talk with Tom Carroll. "Sammy, want to come over to my house today? I just got a new Monopoly game."

"Cool," said Sammy. "Where do ya live?"

"At 476 88th Street."

"That's across the street from my house. If it's OK with Mom, I'll be there."

"I'll be in the courtyard playing ball. When you get there, we'll go upstairs."

"Cool," Sammy replied.

That afternoon, Peter waited by the door to his apartment for two hours until Sally, frantic, opened the door. After a double take she asked, "What are you doing here?"

"My key didn't work."

Sally checked the key herself, let Peter in, and said, "I guess I'll have to change the locks tomorrow." With that, Peter went to his room. Sally cleared the table, throwing out the milk and cookies already set there.

11

Otto

That Sunday, Peter woke up early, opened up his new copy of *American Horseman,* and masturbated to the picture of a brown American saddle horse. Peter thought that horse seemed sensitive. His orgasm scored 7 with a positive valence, bringing the total score for this new magazine to a positive 1, compensating for the two negative but less intense orgasms he already had looking at the other horses.

Later that day, Peter left the apartment and walked to Aunt Cindy's brownstone, where he found the front door open. For five minutes he stood by the door, not knowing what to do. With the door open, he would either have to enter the vestibule, crossing the door jamb, without Aunt Cindy's permission, or lean over at a 70° angle to reach the door at the proper point of contact. Peter strongly believed that doors should be knocked at a 90° angle to the ground. And there was no way to keep an open door from moving with the knock. As Peter pondered his dilemma, a large man with blond hair in work clothes came to the door, opened his mouth wide with surprise, and said,

"Well, I'll be a sonofabitch. Where the hell have you been? My God. Little Georgie Branstill."

The man quickly leaned forward, smiling, holding his hand to his mouth in a fake whisker, "I can call you George. She's dead."

Peter was shocked to see his cousin Otto standing in front of him. Otto looked Peter up and down before going on.

"My God, George. Where the hell have you been? No one knew you were around, and now, today, of all days, you come by, one week late. You missed the funeral. I'm sure the old bitch, I mean Aunt Cindy would've wanted you there. Well, can't do nothing about that now. She died last Sunday night. Seems she had some company." Otto beamed a knowing smile. "Well, that's the way she would've wanted it. Everyone knew she always whored around, but at her age. Must have been some strange dude. Left this weird plate of food, everything cut up in cubes and pyramids, laid out perfectly on the plate. We found her dead on Monday, had her burned on Tuesday. So, how you doing?"

Before Peter could answer, Otto continued, "Listen, I've always wanted to ask you: Was that shit true? Was your mom really a virgin? I mean, I know she couldn't have been one and had you, but they always said your mom and dad never did it the first ten years they were married." Peter looked down. "I know, man. We had some laughs but we were fucking cruel, and not just to your mom and dad, but to you, too. Remember the time George Quincy stole your pants. I bet that was the last time you took a crap at school." Otto touched Peter's shoulder, adding, "Now how about helping me with some of these boxes?"

Otto and Peter each picked up a box and walked to the open U-Haul truck, parked on the street. Squeezing the boxes in a small space left in the back of the truck, Otto said, "I never knew what Aunt Cindy had against your dad. Sure, he was simple and everyone knew he was retarded, but he was still a nice guy. Kind of sad watching him sit by himself in the kitchen."

Peter looked at Aunt Cindy's furniture inside the U-Haul as Otto pulled down the rear gate. "Well, you look like you've done well for yourself. What do you do? An undertaker?" Otto laughed. "Just kidding, but you gotta do something about those duds, not that you were ever much of a dresser. I always told ya, you gotta dress sharp if you wanna be popular.

"Well, I'm done. Most of her shit's out, but if there's something you'd like, feel free. Anyway, stop by sometime. Don't be such a stranger. Marge would love to see you." Otto opened the door to the driver's seat, started the truck, and drove away.

Peter walked back up the steps and stood by the door for another two minutes, still in a quandary about how to knock on the door. He decided it was better to lean 70° and did so, making a strong 2-1-2 knocking sound. Peter shuddered as the door moved about 7 inches. After waiting another four minutes, Peter knocked on the door again, now having to lean at a 67° angle, accounting for the door's new position following the last knock, this time knocking softly enough to prevent more than another 1-inch additional movement. Peter stood pleased about his better knock, a feeling that quickly left when no one answered the door. Peter thought back to Otto's words, "She's dead," and realized that there was no one home to answer, so he walked in.

The apartment was virtually bare. The pictures were removed from the walls, Aunt Cindy's fine furniture gone, even the fixture holding the bulb he changed last week, and the bulb, were gone. All that was left were three old bridge chairs and a pile of magazines. Peter sat on one of the chairs, realizing that his record of dinners with Aunt Cindy ended at twenty-two hundred.

■ ■ ■

"Remember the time George Quincy stole your pants," thought Peter. But the memory didn't come. George Quincy. Stole your pants. George Quincy. Stole my pants. George Quincy. Crap at school. George Quincy. King George. Staring at the wall, Peter pictured PS 23, the school near Aunt Cindy's brownstone. Dad had just died and Mom was in the hospital. The first night staying with Aunt Cindy, she made Peter take off his shirt and lie face down on her bed.

"What's your name?" she yelled. "George," Peter replied. A loud crack, the belt buckle striking him three-eighths of the way down from the top of his back, Peter screamed. "Shut up. Don't make a sound. I don't want anyone to hear. Now damn you, what's your name?"

Again, Peter answered, "George," followed by another sharp crack of the belt, this time 2 inches to the right of the last one. Without a sound, tears dribbling down his cheeks, Peter waited until Aunt Cindy asked again, "What's your name?" Four beltings later, Peter replied, "What is my name?"

"Peter. You're Peter Alfred Branstill. I'll go to court and change your last name, too. You should never have been named for that dog of a father you had. If I ever hear you using the name George again, I'll beat you ten times harder, like this." Again, Aunt Cindy whips the belt against Peter's back. "I'll stuff your mouth with food till you die, just like that dog."

The next morning before Peter left for school, Aunt Cindy told him, "Today's your first day of school since the dog died. I'm putting you in a different school until your mother comes home. Your name is Peter. Otto's in this school, too. He knows your name. Don't ever say the dog's name again, or I'll kill you."

Breaking from these thoughts, Peter looked around the room. Otto took the table. *Where are we going to have dinner?* He looked at his watch, 3:18 p.m., too early to go home. As he sat, he thought more about PS 23 and George Quincy, the boy who had his name.

A popular, good-looking, strong youngster, a class leader, George Quincy, known as King George, was a savvy bully who rarely got into fights himself. During recess, he sat under a tree, with the girls around him offering him snacks from their lunch boxes. King George carefully made his selection, the lucky girl feeding him personally. Watching King George from afar, Peter longed for his name and to be fed. Even as an adult, he sometimes thought back to that scene, masturbating to fantasies of the girls feeding him.

The boys King George liked became warriors. The others were his enemies. While King George sat with the girls, his warriors circled the playground, spying on the enemies, returning periodically with scouting reports and to receive new orders. When King George ordered Peter's arrest, he came.

"We've arrested Peter Branstill," one of the boys said, saluting King George as he talked. Shocked by how quickly they captured Peter, King George asked about the chase. "He didn't run, sir. He just came."

"What a dork. OK, Peter, bow down." Peter bowed down. "Pray for my mercy." Peter held his hands together in silent prayer. "Not a church prayer: Say, 'Sire, grant me mercy.'" Peter said, "Sire, grant me mercy."

"Okay, now say 'Long live King George.'" Peter replied, "Long live the King."

"I said, say 'Long live King George,'" King George said. "Long live the King," said Peter. "King George! I said," shouted the King. His lips quivering, tears in his eyes, Peter said nothing. King George looked at the others; they silently awaited his next move. Nancy, who was feeding the King before Peter's arrest, said, "Aw, he's scared. Leave him alone."

An angry look in his eyes, King George hit the ground with his baseball glove and shouted to the warriors. "Kick him in the balls."

"In the balls?" Stanley said. "Cluck, cluck, cluck," Ted responded, his hands at his armpits prancing like a chicken, as the others started a tense round of dares and double dares, arguing among themselves about who was too afraid to kick Peter in the balls. Finally Margaret, who had been sulking ever since King George took Nancy's treat over hers, said, "Oh, for God's sake. I'll do it myself."

At that moment Simon Minsky stepped forward and kicked toward Peter's balls. An uncoordinated youngster known for striking out at kickball, Simon's actions shocked the children. He predictably missed the mark.

"Eek!" squealed Peter, catching the playground monitor's attention. Quickly, Margaret pointed her finger toward Simon, saying, "He did it." Simon pointed his finger at George. "He ordered it."

The monitor made the children stand against the wall of the school building while she sent Peter to the school nurse. The nurse made Peter strip so she could carefully inspect his genitals: No marks, the kick never landed. "You're lucky," she said. "There's nothing there."

Later that day, the principal met with Peter, Simon, and King George. "Children," he said. "Peter's father just died and his mother is in a mental hospital. Please don't taunt him anymore. He's a very sensitive boy and needs a lot of understanding. Now let's shake hands." Following a hearty round of handshakes and a promise to be Peter's friend, the boys left. Proudly, the principal watched the children go down the hall. After turning the corner, too far to be heard, King George said to Peter: "You're dead meat."

That evening words swirled in Peter's head. *Dead meat. Dad died eating meat. George is dead. Pete is meat.* Peter could not sleep anticipating the end of his life the next day. He prayed for a miracle. His prayers were answered when he awoke to a hard rain. Recess was indoors.

It rained the rest of the week. By Monday the sun was out. Terrified, Peter watched the clock tick minute by minute toward recess. After the bell rang, he walked out slowly, expecting to meet his destiny. Across the playground, he saw King George playing baseball. For the next week George and the other boys played baseball while the girls played jumprope and jacks, as Peter stood pensively by the sidelines, appreciating his reprieve.

■ ■ ■

Peter looked at his watch, 5:00 p.m., and got up. He looked at the magazines and chairs: *Where's the table? What did we have for dinner?* Looking around, seeing that Aunt Cindy was not there, he left Aunt Cindy's apartment.

Once home, Peter thought: *George Quincy, stole your pants. When did King George steal my pants? What did Otto mean? I never used the bathroom at school.*

Peter went to his file cabinet, opened the drawer marked G through L, and retrieved a large folder marked History of My Life. In the folder, there were five notebooks, Birth through 10 years, 10 years through 20 years, 20 years through 30 years, 30 years through 40 years, 40 years through 50 years. Peter opened the last notebook, removing the last page, *Peter died today, July 23, 1995* and replaced it with a new page, *Peter died either today, July 23, 1995, or in his sleep the night of July 24, 1995, possibly the next day after midnight.* Then on another page, he wrote *July 23, 1995, Peter masturbated once today. He did not think he went mad waking in the morning, he wore clothing combination 36273* (the digits respectively identifying which suit, shirt, tie, socks, and shoes he wore). *I learned that Aunt Cindy was dead from Cousin Otto, the first time I've seen him in 5 years, 2 months, 3 days since Mom's funeral, and the* – Peter stops to check another book that referenced the number of contacts he had with each person in his life – *1,587th time I've seen Cousin Otto during my life.* He then returned to the page documenting last Sunday's activities, adding: *Aunt Cindy died today. She may have died while I was there.*

After putting this volume away, Peter pulled out the notebook

Birth Through 10 Years, opened to the section on seven years of age, turned to Living with Aunt Cindy, and added, *George Quincy took my pants while at school.* On the line below he wrote: *Last known time to have used the bathroom at school.*

That night, Peter dreamt he was surrounded by beautiful girls feeding him sumptuous treats, surgical gloves on their hands. Long live King Peter, they shout. The crowd lifts the legs of Peter's throne. High in the air, the crowd chants: Go to the bathroom. We want a crap. Peter pushes hard, a baby comes out of his rectum. Under a shining star, Otto asks, What's its name? With a twisted face, Aunt Cindy screams: You're fucking dead. Peter looks up and sees his pants flying from a cross.

12

Kids

On Monday, Peter walked to the bench still asking himself, *When did King George take my pants?* His thoughts broke when he saw John already at the bench. John calls out, "Hey, Petey. Look, I'm respectable now. Got my own smokes. I ain't gonna bum no more. Watch."

John gets off the bench and calls to the first passerby, "Hey buddy, gotta light?"

The man takes a lighter out from his coat pocket. John reaches for the pack rolled in the sleeve of his shirt, pulls out a cigarette, and says, "Thanks, man," as he lights the cigarette. Then he offers one to the man, who refuses and goes hurriedly on his way.

John comes back to the bench. Instead of propping himself on the back as he did as Peter arrived, he simply sits down, seeming mellow, asking Peter, "Ya got kids?"

Not waiting for an answer, John goes on. "Yeah, man, I'd really like to have a family. I'm real lonely. Could use a wife. Ya get tired of a piece of ass here, a whore there. No, I could use a good wife. And kids. Lotsa kids: 10, 20, 30 kids. Barefoot and pregnant. Yeah, keep 'em barefoot and pregnant.

"Really man, I'm serious. I've been thinkin' a lot about havin' kids. Life ain't mean nothin' without 'em. Ya know, people say ya go to heaven when ya die. Some folks say I'm goin' the other way. Shit, my life's hell now, so how could it be worse?

"I don't know 'bout heaven and hell. Maybe they got it right in India: Ya ain't no mental patient, you're just fuckin' untouchable. Everybody thinks I'm untouchable anyway. Ya saw that guy. Gave me a light but wouldn't take a smoke from me. Everyone but you.

You're OK, man. Ya even shook my hand when we met."

John turns to Peter asking, "Your kids okay? Stayin' outta trouble. Bet they don't use drugs. Good schools? That's the way it should be." For a few minutes there is silence as John drifts off into thought.

Peter was puzzled. He liked John and appreciated his interest, and it usually didn't bother him that John never waited for an answer. But kids. Why would he think I have kids?

"I think that's how you face death," John goes on. "Children, lotsa children. Kids that look like ya. Kids who take care of ya. I sure hope they don't act like me. Ya know I'm really fucked up. It's the drugs. Well, who knows? I mighta turned out just the same without 'em. But I could use a kid. Otherwise, it don't make no sense." John gets up to leave.

"Listen, I can't stay. I just gotta be alone before I go back... ya know, I think I'll just walk around and go home. I can't go back there."

As John left, Peter sat and thought a while. John had been edgy today, and Peter thought it might have been something he had said or done earlier. He felt guilty that he might have upset John. *John doesn't really care if I have any kids or not.*

Peter then pictured himself with a child who looked much like John. He and the child ate lunch together, the child's sandwich cut in the form of a perfect six-point star, his an isosceles triangle. They are joined by an obese woman named Shirley. She lifts her dress, and twenty-nine children drop from her crotch. She turns to Peter and says, "I always loved you." Peter takes a bite of his sandwich: *a strange taste.* He lifts the top piece of bread. The sandwich is made of snot.

Suddenly, jarring Peter from his thoughts, John reappears, agitated and angry. "Those motherfuckers, Petey. Those fuckin' motherfuckers. How dare they. How goddamn dare they tell me I ain't a good father. I didn't leave that kid. It was them welfare assholes. They goddamn fuckin' took that kid. I don't care how stoned I was. Sure I was messed up but they goddamn fuckin' took the kid from me. They say they want to help. Well, fuck 'em. Sure I let 'em have her. What the fuck was I supposed to do? Her mom was in jail and I was fucked up. But she was my goddamn daughter and they took her and they – they fuckin' kidnapped her right under my nose, in front of a judge.

Acted like they were gonna help me out. I straightened up, I did everything they told me to do, and they fuckin' took her away from me.

"I went through a program but they wanted another thirty days, to be sure, and then maybe another sixty days, and then I needed a better place to stay, and then it wasn't fuckin' clean enough, and then how come I ain't got no job, so I get a job, and how can I take care of her if I ain't home, workin' at my job? So I get me a girlfriend who'll stay home and take care of her and they say, well, what if it don't work out. Whatever I did, it was wrong, it was goddamn wrong. Because they decided. They wanted my daughter to stay in the fuckin' foster home. They didn't even have the goddamn decency to tell me where she was stayin' or who the foster parents were or even let me take her out to eat. No, they had to supervise every fuckin' visit. What the hell were they 'fraid of, that I'd fuck my own daughter?

"And now I gotta sit in a goddamn group with some motherfuckin' psycho tellin' me I ain't a good parent, because *his* whore of a mother was on drugs and fucked *him* up. Man, I ain't gonna take it. I'll hurt someone. I tell ya man, I'm gonna hurt somebody. I don't wanna do that. Just chill out. Just chill out. Man, I'm really fucked up today." His face beet red, John gets up and says, "I'm gonna call my sponsor. I ain't goin' back there, never. Listen man, thanks for the ear. You're a good friend. I gotta go."

Peter watched John as he backed away, kicking a bench and punching a tree on his way. After John faded from sight, he thought about John's kid. *Confusing. How could John care for a child?* He smiled to himself, thinking about Mom. Then images of Aunt Cindy, Ma Burns, and Beaver Camp came to mind. *Ugh!* Peter looked at his watch: Lunch is over. As he walked back to work, cringing all the way, he knew for sure that his mother was far better than any of the places they put him while she was away.

■ ■ ■

Peter remembered being placed in a foster home when he was ten years old. Cindy and her brothers – Peter's uncles Mike and Peter – went on a family vacation to a resort hotel, leaving Sally and Peter behind. Before leaving, Cindy told Sally that she and Peter were an embarrassment to the family and that they were going away without them. She lied, saying that their two brothers agreed with her. Without leaving any information about their destination, the rest of the family took off without the Branstills.

Throughout the week, Sally talked on and on, paced endlessly, cried for no apparent reason, and screamed often. By Friday she called Peter's psychologist, Dr. Kline, for help.

With Dr. Kline away for the weekend, his calls were handled by his associate, Dr. Levitt, who didn't know Peter or Sally. Sally babbled on, telling Dr. Levitt she couldn't make it through the weekend, referring mostly to the fact that they were out of food and Cindy left her without money. Thinking she was suicidal, Dr. Levitt called the police, who took Sally away, leaving Peter's care over the weekend to the Bureau of Child Welfare.

■ ■ ■

Jenny Myers, a fashionably dressed 28-year-old social worker, a woman with heavy makeup, lavish jewelry, a strong Long Island accent, came for Peter. Three months pregnant, waiting for her baby's birth and her husband's graduation from medical school to leave her job, she took Peter in her Porsche to her office. Without talking with Peter, she made the necessary arrangements to place him in Suzie Burns' foster home.

Suzie's house had eight extra beds for foster children. Peter shared a room with three other boys; four girls stayed in another bedroom. Except for Peter, all the children talked about sex constantly. "I'll wash out your fucking mouths with soap," Suzie often screamed to no avail. Throughout, Peter tried to visualize how Suzie would divide a six-pack of soap between the eight children. *That's three bars for the four boys, three bars for the four girls. If three boys and three girls get 3/4 of a bar each, then there are three 1/4 bars left for the other boy and the other girl, assuming they count me even though I never curse. If she doesn't count me, then each boy gets a full bar of soap and each girl gets 3/4 of a bar of soap. I wonder if she'll divide the bars equally among all four girls. Mary and Samatha don't really curse that much. I guess they could share a bar.*

Peter hardly ate during the five months with Mrs. Burns, afraid he would die eating from Suzie's communal serving trays. With meals served family style, the bravest and strongest took most of the meager portions. Seven pairs of hands fought over each morsel, while Peter sat quietly, thinking about the cylindrical piece of stew meat that killed his father.

After months in the Burns home, Peter had given up all hope of ever leaving or seeing his mother again. One day, Jenny visited Peter in the home. Leaving his case record in her office, she forgot who he was, referring to him as Larry, a similarly built youngster she had visited the week before. Larry's parents had recently died. His father was bisexual and had been murdered trying to solicit another man. His mother committed suicide the next day. As soon as she arrived, without asking Peter questions, Jenny started telling him about her efforts to find a permanent adoptive home.

"Listen, Larry. You're gonna have to be strong. Your parents are dead and you gotta accept that. There's no one out there who loves you. I'm trying the best I can but there's a lot of kids who need homes as much as you. We gotta be fair. We're trying, but remember, it's gonna be hard to find a home for a kid whose father was a fag and whose mother blew her brains out. I still can't believe your dad was such a jerk, cheating on your mom, taking it up the ass. My husband would never do that. He's a true man. Hmmm, he's good. No limp wrist for me. It's not that I haven't had lovers, but Irv. No. He's quite a guy. Got me pregnant on the first try. Well, you just be careful. You don't want to be queer yourself. So don't turn your back on anyone."

As Jenny talked, Peter thought: *Larry, that's not bad. It's got five letters just like Peter. George has six letters. Larry's a nickname and Peter's a full name. Pete is short for Peter and that has four letters. I think Larry's a nickname for Lawrence: eight letters. OK, Pete is four. Peter and Larry: five. George has six. Lawrence has eight. Four for Pete plus five each for Peter and Larry: 14. Add six for George, twenty, and another eight for Lawrence is twenty-eight.* Peter wistfully pictured Howdy at home on the dresser with Buffalo Bob and Clarabelle Clown. *Five for Howdy, three for Bob, Clarabelle is ten. Five plus three plus ten plus twenty-eight is forty-six.*

"Well, let's talk with Ma Burns now." Peter and Jenny went to the kitchen where Ma was sitting, drinking coffee. They sat at the table. Jenny asked, "Is Larry being good?"

Ma started to answer, "Yeah, he's OK. Don't eat too much but…"

Before she could finish Jenny blurted out, "Oh, don't let me forget. I have to pick up dinner on the way home. Irv won't mind. We'll have pizza. Well, I'm glad Larry's doing well. You know, some of these parents are out of sight, really bad. I'm getting sick and tired of picking up the pieces. I tell you, I'm really gonna feel better after I go out on maternity leave. Don't tell anyone, but I'm not coming back."

As Jenny talked, Peter noticed a small blue spot on the right sleeve of her dark green jacket. Curious if it was a speck or a stain, but afraid to be seen staring at her, he quickly picked six locations in the room, Jenny's right sleeve, the top of her chair, a clock on the wall, the refrigerator handle, the left lens on Ma Burns' glasses, and the toaster on the kitchen counter, and systematically shifted his view from one location to the other while counting to ten in his head. Studying the spot during the ten seconds he looked there each minute, he confirmed it was a blue stain, approximately 1/8 inch across. He estimated the length by picturing the ruler in his desk at school against the stain. Years later, Peter developed the Graduated Dirt Rating Scale, crediting Jenny for helping him identify color and size as significant variables when evaluating dirt.

Jenny looked at her watch and said, "Look, I've gotta go. It's Irv's birthday tomorrow. I'll be in the office and won't have a chance to get out and buy him a gift. That's one of the good things about working in the field. You can get out early. Well, it's been good to see you, Mrs. Burns. Keep your spirits up, Larry. We'll find you a permanent home."

While Peter stayed in foster care, Sally sat home waiting for his return. She never considered contacting the authorities to speed up the process, and of course no one contacted her because Jenny thought she was dead. Meanwhile Cindy, who was irate that Sally couldn't handle one week alone, and accustomed to Peter isolating himself in his room, failed to notice that he was not at home. Finally, Jenny left the agency to deliver her baby and Peter's case was reassigned. The new caseworker was shocked to learn that Peter continued to live in foster care while his mother was home, with no plan. She quickly went to Ma Burns' house, picked Peter up, and brought him home. Peter went directly to his room after warmly shaking hands with his mother.

13

Shirley

On Thursday, Peter was back on the bench having lunch when John approached, with a big smile on his face, bellowing out, "Hey Petey. Did I ever tell ya 'bout the violent ward?

"Ya know, I once knew this guy at State. Real weird dude. They said he cut his prick off with a knife, so they locked him up in the violent ward. Fuckin' strange if you ask me! The violent ward? Ain't like he cut nobody else's prick off. And he ain't got no more pricks of his own left to cut.

"Heard he'd been there for years. Doped him up real bad. I heard they cut out a piece of his brain, ya know, a lobotomy. They used to do that to psychos. Can't figure it out. He cuts his own prick, they cut his brain. What's that thing they'd say in church? An eye for an eye. Imagine: a brain for a prick, and both the brain and prick were his.

"Anyways, one day I get real mad. I mean like real fuckin' mad, so I start this big fight. You shoulda seen me, throwin' chairs and screamin' like all hell broke loose. Them other patients were scared shitless, didn't know what hit 'em, half of 'em hid in a corner. Now, it ain't like I don't know what's gonna happen. Ya can't do that long without gettin' sent up, to the violent ward, ya know. I didn't wanna go, at first, and I tried real hard to hold back. But then I saw it in the shrink's eyes. I'm sure I was pissed off at him, so he's thinkin' 'bout his rep. Shit, I know I'm goin' so what the hell? I figures I may's well hurt someone, so I do."

John stops for a moment, saying wistfully, "Didn't wanna hurt her." Following a pause, he adds, "Shoulda clocked the fuckin' shrink instead."

He shakes his head and says, "Before ya know it, one thing leads to another and there's little old me on that violent ward. Now I'm really fuckin' mad. But they shoot me up with all kinds of shit and I calm down. It's my first time there. Real weird, dark, smells like shit, quiet, real tense. Then I remember they got this dude who cut his prick off. I figure I'll look him up, so I ask 'round and find out who he is. The guy's pacin' back and forth, really burnt out. Looks like a lifer. So, I go right up to him and say, 'Hey, ain't you the guy who cut off his prick?'

"He tries to ignore me but he looks kinda mad. A little scary, not that I ain't scared of nobody: I can handle myself cause I'm Street. And I get a feelin' the shrink's got him up there for a good reason. Probably some real sonofabitch when he was younger, but now he's got no prick, half a brain, doped up with meds so I figure he can't do nothing to me. So I goes up real easy and says, 'No, really man. I wanna know if you're the guy who cut off his prick.'

"He still don't answer. I figure I gotta let him know that I ain't gonna hurt him. Ain't gonna tease him. I just wanna know.

"I see him pacin' up and down the ward, exactly the same way every time. So I get up real close to him and start walkin' up and down the ward just like him. We keep walkin' up and down the ward together for a long time before I make my move. When we get near the wall, I drop back and move to the side. He hits the wall, turns 'round, and I'm right in his face. I says, 'Really man, I'm only askin' cause I heard ya did it and I just wanna know if ya thought it was a good idea.'

"He stopped pacin' and paused. I don't think nobody ever asked him that before. He looked me right in the eye and said, 'No, I wish I hadn't of done it.'

"I said, 'I understand man. Sometimes, somethin' seems like a good idea at the time but it just don't work out the way ya thought it would. I count to ten before I do anything. It sure helps me not make a whole lotta mistakes.'

"I thought I really helped him. Shame I didn't know him before. It's that simple. Ya wanna cut your prick off, ya count to ten. Before ya know it, ya change your mind."

"Well, we're havin' a party today. Sure wish I could invite ya but they got a rule: fruitcakes only." John slaps himself jokingly and smiles at Peter, "that's patients only," adding as he left, "See ya tomorrow."

■ ■ ■

Peter finished his lunch, and after placing the refuse neatly in the lunchbag and folding the bag into an isosceles triangle with two 70° angles and one 40° angle, he stood up, walked past a nearly empty trash can, dropped the bag precisely in the middle of the container, and went back to work.

Peter repeated John's words over and over again in his mind: *It's that simple. Ya wanna cut your prick off, ya count to ten. Before ya know it, ya change your mind.*

Peter hated masturbating, the peep shows, horses, and the notebooks he kept. He understood little about his penis except that it tormented him daily. He studied anatomy books, sex guides, *National Geographic* magazines, and photographs of victims of the Holocaust, all in an effort to better understand his sex organ. While he owned a large and lush collection of pornographic materials and used it regularly, he still could not describe the parts or the acts. He could never remember what he saw. *God, I should just cut it off,* he often thought. Now John tells him he met a man who cut his own penis off, confined to the violent ward, pacing back and forth, his brain cut too. Peter sat in the living room, looking toward the kitchen. *Knives,* he thought. *In a moment, it could be off.* Peter got up and walked toward the large window in his living room, touched it, and walked back to the other side of the room. Pacing back and forth touching the wall on one side, the window on the other, Peter thought, *"It's that simple. Ya wanna cut your prick off, ya count to ten. Before ya know it, ya change your mind."*

John's an idiot. What does he know? Count to ten and you won't cut it off. Simple for him but it's not his penis. I should cut it off just to spite him. Here John, take it, and by the way I counted to ten.

What if John knows I'm angry? CAN'T KEEP A FRIEND YOU LITTLE NERD. *Yes I can.* NO YOU CAN'T. PETER'S GETTING MAD. PETER'S GETTING MAD. Through the rest of the day and evening, Peter practiced how he would greet John the next day. *Hi. How are you doing? I'm not angry.* Too direct. *John, I just wanted to tell you that I was a little upset yesterday.* IDIOT. *I tried counting, it worked.* NOTHING'LL WORK FOR YOU. *One Potato, Two Potato, Three Potato, Four...* No, that won't do. *One, two, buckle my shoe. Three, four, your prick's in the door.* MISS WEINTRAUB. PETER SAID A BAD WORD.

That night, Peter dreamt that he showed up at the hospital emergency room, penis in hand. The nurse behind the counter told him they were busy, he would have to wait. He tried to be patient but became concerned as the wait continued and the penis began decomposing in his hands.

Approaching the nurse again, he demanded immediate service. Angrily, she told him to go back to the waiting room, which was now occupied by the boys from junior high school, penises in hand, also waiting for reattachment procedures. Many of them were accompanied by the girls from the class, just as eager for successful operations as the boys.

"You'll simply have to wait," the nurse repeated. "We're very busy. The people with the biggest penises go first."

Returning to his seat, he watched his penis slowly wither away. Then Shirley Parker – a girl from junior high school – came up to him. She told him that she always loved him and gave him a hug. She looked at the penis in his hand. "Oh. I didn't know it was so small!" She smiled as she walked away.

"Tom Carroll, you're next," the nurse called.

Still a jock, Tom – also from junior high school – sauntered over toward the operating room, a large penis in hand. Looking back at Peter as he left, he said, "You should've fucked her then. I told you: She wanted you, man."

Tom then turned to the nurse who was asking him what had happened. "My girl and I were really getting it on, you know, just one of those things," he said. "Cut it off in the heat of the moment. Anyway, I'm bleeding an awful lot. Thought you might be able to sew it back up... And could you do it quickly? She's waiting for me in the car."

■ ■ ■

Peter woke up in a sweat. *My God, Shirley and Tom. Where did they come from? And Shirley, what did she mean?* He jumped out of bed, went to his file, and pulled out the folder History of My Life, retrieving a small notebook at the end:

Index, PARKER, SHIRLEY:
   1. BERNIE HOFFMAN'S BAR MITZVAH
   2. STUDY HALL INCIDENT
   3. GIRLS THAT WOULD HAVE HAD SEX WITH ME

Peter quickly leafed through his notebooks, reading everything he wrote about Shirley. After putting the books away, he went back to bed, and thought about her.

■ ■ ■

"Shalom," the old bearded man said to Peter, offering his hand and a yarmulke at the same time. "Welcome to Temple Beth Zion." Peter looked at the shiny silver-gray object, six pieces of material forming the polar cap to 30° latitude of an imaginary globe, inside the engraved words: *Bernard Hoffman's Bar Mitzvah, October 9, 1965.* Folding the object, placing it in his pocket, Peter walked into the grand hall of the temple, where he was stopped by another old man, "Did you get a yarmulke?" Staring at the synagogue's large stained-glass windows, categorizing the multicolored pieces by their shapes, Peter failed to hear him until he sharply said, "Son, you must wear a hat in a synagogue." YOU IDIOT! YOUR HAT'S AT HOME.

"I'm sorry. It's at home."

"At home?" the man laughed. "We always have a yarmulke here. You know that." The man looked at Peter and asked, "A goy?" Peter did not answer but glanced at the wall, looking for a mirror, wanting to check that he was still a boy. "Please, put this on?" the man said, returning with another silver-gray yarmulke similar to the one in his pocket. Placing it directly on Peter's head, the man said, "Come in." YOU FOOL. HE KNOWS YOU'RE A GIRL. THERE'S DIRT ON THAT HAT. IT'S ASYMMETRICAL. As he walked to his seat,

Peter pictured Mom's reaction when he showed her the invitation to Bernie Hoffman's bar mitzvah.

"A birthday party! This is wonderful. We'll have to get a gift. I was invited to Jerry Schulman's bar mitzvah but Mom wouldn't let me go. She made me stay away from Jews. I didn't know why. We always had Jewish customers and they were very nice. They seemed just like us except their names ended with 'berg' or 'stein' or they had some names that didn't end with anything in particular but were still different like Cohen and Levy, or Levine, or Levin, while Irish names started with O', sometimes a Mc, but Mac's a more Scottish name. Now Branstill is an English name and it doesn't have any of those special things that make it sound like one type of name or another, but I think most people know that it's an English name. English and Irish names often mix together just like George and I mixed together, hee hee hee, but that's something else you have to stay away from. You're too young to actually, well you know, mix together with a girl, but a bar mitzvah is a nice party. They'll have a cake and you'll wear a party hat. You should have a lot of fun." Peter looked around and saw that all the men wore party hats just like his, different from the brightly colored, conical hat he wore at the only other birthday party he went to. That was a third-grade bowling party and Peter remembered that everyone laughed at him as he methodically placed the balls in the gutter, not wanting to disrupt the symmetry of the standing pins.

■ ■ ■

After the service, Peter was directed to another room, a large dining hall filled mostly with adults, where the bar mitzvah boy and his friends sat at a special table. The caterers served enormous portions of traditional Jewish food, and even though he was hungry, Peter could not eat. Watching the gluttonous crowd, thinking about his tainted head, Peter expected them all to choke to death like his father. But of all the gluttons, one, a girl his age from his school, stood out. Shirley Parker, an obese, slovenly young lady, Bernie's other non-Jewish guest from school, seemed to eat nonstop throughout the afternoon. Unbeknownst to Peter, Shirley watched him often between bites.

As Peter stood petrified, and Shirley ate, they never joined the other youngsters who ran around and acted silly. And those children did not notice Peter until the bartender started serving the boys 7 and 7s on the rocks. With Bernie's mother's covert approval, the bartender served mixed drinks filled with 90 percent 7-Up and the rest Seagram's 7. The boys acted as if they were totally intoxicated, walking in staggering lines and toasting each other. Bernie brought a drink to Peter, who refused to drink it, noticing a slight smudge on the rim of the glass and certain there'd be a second smudge caused by Bernie's fingers holding the glass. Peter just wanted to flee. Bernie taunted him for being a sissy and the group laughed at Peter but eventually went on its way, gallivanting "drunkenly" through the hall.

On Monday, Bernie could not wait to tell everybody about his Bar Mitzvah. Going up to the most popular kids in class, he said, "Boy, you missed a great party. I mean a really GREAT party. The bartender, I mean this guy was really COOL. Gave us all drinks. We got drunk as skunks. And did I rake it in? I've got some really rich relatives. I mean like mucho money, thousands. Got some nice gifts from the other kids, too. But you want to hear something really funny: Peter Branstill. Guess what he gave me. Can you believe… Lincoln Logs. Yeah, that's what he did." Bernie laughed out loud as he shared this story, never getting the response he wanted. Instead, he heard, "You know, I'd give you Lincoln Logs too, you dork."

But that wasn't the end for Peter. The story about his gift passed around school, and Peter soon became known as the Lincoln Log Boy. Deeply regretting his gaffe, Peter vowed to always avoid the other teens. And he might have succeeded if Shirley Parker had not made her own vow at Bernie's bar mitzvah, to make Peter hers.

■ ■ ■

Despite her weight and reputation among the boys as a "dog," Shirley was a pretty girl who seemed to know how to bring out the very worst in herself, wearing mismatched clothes and poorly applied makeup, seen often with her finger in her nose. Short with a stocky build, a face ravaged by pimples, and stringy hair, painfully shy, she never went to parties or hung around boys. But adolescence being what it is, she felt the same urges that most young people feel and set her sights on Peter.

She wrote "Peter and Shirley" all over her book covers. She drew hearts with Peter's name through them. She giggled whenever they passed in the hall, and she told her friends she was "in love" with him. For hours, Shirley and her best friend, Joan, plotted how to get Peter to ask her out. Realizing that Peter would never make the first move, Shirley finally decided she would have to do it herself. But unpracticed in the art, when she finally made her move, she chose – paradoxically and inexplicably – not the safety of a secluded spot but the middle of study hall. Seated three students away, she leaned toward Peter. Trying to whisper, she modulated her voice poorly and produced a booming and unintelligible noise instead. Annoyed by the disruption, the study hall monitor called out to Shirley. "Miss Parker, is there something you wanted to tell the class? Something important enough to interrupt study hall? Let's hear it, Miss Parker."

Now she was stuck. She did not know what to do. She had planned a private communication with Peter, but now Mrs. Bernstein was demanding a full confession of her private intention before the entire class. At this point, most students would act dumb. A simple "Nothing" would have sufficed. What could Mrs. Bernstein have done? Call Shirley to the front of the class? Send her to the principal's office? Most likely, Mrs. Bernstein would have grumbled and let it be. Acting dumb was the logical, typically teenage thing to do.

But Shirley was not a typical teenager. She was awkward and nerdy, fat and unpopular, and she listened to her parents. They told her not to use curse words, so she plugged her ears whenever she heard them; they told her to do her homework, so she never went out with friends until it was done. And Shirley's parents told her not to lie. Instead of acting dumb or lying, Shirley blurted out, "I wanted to ask him to study with me this afternoon. I'm in love with Peter." As Mrs. Bernstein and the class broke out in laughter, Shirley raced out of the room in tears.

Peter was confused. He thought Shirley had dropped her glove by him and scanned the floor while the class roared.

The next week, Tom Carroll – one of the most popular, athletic kids in school – walked up to Peter and asked, "So did you fuck her, man?" Peter said nothing.

"Really, man. Did you fuck Shirley? She was really hot for you."

Peter felt embarrassed and ashamed: He had not understood Shirley's outburst and could not answer Tom's question. But now, he watched her from afar, studying her movements, memorizing her schedule, hoping to have another chance. At first, Shirley still looked at Peter, waiting for him to make a move. For months, they would glance at each other. Shirley would smile, then Peter looked away. After a while, Shirley's smiles stopped, and she began spending time with Bernie Hoffman.

Over the next few years, Peter thought constantly about Shirley, knowing she wanted him, not Bernie. He had fallen in love with her but assuming Shirley would not remember what she had said or felt toward Peter, it was now too late to act. Instead, for years, he pictured himself with her, each night, as he masturbated, often after looking at the invitation he saved for Shirley and Bernie's wedding.

14

Seventy-Two Percent

On Friday, Peter went to work, still afraid he'd divulge his angry feelings to John. Hoping he would calm down in a few days, he decided to skip lunch. As he buckled down to work, he pictured himself lying on the analyst's couch, as Dr. Johnson asked, *I wonder what's going on?* Peter lay still, waiting for Dr. Johnson's next remark. *You're being very quiet today. Shhh,* thought Peter. *You've got to be quiet. I wonder what you are blocking today?* BLOCKHEAD. Finally, Peter asks, *Would you like to play a game of checkers?*

With a thunderbolt, Dr. Johnson shouts, *Ah-ha! Why do you want to play checkers with me? What are you really trying to say by asking to play checkers? What are you really feeling that you asked to play checkers instead? You're not angry at John. Are you!?* Peter begins to count, one, two, three. *Perhaps you want to play, with me, the checkers game you never got to play with your father. Fier, funf, sext. Dammit!* shouts Dr. Johnson, *I'm going to cut off your penis if you ever play checkers with your mommy!* Peter turns around and sees John sitting in Dr. Johnson's seat. *John? It's John-son!* With the word *son,* John chokes, falling to the floor dead.

A chime sounds as Peter looks at his watch: Noon. His morning's work done, he put his papers away, picked up his lunchbag, and walked to the park. But by 1:00 p.m. John had not come despite his parting words, "See ya tomorrow." Relieved, Peter went back to work sure his anger would dissipate by Monday.

■ ■ ■

That night, Peter dreamt that as he went to school, he looked up and saw a pair of pants flying from the flagpole. Looking at his body, he realizes that he's naked from the shirt down. Throughout the day, Peter slinks through his classes, hoping no one will see that he has nothing on. By now even the shirt is gone. At recess, he stands outside watching the other children play, hearing King George say, *Peter's cool. He can play with us today.* The warriors take off to bring Peter back – to honor, not humiliate him. But without his pants, Peter must hide. He backs up against the school building, his pink flesh blending with the red bricks, until all that is left are two eyes, wide open, imbedded in the mortar. Peter wakes up, Howdy calls out: *It's your last chance, jerk. Come out of the wall if you want to play.* His eyes cross the room, taking a place between Howdy and Buffalo Bob. They look back at Peter's jelly-like body, forming a growing stain on the bed: PETER CRAPPED HIS BED. PETER CRAPPED HIS PANTS.

■ ■ ■

On the train to his mother's grave, Peter recalled Otto's words: "Remember the time George Quincy stole your pants. I bet that was the last time you took a crap at school." He pictured the pants on the flagpole: *They can't be mine. They're not symmetrical. One leg is shorter than the other.*

Peter scans the school yard, looking for a child with one short leg: *King George, two equal legs, Cousin Otto, the same.* Peter passes the kickball game. It's Simon's turn. With three swift kicks, Simon strikes out. The kids shout, YOU MISSED HIS BALLS. Peter looks at Simon. *No wonder he missed, his right leg's too short.*

■ ■ ■

Sitting by his mother's grave, Peter thought about Otto's words again: "Remember the time George Quincy stole your pants. I bet that was the last time you took a crap at school." *It didn't happen. I never used the bathroom at school. Why did I take the blame? And for Simon, he tried to kick me in the balls.*

Looking at his chair, Peter saw it was positioned at the short angle of the right triangle formed with Mom's and Dad's graves. Unable to recall working on his formulas for housecleaning, he quickly opened his suitcase, pulled out the notebook Housecleaning Review,

and read:
> Dishes, begin stacking dishes with the rightmost rose at 4:00.
> Research dishwashers for replacement on November 6.
> Change dusting angle to 37°.
> Leave all other procedures unchanged.

Putting the notebook back, he looked at Mom's grave, then in the direction of Dad's grave and thought: *Why don't I ever visit Dad?* HE'S A PIECE OF SHIT! Aunt Cindy screams. *She's dead,* thought Peter. Hesitantly, he got up, folded his chair, and with the suitcase in his left hand, the chair in his right, walked to his father's grave. HE'S A SLOB. HE'S AN IDIOT. LOOK AT HIS GODDAMN GRAVY-STAINED SHIRT. SHIT! GET THAT BOWL AWAY FROM HIM. HE'S EATING LIKE A DOG. Peter continued toward his father's grave, calculating the number of days lived by each of the people commemorated on the gravestones. *Hey, George. How's your sex life? Let's see, Christmas is coming up. I know: bunk beds.* At the grave, Peter looked at his father's tombstone. Never having scrutinized it before, he read, George Alfred Branstill, Sr. Born November 3, 1911, Died March 23, 1959, nothing else. Peter looked at another grave, reading the words: Loving Husband, Father, Grandfather, Great-grandfather. Turning back to his father's grave, Peter took out his tape to measure the stone's horizontal expanse: 3 feet. Placing a pebble at the midpoint of the base, he marked a perpendicular line with a right edge and string, from the grave to a spot on the ground, 6½ feet away, where he centered his chair. Sitting in the chair, looking at the grave, he imagined Aunt Cindy saying, "Dr. Kelly had me laughing on the floor when he said, 'Maybe I'll be the first obstetrician to deliver a baby from a virgin mother since the guy that delivered Jesus.'" Then, imagining himself in the kitchen, at the far end of the triangle with Dad, Peter repeated to himself: *Why did I take the blame? And for Simon, he tried to kick me in the balls.*

∎ ∎ ∎

The next day, Peter left his apartment, taking off for Aunt Cindy's house, half expecting to have dinner although she was dead. He walked up the stairs and knocked in 2-1-2 fashion on her front door. A minute later, a man with paint-spattered overalls, an old baseball cap, and workboots answered the door.

"Can I help you?" As Peter stood blankly, not answering, the man added, "Who are you?"

"Peter."

"Listen, Peter. The apartment's not ready yet. I'm fixing it, painting, finishing some things. It'll be ready by the end of the month. The last tenant died. We'll have an open house next Sunday. Then we'll rent it." When Peter continued to stand speechless, the man finally said, "OK, I'll let you see it now."

Peter walked in, feeling regret when he saw that the chairs and magazines were gone. *I should have taken them,* he thought. With only his memories left, Peter looked at the kitchen, thinking about the bulb he changed two weeks ago. He walked into the parlor and pictured the family there, except his father, still in the kitchen wiping gravy off the front of his shirt. Peter walked into the bedroom, spying the northwest corner. He could almost hear the loud snap of Aunt Cindy's belt as it cracked across his back.

■ ■ ■

As Peter lay across Aunt Cindy's bed, his mind delicately off in a world of squares and triangles, interesting rhombi, unusual parallelograms, and pyramids with many different-sized bases, he heard the snap of the belt, CRACK. No pain. There was no need for the beatings anymore: George is dead.

"I'm sorry," Aunt Cindy cried, as she whipped him again, CRACK. "You've been a good boy. You've learned well. But your mom's coming home tomorrow. We've got to make sure."

The next day Peter waited in the apartment alone while Aunt Cindy went to get Sally from the hospital. "Don't pick up the phone. Don't answer the door. Sit here, still," she said, pointing to a wooden chair in the kitchen. "Don't make a move until I get back."

Gone for three hours, Peter sat still in the chair, now able to feel the sting of the fresh belt marks as he sat erect, his back evenly distributed against the back of the wooden chair. Knowing his face was slightly asymmetrical, his nose crooked, off by $1/16$ of an inch, he figured that the mass on the right side of his face was slightly greater than the left side. Too young to make the precise mathematical calculation he completed years later, Peter still knew he had better balance if he leaned slightly to the left. Unsure whether he should be symmetrical to the chair with respect to the shape or the mass of his head, Peter shifted every five minutes between these two positions. I TOLD YOU TO SIT STILL he heard with each move.

Upon their return, Sally and Cindy walked into the apartment. With Peter still in the kitchen, his back to his mother, not free to move, Sally failed to notice him as Cindy told her, "Sally, I changed his name to Peter. Don't give me any shit about it. You got a problem?" Sally just replied, "That's fine." With that agreement, Cindy called Peter. As he turned around, she told Sally, "Here's Peter."

"You look a lot like my son," Sally replied.

"He is, you idiot," Cindy scowled.

"Oh, that's right. You just told me."

"Now listen straight, Sally. If I ever hear you call him anything but Peter, if I ever hear him call himself George, if he even talks with a kid named George, I'm going to kill him and I'm going to kill you, too. You got that?"

"It's okay. We'll call him Peter."

The next hurdle was his former school. It was easy to convince the new school that Peter was his nickname, but his former teachers and classmates would find learning a new name a little strange. Cindy decided to get a professional opinion in her favor.

She told Sally that Peter needed professional help before he returned to his old school, so at her sister's suggestion, Sally sought a consultation with Dr. Richard Kline, the psychologist Peter later saw for therapy. Not knowing that Peter's real name was George but easily recognizing Peter's great distress, Dr. Kline recommended therapy. And at Cindy's request, he wrote the recommendation on letterhead.

With letter in hand, Cindy took Peter back to his old school and met with his principal and teacher. She explained that strangely Peter had rejected his given name, George. She assured them that while she was personally against recognizing this new name, Dr. Richard Kline, a well-known psychologist, had advised them to call him whatever he wanted. She told them Dr. Kline had strong opinions about letting Peter have his own way, that there could be great psychological damage should they act otherwise. Cindy thoughtfully produced Dr. Kline's letter to support her contention.

The principal, a conservative and tastefully dressed woman, had heard of Dr. Kline and acted as if she knew him well. She was so caught up with impressing Cindy that she didn't notice that the letter made no specific reference to the name change.

Peter's teacher, Miss Weintraub, was much more cynical. Not objecting in front of her boss, she waited until she got back to her class, took Peter aside, and said, "George, they tell me you want to be called Peter. Is that true?" Peter stood in silence, a pained expression on his face.

"That's what I thought. We'll call you by your name." She patted him on the back and said, "You can go to your seat now." As he left, she mumbled to herself, thinking about Cindy, "What a fruitcake!"

Miss Weintraub began class by welcoming George back. There was a round of applause and one of the kids shouted out, "Speech, speech!"

Normally, Miss Weintraub was very strict about behavior and would have scolded a child who called out. But today she was much too concerned about George's well-being to squabble over the infraction. Instead, she encouraged George to get up and make a speech.

Generally shy and hesitant, George usually refused to talk in front of the class. This time, however, to Miss Weintraub's great surprise, George got up, faced the class, and said, "My name is Peter."

Everyone laughed as Peter sat down.

No one knew how to respond to his declaration. Miss Weintraub decided to ignore it, continuing to address him as George. After calling on him many times with no response, she became angry. By the end of the day, Miss Weintraub, no longer sympathetic, was yelling at him for his misbehavior.

On the playground, several children came up to tell him how glad they were to see him. One thought he was very funny for saying his name was Peter as other children tried to one-up each other.

"Hi, my name is Harold."

"Hi, my name is Arthur."

"Hi, my name is John."

"Hi, my name is Bartholomew."

"Hi, my name is Coca Cola."

While the children laughed on, trying to come up with sillier and sillier names, Peter stood motionless. His mind felt heavy, cluttered with a whirlwind of thoughts: *George, Peter, Dad, meat, King George, Aunt Cindy, the nurse, beatings, the police.*

Noticing that Peter was not laughing, the children turned on him, changing now from funny names to "Peter's names."

"OK troops, follow me across the Delaware; I'm Peter Washington."

Another child scrunched his nose and made rabbit motions. "Hi, I'm George Rabbit."

"Peter, Peter, pumpkin eater, had a wife and couldn't keep her, so he named her George."

"Georgie, Porgie, puddin' and pie. Made the girls touch his Peter."

One girl screamed out, "George Branstill, you're a jerk." A boy added, "No, Peter Branstill's the jerk." The children laughed until they were called in by the recess bell.

Miss Weintraub continued to use George, and Peter refused to respond. Forgetting the reason for George's belligerence, she sent him to the principal's office. The principal saw the note recommending discipline for George Branstill and sent Peter back to class. Later, the principal called Miss Weintraub into her office, screamed at her for not accepting Dr. Kline's recommendations, and threatened to cite her in her personnel file.

From that day forward, Miss Weintraub recognized George as Peter Branstill – and vowed to make his life hell.

■ ■ ■

Two weeks later the school received the results of its annual standardized achievement tests. Peter scored top in his school, in the 99th percentile, in mathematics. Unable to stand the thought of Peter succeeding, Miss Weintraub proceeded to thwart his success at every chance.

When Peter answered a question correctly, she challenged his method and accused him of cheating off another, obviously less gifted student. She tore up his scratch work before taking points off for not showing the calculations. She took points off for poor handwriting regardless of how compulsive and meticulous his script became. At times she erased his answers, replaced them with wrong ones, and took points off. No matter how well Peter did, he was destined for mediocrity in Rebecca Weintraub's eyes. A hundred became a seventy-two, a ninety-five became a seventy-two. Test after test became seventy-twos. Before long, Peter began changing his responses to score exactly seventy-two, no more, no less. Each test, Peter provided exactly the right number of errors to score a perfect seventy-two, often finding creative ways to lose enough partial credit to score exactly seventy-two.

Meanwhile, Rebecca became more and more bold in her assaults on Peter's performance. Each time she altered a grade, Peter took it without response. There were no complaints from Peter, no irate calls from his mother. Her successes were addictive, as she gloried in the knowledge that she could ruin his life without resistance.

Four weeks before school ended, the faculty met to plan the next year. When Dr. Prindle indicated that changes in the district's demographics meant that one of the second grade teachers would have to teach a third grade instead, Rebecca volunteered, knowing this would give her a chance to get back at Peter for another full year.

Over the summer, Rebecca spent two weeks at a religious retreat, in a camp by a beautiful lake, in the Green Mountains of Vermont, where she thought about Peter often. During prayer, she prayed to be forgiven for the way she treated him. And during breaks while the others talked, she'd simply walk around the lake, feeling ashamed of herself. By the time she went home, she felt Deeply Changed.

Yet when Peter showed up the first day in her third grade class, Rebecca realized that nothing had changed. Overwhelmed by rage, she tried once more to destroy him, changing his grades, standing him in the corner, keeping him in for recess, commenting on his hygiene, and yelling at him for "misbehaviors." At night when Rebecca went home, she prayed to God, hoping to change. Yet each day, as soon as she saw Peter, she started up again.

Finally one day, Rebecca started class saying, "Children, there's something I have to tell you. When I was a young girl, I fell very much in love with a young man. There was a war going on. He was in the service and was about to go overseas to fight in this war. I knew I might never see him again. I loved him very much. We spent as much time as we could together. After he left, I learned that I was pregnant. I wanted to keep the baby, but my parents made me have an abortion. They took me somewhere to get the abortion. I bled a lot and had a terrible fever. I thought I was going to die.

"The boy came back, but he didn't want to see me anymore. I never told him about our child. By then, I finished school and had become a teacher. I had two other boyfriends but never got pregnant again. I got real depressed, knowing how much I wanted a child. Sometimes I barely made it to class. But I did, and I'll tell you, I did a damn good job, too. You kids were the only thing that kept me going. You really mattered to me."

The class sat still as Rebecca paused in deep thought. "You know, I was OK until last year," she said softly. Then, with tears in her eyes, she turned to Peter and cried, "Why'd you do this to me, George? Why?" She sobbed for several minutes. Then her mournful face stiffened, the cheek muscles tightened into a sinister grin, her eyes glazed, and, her face red with fury, she stood up, snapped a ruler against her desk, and bellowed,

"Today, children you will have my last and best lesson ever. Stand up!" As the children rose, one slow in rising, she snapped the ruler once more against the desk, breaking it in two, shouting, "Now!" With the offending child still not fully erect, she screamed, "George, stand up now!" even though this child was not Peter, nor himself named George.

"You will stand for the entire lesson. You will be tested on what I say at the end of the day. No one will move. No one will leave. There will be no lunch, no recess. You will hold your water all day and learn. Do you hear me class, learn, learn, learn."

With that, Rebecca bent down and lifted several books from a box on the floor. She began reading selections from *Silas Marner, The Iliad, The Merchant of Venice, Cannery Row, Madame Bovary,* and *The Sound and the Fury*. Throughout, Rebecca demanded perfect obedience, periodically reminding the class that George was responsible for today's ordeal, and that he would also be responsible for the end of her career and her life. As Rebecca went on, the class stood in deadly silence, trembling with fear. By lunchtime, Dr. Prindle realized that Rebecca's class had not come to the cafeteria, and walked over to her class. Entering the classroom, she saw the entire group standing at attention while Rebecca walked up and down the aisles, another ruler in hand, snapping it sharply and methodically against her other hand, and reciting over and over again the 23rd Psalm.

Dr. Prindle stayed with the class after having Rebecca removed. They talked first before spending the rest of the afternoon playing games. The next morning when they came to school, Dr. Kline was there to provide group and individual Crisis Counseling. He greeted Peter warmly, remembering him from their consultation the year before. He met with the faculty at other times during the day and conducted a special meeting for the parents that evening. Afterwards, he recommended that some of the students seek additional counseling outside school; Peter was one of those students. With that, Peter started to attend weekly sessions with Dr. Kline for the next two years.

15

Cutting It Off

"Hey buddy. You still here? I almost locked you in," the man Peter met when he entered the apartment said. "Listen, if you really like the place that much, you can have it." Handing Peter a business card, he added, "Call me tomorrow and I'll draw up a lease."

Peter walked to the front door, turned around, and quietly said good-bye to Aunt Cindy's apartment, then walked down the stairs, reached the street, and made a perfect 90° turn to the right before walking home.

■ ■ ■

That evening, Peter found himself getting angry at John again. *What does he mean? You won't cut your penis off by counting to ten. He has no idea. God, I wish I could just get it over with.* Peter pictured himself pacing back and forth on the violent ward. *I've gotta tell him how I feel.* HA-HA-HA laughed the children. NOW HE'LL KNOW YOU'RE A JERK.

John, it's really not that easy. Peter thought, *No, let's be firm. John, you don't know what you're saying.* HE'S MAD NOW. LET'S GET HIM, GUYS. *John, it's not like you think. You don't count to ten. You, uh, count to eleven.*

That's it! thought Peter. *Of course. You don't count to ten. You count to eleven. Sure, eleven has two lines, ten has a line and a circle. If you rotate eleven 90°, it's an equal sign: Equals a whole penis. A ten on its side is like a line with a ball over it, like a steam roller crushing your penis. Unless you rotate it the other way and the line's over the ball. Then the line will bend like a soft penis. And anyway, eleven's a prime number. Ten factors into five and two. You can't protect your penis with a number like that.* Pleased with his discovery, Peter spent the rest of the evening thinking of more and more arguments he could use to prove to John that you can't save your penis counting to ten. You've got to count to eleven.

▪ ▪ ▪

By Monday, Peter no longer felt angry. Instead, he was ready for a lively debate. But John did not come, and when he failed to come the next week either, Peter became anxious and worried. And after several weeks without seeing John, Peter knew he was not coming back. As time passed, he felt more and more guilty, certain that John left because he was angry.

Two months after his last contact with John, while eating dinner, Peter felt an intense urge to cut off his penis. And although he had always lived with the fear that he would castrate himself, this time he thought he might really do it. He struggled to finish cutting his chicken breast in perfect geometric shapes, almost certain he saw himself slicing cross-sections of his penis. As soon as he finished cutting, he raced downstairs to drop the knife in a garbage can. And although he was usually careful to wrap his refuse to keep it separate from other tenants' trash, this time he placed the knife directly into someone else's trashbag to ensure he would not retrieve it later and cut off his penis.

Peter returned to his apartment to finish his meal. As he cleaned up, he noticed the knife rack, which held a large collection of cutting implements. He quickly removed all of the other knives from his apartment as well.

Over the next several months, Peter progressively discarded all implements that could be used to harm himself. He threw out scissors, staples, and products, such as Scotch tape and Saran Wrap, packaged with serrated edges. He discarded his razor and blades, purchasing an electric shaver to take its place. He installed door closers on all the doors to prevent him from slamming them shut on his penis.

Peter fought a daily battle to protect his penis. And it was not that he feared castration itself, for Peter believed he would find comfort by removing the organ that haunted him. But he feared commitment to the insane asylum, and now, according to John, its violent ward.

One night, Peter dreamt that he had sliced off his penis. He waited fearfully in his apartment, knowing that he would be taken away. When the ambulance came, the attendants quickly approached Peter, and without saying a word, bound him in a straitjacket before putting him alone in the back of the padded wagon. While riding he overheard the two attendants talking to each other about left-lunged smoking.

They arrived at a large gray building built with heavy cinderblock. He noticed his mother wandering aimlessly, along with Shirley Parker. Mom was telling Shirley that Peter would be here soon, and that they could marry, now that Peter had lost his penis.

The attendants took Peter directly to the operating room where a doctor was waiting ready to perform a lobotomy. Peter remained awake through the operation as the doctor cut deeply into his brain and removed a penis, announcing, "Here's the problem. No wonder he's so fucked up." The dream ended with Peter pacing endlessly up and down the violent ward with John.

The next day at work, Peter came across a ledger entry for $123.45. In his mind, he completed the sequence, *six, seven, eight, nine, ten,* and for a moment felt relieved. The relief was short-lived as he found himself again thinking about cutting off his penis. So Peter said to himself, *one, two, three, four, five, six, seven, eight, nine, ten,* and again there was a moment's peace. Throughout the day, he counted to ten over and over again, and although it disturbed him to have to count, he felt confident that he would not castrate himself.

That night, he lay awake remembering John's words, "I thought I really helped him. Shame I didn't know him before. It's that simple. Ya wanna cut your prick off, ya count to ten. Before ya know it, ya change your mind." Knowing he would have his first peaceful night's sleep in several months, Peter reached over to his night table. He picked up his calculator, notepad, blue pen, and pencil, and calculated the number of days he had lived tormented by castration fears.

One Year Later

16

Homecoming

On Tuesday, June 25, the next year, a hot, sunny day, Peter sat on his bench, a napkin neatly folded on his lap, in his left hand a sandwich from which he had just severed a triangular bite. As he chewed, first with the left side of his mouth, then the right, carefully ensuring that the bite passed over each of the four taste zones of his tongue, Peter pulled out a note he received from Andrew that morning.

From the Office of Andrew Lerner

The Sterling and Warner audit is scheduled for the week of July 22nd, next month. Harold Sterling asked if you would be there. This is a great opportunity for your career. The company's grown, so we'll be there all week. He's promised to find a restaurant you like this time: said he's going to have all his meals with you until you eat. Wanted to give you plenty of notice.
Andrew

Cringing, Peter pictured himself spending an entire week hungry, as Harold looked over his plate. Before long, Harold transformed into Danny McGraw.

∎ ∎ ∎

During the summers, the cousins attended Beaver Christian Camp where Maureen and Hal were co-directors. Situated on 70 acres of wooded land on a small lake, with log cottages, a central dining hall, a snack shop, the administration building for Maureen's and Hal's offices, the counselor lounge, and a nursing station, campers entered Beaver through a wooden archway boasting the motto: Camping for Christ. So that summer Peter, who was starting to feel comfortable with the name George, enrolled in the camp, too. Right off, he heard rumors about a boy whose mother was insane. And after a while, he learned that he was that boy.

Not surprisingly, George was a poor candidate for summer camp, hating dirt, socializing poorly, terrified to bunk with the other campers. During the day, he carefully watched for dirt that was all around, observations that later helped him create the Graduated Dirt Rating Scale. It was at camp that he first learned to distinguish the color of dirt from its discoloration, and that there was an inverse relationship between the dirt's texture and its potential harm. At night, he lay for hours, terrified, awake in his bunk, sure that a bug or another boy would get in his bed and hurt him. During the day, he thought constantly about how to keep himself clean without being exposed in the communal bathroom and showers. At times, he held his bowels to the point of potentially dangerous constipation, hoping for the right moment to go to the bathroom.

Aunt Maureen, who sensed George's great discomfort, made a special effort to introduce him to all the counselors and staff. The counselors were college students, many of whom had attended Beaver when they were younger. The cooks were two local women who worked in the school cafeteria. Mrs. Cooper worked Sunday through Wednesday morning and Mrs. Campbell worked Wednesday afternoon through Saturday. During the tour, George noticed Mrs. Cooper pick her nose. Repulsed, he vowed he would not eat food that Mrs. Cooper had cooked. It never occurred to George that Mrs. Cooper might not always pick her nose or that Mrs. Campbell might occasionally pick hers, too. He also failed to notice that despite eating her snot-laden food, the other campers and staff were healthy and well. So from Sunday to Wednesday, unnoticed for the most part by the other campers, George starved, waiting for Mrs. Campbell's shift.

This all changed on the sixth week when Danny McGraw showed up. A burly youngster with a voracious appetite, he always wanted second and third portions and kept a watchful eye on everyone else's plate, stalking for leftovers. But leftovers were rare at Aunt Maureen's camp. Because the philosophy was staunchly Christian and frowned on waste, campers usually took only what they could eat. And while George struggled to disguise his plate during Mrs. Cooper's shift, pushing the food around to look partly eaten, Danny could not be so easily deceived.

As far as Danny was concerned, he had hit paydirt. For the first three days of camp, he willingly cleaned George's plate for him. This arrangement worked well: Danny got all the food he could eat and George kept his secret. On Wednesday, however, everything changed: Starving, George finished his meal. Danny was disappointed but assumed that George might have been sick earlier in the week. He did not give it much more thought until his second week of camp. On Sunday, George's plate again provided Danny with plentiful pickings.

Danny questioned George about this. At first, George said nothing, but Danny kept after him. So in what he thought was a bid for popularity but in reality turned out to be a disastrous lapse in judgment, George let down his guard and decided to answer Danny's questions by giving an exposé, on Mrs. Cooper's unsanitary habits. Danny just laughed out loud at George's story. His laughter caught the attention of the other boys and, playing to the crowd at their table, Danny grabbed George's uneaten hamburger, bit deeply into it, and said, "Boy, that's a great snotburger."

The other kids chimed in with one snot joke after another. There were snotburgers, snot-fried potatoes, snotcholate chip cookies, snot beans, snot-style corn, and snotaronis on pizza. Each camper tried to outdo the others. Most jokes were repeated four or five times by different children hoping to get a laugh. The boys made all sorts of fake nose-picking gestures and pretended to eat their own snot or to smear it on another camper. George became known as snot-boy and Mrs. Cooper became known as the snot-cook. And to George's amazement, everyone kept on eating.

Meanwhile, Mrs. Cooper became so upset that she was ready to quit. To rescue her reputation, Aunt Maureen publicly admonished George for his awful rumors and prayed for his forgiveness. In the end, the entire incident was blamed on Satan.

On Thursday, Danny and several other campers came up to George with great excitement. "George, you missed mail call." Sally never wrote, so George never waited for mail.

"Your mom sent a package. You weren't there so I picked it up for you, buddy."

Danny handed George a box. George opened it up. In it was the condom he had purchased on the ride up. It was stuffed like a balloon with a variety of used handkerchiefs, tissues, and other nasal byproducts. There were also nose pickings, snot which had been blown into the box, and a toy nose from a Mr. Potato Head set, also covered with snot. On the package was a note: "To my son, Snot-boy. Love, Mom. From the insane asylum."

As the boys rolled with laughter, and George sat quietly with no expression, Aunt Maureen came up and said, "George, I've got great news." She stopped, noticing the laughter. "Glad you guys are having such a great time.

"Anyway, I just talked with your mom. She's out of the hospital and feeling a whole lot better. I told her you love camp, so she said you can stay the rest of the summer." As she walked away, George's mind turned black. He could hardly hear the laughter anymore.

■ ■ ■

Camping for Christ, thought Peter, picturing the sign above the entrance to Beaver. Remembering he was in the park eating his lunch, Peter looked back over his right shoulder, 4° north of north northwest, where Savior Man stood each day warning that the world would end: Christ the only salvation. Peter often saw children running to the play area, and worried they would stop and taunt him, as if he were condemned to hell. Rotating his head in a steady, continuous motion, keeping his body perfectly erect, Peter turned to look over his left shoulder, where by looking out the leftmost corner of his eyes, without disturbing the symmetry he formed between his right and left turns, he could see children playing. As they jumped and ran, laughed and shouted, Peter pictured himself stationed by the edge of the playground, standing over a German machine gun. "Fire!" shouts Savior Man. The children fall as Peter laces rounds of ammunition into them, Savior Man singing "Onward, Christian Soldiers" by his side. King George shouts, CUT IT OFF BEFORE HE HURTS ANYONE ELSE.

Glancing at his watch, realizing he spent twenty-nine seconds looking at Savior Man, ninety-three at the children, Peter turned back to the right for another sixty-four seconds before facing forward, ready for another bite of his sandwich. Having taken his eyes off the sandwich for 186 seconds, Peter lifted the top slice of bread, checking for sabotage: No snot. As he opened his mouth, preparing for his next bite, he heard a loud, cheerful, bellowing voice call out, "Hey Petey. What's up? Haven't seen ya for a long time. What's happenin'?"

Chills down his spine, doing all he could to suppress a smile, Peter looked up to see John loping over to his bench. Before he could respond, John went straight to the story of what had happened during their separation.

"Ya wouldn't believe, Petey. I had the most amazin' time. Thought 'bout ya the whole time. Wish I had your phone number. Probably woulda called ya a hundred times. Ya should gimme your beeper number sometime."

Peter smiled to himself. John was really here; he never changed. He thinks I'm some big executive. Not knowing why he needed "Petey" to be so successful, but willing to be the illusion, Peter looked back at his sandwich, checking it carefully before taking the next bite.

"Anyways, there's this chick in the program. Real plain-looking girl, maybe 30, 35. Remember, I told ya. Hanna Banana. Been in the program for a long time. Real quiet, kinda plain; hardly says nothin'. I musta sat through a thousand groups with her. Can't think of one word comin' outta her mouth."

If John goes to his program five days a week, fifty-two weeks of the year, closed eleven major holidays, he must attend two hundred forty-nine days each year. If they have group every day, and if Hanna Banana goes every day, that's four years and four days in his program. John's known her for a long time.

"Every year, in the summer, she seems to go off. This year's no different. Ya see it in her face. First, she's smilin', talkin' a bit, wearin' makeup. Not too good-lookin' but catches your eye. Anyways it's August and I notice she's startin' up again. Talkin' a lot, laughin' all the time. The newer staff seem to like it, but the ones who've been 'round awhile seem worried. Guess they've seen her go off too many times before, they know the signs. I've seen the signs before, too. But this time it's different. Just like I thought, she's comin' on to me. Whatdaya know. One Friday afternoon she says to me, 'Let's get the hell outta here.'"

Savior Man knows lots about hell.

"I says, 'Sure. Where ya wanna go?'"

"And she says, 'It's a surprise.'"

"Well, I always like surprises, particularly from hot women who look like they really want it. Anyways, we get outside and she calls a cab. Now, I ain't got no money for no cab but she tells me not to worry. She's got lotsa money. Then she gives me $300; tells me it's pocket money for our trip."

John's been gone a year, 365 days. Looking at his watch, checking the exact date, June 25, *last time I saw John was July 27, 334 days. 300 divided by 334 is .8982 or 90 cents per day. They were selling chicken for 69 cents a pound last week. If chicken was on sale wherever John went, he could have had 1 pound, 5 ounces of chicken every day.*

"We go to Port Authority and before ya know it, we're on a bus to California. Hey man. I ain't ready for this; left my meds at home. I got no clothes, no toothbrush, no nothin'. But I got $300 and a hot chick so I figures it can't be too bad. I can handle it. We're sittin' on this bus and she's got her hands all over me. We're kissin', makin' out, but the first night nothin' really happens. We just fall asleep.

"By the second night, we're somewhere in Nebraska and it's dark and everyone else is asleep. She reaches down for my crotch, pulls down my fly, and starts suckin' on my dick! Man, I gotta tell ya. This girl ain't never given no head before. She don't know what the hell she's doin'. Thought she was gonna fuckin' bite it off. But what the hell; ya can't pass up a blow job on a bus, even from a beginner. I figure I'll never get a chance like this again, so I go for the gold and come right in her mouth.

"All of a sudden, the bitch is screamin' at the top of her lungs, 'Rape, rape, rape!' Wakes up the whole fuckin' bus. Shit, it's fuckin' embarrassin'. Scary, too. Ya know, there I am, I've got a record, and she's fuckin' out of control; a fuckin' nutcase.

"The bus driver don't know what the hell to do. He pulls off at the first exit, into some hick town. When the police come, I swear I thought it was Andy and Barney themselves. They grab her and take her into the police car and I figure I'm in the can for sure. So I try to speak to them. Tell 'em I'm innocent. But they're too busy with her. Finally, she's in the cop car and Barney comes back to the bus.

"I run right up to him and says, 'Listen man, I didn't rape her. No way she's gonna pin that on me.'

"He looks at me real puzzled. 'Who said ya raped her?'

"I says, 'Listen to her, she's fuckin' out of her mind. Ya heard what she said.'

"He looks at me for a long time, not sayin' nothin'. Then he just breaks up laughin'. I ain't never heard no one laugh so hard. Couldn't hardly get a grip on himself.

"Finally, he looks at me and says, 'Listen, pal. Next time ya want a little head, get yourself a nice Christian whore. Don't go messin' with no crazy Jew girl.'

"Anyways, Petey. I got lotsa things I wanna tell ya 'bout Nebraska. But I gotta get back to the program. They wanna re-evaluate me since I've been gone so long. Need to see the shrink. I told 'em, 'No way I'm gonna do that 'til I first see my old buddy Petey.' Anyways, I'll see ya tomorrow."

■ ■ ■

Feeling faint with a pounding headache coming on, Peter was not sure he could walk back to the office without falling down. As he slowly staggered back, he conjured up an image of Anna in the form of the girl he saw at the peep show last night, her mouth open, John's penis just outside, a stream of semen spurting out, her nose, mouth, chin covered with the sticky substance. *The semen's white, a good color – 2; mostly white throughout, discoloration – 2; a lot of semen, size – 4; unevenly spread, symmetry – 5; the telltale odor of semen – 4.* Having divided the texture scale into texture and moisture last year, but also having created a special standard for sticky substances, texture/moisture(sticky) rates a combined 4. *In total, the GDRS score for this semen is 2 x 2 + 4 x 2 + 3 x 4 + 1 x 5 + 6 x 4 + 4 x 4 = 69, major dirt.*

■ ■ ■

When Peter got back to work, he went straight to Andrew Lerner's office and asked, "Mr. Lerner, I don't feel well. Can I take the rest of the day off?"

"Anything serious, Peter? Do you need to see a doctor?"

Peter stood speechless in front of Andrew until Andrew said, "No problem, Peter. Hope you feel better."

Andrew tapped his fingers, slightly, on his desk as he watched Peter leave. "Can I take the rest of the day off?" he said, repeating Peter's words. "Wow! I've got to check his file. I think that's the first time he's missed work." Picturing the day Cal Ripken Jr. broke Lou Gehrig's streak, he sighed, "Peter Branstill, the Iron Man of Accounting."

17

Anna

Anna was taken from the bus to a nearby emergency room. The doctor gave her Thorazine, which calmed her down. She talked with a social worker who, after they met, called Sol, Anna's husband, in New York. Angered at the call, tired of Anna's trips, no longer worried that she had been gone, Sol hesitated before doing what he knew he'd have to do – fly to Nebraska to get her. *G-d help me,* he thought. *It's been the same damn thing for years. Who would've known?*

Waiting for Sol, remembering what she had just done, her head ached as she heard G-d scream and pictured Sol lashing out, his closed fist descending toward her right temple. *He won't do it in front of the doctors. He'll wait 'til we're alone.* Her thoughts shifted to the bus. Picturing herself with John, her head in his crotch, a slight smile crossed her lips as she thought: *You finally did it.*

■ ■ ■

Anna and Sol met through a matchmaker, the custom of their strictly observant Hasidic Jewish community. Moving rapidly from engagement to wedding, they hardly knew each other at their wedding six months later. Anna did not know that Sol was an angry, hateful man who would berate and assault her. Stuck, married to a man she loathed, she spent hours by herself, rocking back and forth, lost in thought. Several times, she tried to take her life. Sol didn't care. He ignored her except on Friday night, when regardless of how she felt, as long as she was clean, he demanded the marital ritual. It was inevitable that one Friday afternoon, in violation of her religious beliefs, anticipating a sexual advance by Sol, several years before taking off with John, Anna boarded a bus with no destination in mind, to get away from Sol. On the bus, she met Ed.

Ed Thompson boarded the bus in Philadelphia. Taking a vacant seat toward the back, he noticed Anna. For the first half-hour, he thought about nothing except the pretty, plain, timid woman who sat alone in the seventh row.

Ed lived by himself and although he was shy by nature, he had always wanted to meet girls, which was why he had weekly psychotherapy sessions with Dr. Sherman of Elkins Park, Pennsylvania, a suburb north of Philadelphia. In the past, Ed had two brief relationships, one with a dental hygienist, the other a secretary. Both were outgoing, emotional women who picked him up in bars. Ed, who longed for quiet evenings at home, had nothing in common with either woman; the relationships ended in disaster. Dr. Sherman often confronted Ed for choosing bars – a place he didn't enjoy – to meet women he didn't like.

"The problem for shy people like you, Ed, is that you would really be happiest with other shy people. Unfortunately, you're too shy to ask the girl out, and she's too shy to ask you out. And since men are supposed to do the asking, you only meet women who are bold, unconventional, and outgoing. For all you know, you may pass by several women each week who would be perfect for you. If you're going to be happy, you will have to learn how to make the first move. And learn is what I mean. You have to find someplace to practice asking women out."

"How about a bus?" Ed asked. Groaning at the thought, picturing Ed asking a girl out wedged in a packed city bus, Dr. Sherman stifled his response, asking Ed to further explain his idea.

"I could take the bus to Los Angeles. It's a three-day ride, which means there will be three quiet nights to plan my move. Then I ask the girl if she's going out West, too, and suggest a date when we get there."

Picturing Ed criss-crossing the country trying to meet girls, while Ed beamed over his creative idea, Dr. Sherman finally suggested a test run, the night bus to Pittsburgh. In preparation, Dr. Sherman taught Ed to relax with a twenty-minute taped exercise, suggesting deep breathing, muscle relaxation, peaceful imagery, and positive suggestions: You are strong; you are attractive; women like you; you have the power to have a girl of your own. Each night Ed listened to his tape until Dr. Sherman deemed him ready to board the late bus to Pittsburgh, take a seat next to a woman he wished to meet, and say, Hello.

After boarding the bus, Ed walked slowly down the aisle. He had planned to take the first vacant seat next to a woman, but the first woman was an attractive blond. Ed panicked and went on, spying Anna, plain, frightened-looking, and sitting by herself. He wanted to sit next to her but was too nervous. Instead he took a vacant seat a few rows back, obsessing over his failure to execute his plan. From Philadelphia to Harrisburg, he thought about nothing but Anna.

Ed built up the nerve to approach Anna by the Harrisburg stop. He deboarded the bus, ostensibly to stretch, planning to sit next to her when he returned. Preoccupied, he failed to notice a group of new passengers queue up to board the bus. Suddenly, he realized his seat might be gone. He pictured Dr. Sherman saying: Do it, Ed. Butt in. You'll never see these people again. They won't do anything. Ed shyly walked to the back of the line, sure his chance was lost.

Back on the bus, Ed spied Anna sitting by herself. His heart sank. He now wished that someone took that seat. He almost aborted his plan at the last minute, turning away from her to sit next to a man across the aisle. But looking back, she seemed so shy, he quickly plopped down next to her.

Immediately, his heart started racing and he broke into a sweat. For the next twenty minutes, Ed imagined the full tape in his mind. Calm, he began rehearsing his words of introduction to himself. Finally, he turned to Anna and said, "Hi, I'm Ed."

It was just as he had practiced with his therapist. He remembered Dr. Sherman saying, "Don't worry about her response. Just do what you want to do. If you can introduce yourself, in a direct way, to the woman of your choice – regardless of the result – you'll be a great success."

Anna responded, "Hi, I'm Anna."

Approximately fifty more words passed between them. "Where you going?... Pretty nice bus... New York, oh, I've always lived in Philadelphia... "

Triumphant at the successful execution of his plan, Ed got off the bus halfway between Harrisburg and Pittsburgh to return home.

After Ed left, Anna's mind raced continuously with her thoughts about him. When the thoughts turned erotic, she began to hallucinate. And when the bus reached Pittsburgh, she sat frozen to her seat. When she was the lone passenger left, the bus driver approached her, saying, "Pittsburgh, lady. We're in Pittsburgh." Anna failed to move. Repeating his words, to no avail, he then tried to gently shake her but she still didn't move. "Lady, we're in Pittsburgh. This is the last stop. It's time to get off. You OK?" After waiting a few minutes more, he left the bus, returning ten minutes later with the police, who helped her off the bus and took her to a nearby hospital. There, she became agitated and out of control, needing Thorazine to calm her down.

She recovered shortly and remained stable for about a year. And although Ed stayed on her mind, the Yom Kippur service cleansed her of her guilt. Yet she still thought about Ed, often having lush fantasies while sexually assaulted by Sol. And to Sol's surprise, Anna now responded during lovemaking, with Ed prominently in her mind.

The next summer, Anna abruptly stopped her medications. A few weeks later, she again boarded the Friday afternoon bus to Pittsburgh. This time, a tall blond man sat next to her, opened his newspaper, and read most of the trip. Remembering Ed, she waited for him to talk. When he didn't, after it got dark, she introduced herself, "Hi, I'm Anna." As they talked, she placed her hand on his leg. In Pittsburgh, the man invited her to his home. After she refused, he kissed her good-bye. As he walked away, she ran back to the street and jumped in front of a moving bus, which stopped just in time. After she was predictably taken to the hospital, Sol came out to get her and bring her back home. Again, her feelings of guilt ended at the Yom Kippur service.

Anna's psychiatrist suggested she join a day treatment program. Not wanting her seen entering the local community mental health center, Sol insisted she go to a program in Manhattan, near the Diamond District where he worked. Each weekday, Anna took the subway from her Boro Park, Brooklyn, home to midtown Manhattan, to the program John attended.

To Sol and her rabbi, Anna had sinned. To her psychiatrist, she was ill. But Anna secretly rejoiced, knowing that she could be forgiven for her sins. For the first time ever, she felt happy she was a Jew. Each year, Anna carefully planned her trip, picking the exact day she'd go off her medication in July so that she'd be manic and ready to take off in August, be naughty, and return, stable on medication, in time for the Yom Kippur service. And without knowing it, her psychiatrist played a vital role in the plan by referring her to the day program, the one place where she could get new ideas for her annual trip.

■ ■ ■

The year before leaving with John, Anna had overheard a patient talk about "taking it up the ass." Listening carefully, she learned that homosexual men often engage in anal intercourse. She further learned that heterosexual women sometimes also enjoy the same experience. Longing to "take it up the ass," Anna went off her medication very early and was on the bus by mid-July, looking for a stranger.

The bus, however, offered no good prospects, so she got off in a small rural town near the Ohio-Indiana border and went straight to Sam's Bar, where she sat at the counter, asked the bartender to pour a shot of J&B in a paper cup she took from her purse, ate a package of Planter's salted peanuts, and began flirting with Bill Smith, the man sitting on the barstool next to her. When he asked her to his place, she replied, "Only if you'll come in my ass."

Shocked and excited by her bold comment, Bill stumbled as he stepped off the stool. Balancing himself by holding onto the top of a nearby chair, Bill looked directly at Anna, who responded to his fear-struck look with an affirmative nod. With a broad smile, he took her hand and led her to his car. As they drove to his apartment, he kept repeating the alphabet to himself, afraid he would otherwise climax in his pants. Once there, he directed her straight to his bedroom, pulling his pants down as they went. His feet tied up, still pulling Anna by the arm, he hopped to the bed, pushed her down face first onto the bed with her feet still on the floor, lifted the back of her skirt without taking it off, pulled her underpants down, and without lubrication, rammed his stiff shaft up her behind, climaxing in seconds. "Ow! You're hurting me," Anna screamed. Mistaking her words for shouts of joy as his penis became soft, Bill reached toward his dresser for a large deodorant stick, and shoved it hard where his penis had just been.

Fifteen minutes later, getting erect again, Bill pulled the deodorant stick out of Anna's rectum, ready to insert his penis in her again. But Anna turned around, held up her hand, pulled up her underpants, and without saying a word picked up her purse and walked to the door. She went straight to the local police station where she informed the officer on duty that she had just come to town and was going to kill herself. Following a predictable scenario, she was admitted to the local hospital, where they gave her medications and called Sol.

Following the Yom Kippur service, Anna felt happy and peaceful, forgetting the pain, delighted with herself that she had now had a man's organ in her rectum. But unfortunately, she was also tormented by poor planning: She had gone off medication early in a year when Yom Kippur came late, and she'd had a full four weeks to endure, waiting for the Day of Atonement. The guilt was unbearable: Guilty for what she did. Guilty for wishing she was Catholic.

■ ■ ■

Anna first learned about Catholicism through her day treatment program, her only source of information about religions and cultures other than Orthodox Judaism. Under the protective umbrella of Brooklyn's orthodox community, she learned that Jews were the *chosen people* who had a special covenant with God and were required to live according to a strict moral code. But in treatment, she saw that other people grapple with moral issues, strive to make good decisions, and struggle with conflicts between their values and impulses.

Anna met many guilt-ridden people and – much to her surprise – learned that Jews did not have sole claim to that emotion. In one group therapy session, she recalled hearing a 25-year-old woman of Irish descent, and with a strict Catholic upbringing, describe her several attempts at suicide, saying, "I've been a very bad Catholic. I must die for my sins."

"Are you a bad Catholic or an ambivalent Catholic?" the group's leader asked.

"I'm a terrible Catholic, and I must die."

"Did you ever confess your action to the priest?" the leader continued.

"No, I'd be too ashamed to."

"But you've got to be ambivalent about your Catholicism." the leader said. "Your religion is clear: You sin, you confess; you confess, you are absolved. I once knew a priest who violated his vow of celibacy by sleeping with a woman. The woman, who felt exploited by this man whom she trusted, was troubled for years; the priest stopped feeling guilty once he cleared his conscience by offering confession to a fellow priest. Who do you think is the better Catholic?"

The woman offered no response, so the group leader went on to say, "You're a perfect candidate for forgiveness. You had one out-of-wedlock sexual experience, you regret it, and you have never done it again. You only refuse to confess because you are conflicted over your religion: They can make you feel guilty, but they'll never make you use their sacraments."

While the group went on, several other patients chiming in, Anna sat quietly, picturing herself in schul, a priest leading the Yom Kippur service.

■ ■ ■

Facing four weeks of unbearable guilt while she waited for Yom Kippur, Anna thought back to this group session and decided to seek out a priest. Knowing she could not be seen, she went far from her neighborhood to find a church. That day, she left the day program early so she could receive forgiveness and absolution but still be home on time for her husband. She could not afford questions, and she did not want to lie. She took the subway and exited at a random stop in a Latino neighborhood of Manhattan. Everything about the people and their surroundings was alien to her; signs were in Spanish, not Hebrew or English. She was quite hungry but she knew she would have to wait, as there were no kosher stores or restaurants around. Anna asked a passerby to direct her to the nearest church. When she arrived, two and one-half blocks later, she found the buildings, paintings, and pews strange, with a grandeur missing in the familiar schul. Anna found the confessional booth with a sign stating that confessions would begin soon.

Not knowing the protocol, she simply entered the booth and started blurting out her story. She told the priest about not only her most recent incident but her entire history of indiscretions, omitting only the fact that she was Jewish. She also told the priest about her husband's brutality. She found him comforting in a way she did not think a rabbi could be. The priest accepted that some husbands beat their wives; the rabbi would never believe a good Jewish boy could do that.

Anna finished her confession feeling peaceful and free of shame. The priest gently commented that it had been a long time since she had been in church and then offered her total absolution. Anna realized that for all the cleansing Yom Kippur gave, this was the first time she had received an answer to her pleas for forgiveness. Anna cherished the moment until Father told her she could now receive communion again.

The communion comment jarred Anna back to reality. She was a Jew; she could not take communion. And while confession had been cleansing, communion was frightening. Anna knew that she could take a man who was not her husband into her body. But communion: The body and blood of Christ. Anna shuddered picturing herself swallowing the wafer, Sol's fist crashing into her cheek, Rabbi Sofrin by his side, explaining, "Anna, it's not kosher. It's a Catholic cookie."

For Anna, Kashrath – the Jewish dietary laws – stood inviolate, above all other Jewish laws. Under the guise of her manic state, Anna could travel on the Sabbath and have relations with strangers while unclean, but she never broke the dietary laws. Because of her strict adherence, she often ended her trips exhausted and famished. Her travels took her to strange places with few Jews, and the bus never stopped in Orthodox neighborhoods. At most, she ate a few selections of packaged foods – like the Planter's peanuts – displaying the familiar Ⓤ.

■ ■ ■

The following spring, months before they actually took off together, Anna made her decision to have sex with John while Dr.

Brown talked about the sexual side effects of psychoactive medications in a meeting of his regular weekly group with the patients.

"Last week I described many of the side effects you may have from your medications: dry mouth, blurry vision, stiffness in your joints," Dr. Brown began. "Today, I'd like to talk about sexual side effects some of you may have had. Your medication may inhibit your sex drive. It may make it difficult to have an erection. You may even have retrograde ejaculation, particularly those who are taking Mellaril."

John, who took Mellaril, immediately spoke up: "What the fuck's that?" Never comfortable with obscenities, but wanting to be open, Dr. Brown stiffled a grimace, and, through a forced smile, said, "John, retrograde ejaculation is when you have a normal sexual response, but no semen comes out. The ejaculant empties into your bladder and harmlessly leaves your body when you go to the bathroom. It's really not a problem."

"Wait a fuckin' minute," John shouted. "I've been on this shit for years and it ain't as harmless as ya think. It's damn harmful, fuckin' embarrassin' too. Whatdaya think it's like to pick up a hot chick or a cheap whore and know ya ain't gonna come. Shit, ya just hope she don't notice, don't beg ya to squirt your love juice on her tits. It's easy for you to say it's harmless, but ya ain't on this shit. I thought I had some fuckin' disease 'cause nobody never told me before that Mellaril did this shit to me."

Uncomfortable with John's tirade, Dr. Brown looked at his watch and ended the group early, telling John he would meet with him later that day.

Meanwhile, Anna secretly rejoiced at her good fortune. She had long wanted to perform oral sex on a man but never did because of the laws of Kashrath. Now, Dr. Brown was telling her that she could solve this problem by giving a blow job to a man on Mellaril. When John spoke up, Anna knew she would have him.

■ ■ ■

Anna's plan was to perform fellatio on the first night of their trip, but she had found herself more hesitant than she expected when she realized she would still have to put his penis in her mouth. She struggled with the problem of whether the penis itself was unclean food or just the ejaculant.

Her ruminations took the form of an imaginary audience with her rabbi. "Rabbi Sofrin, is fellatio allowed with a man who cannot ejaculate? Is the penis itself unkosher or just the semen that comes out?" The rabbi responds, "You know it is forbidden to take a man's penis into your mouth. The Code of Jewish Laws prohibits that form of relations between husband and wife."

"But Rabbi, I have a mental illness. When I am ill, I am unable to abide by our laws. I always feel terribly guilty and I always seek God's forgiveness on the Day of Atonement. The only law I have been able to follow is Kashrath. No matter how ill I have been, I always follow our dietary laws."

"Oh, I see," responds the rabbi. "I probably should tell you it's forbidden, by the laws of Kashrath, just to keep you virtuous. But you are an intelligent woman and this is an interesting question. Let me see." Rabbi Sofrin ponders the question and after thinking deeply he responds:

"My child. Many years ago the great rabbis posed a similar question. We are commanded to eat bitter herbs, matzo, and Harosis on Passover. One of these great rabbis, Rabbi Hillel, interpreted the commandment to mean that they should be eaten together. As you know, we first eat the herbs, matzo, and Harosis separately at the Seder table and then we eat them together as Rabbi Hillel said we should. Now let me think, if the great rabbis were asked, should we eat penis with semen together or penis and semen separately... "

At this point, Anna's imaginary dialogue ended. And even though she replayed it in her mind again and again from the beginning, each time with exactly the same ending, she never found the answer to her Talmudic question.

The first night of their trip, Anna just touched John and held him throughout the night. Enjoying him greatly, she felt an increasing desire to make love to him and was almost tempted to abandon her original plan and go straight to intercourse. But Anna needed to try new things, and she had her mind set on fellatio. Anything else would compromise her dreams for petty reasons. While the rest of the year was hell for Anna, these trips were life itself. She knew she could never abandon her roots, but she had to be free.

By the second night, Anna's head was spinning from her own indecision. She could not wait; she had to have him now. So she quickly opened his fly and took his penis in her mouth. To Anna's surprise and revulsion, John came directly in her mouth. She never considered that John would ask to change his medication after the group session. With semen still in her mouth, Anna instantly realized what she had done and in desperation began screaming "Traif, traif, traif," the Jewish word for unclean food.

18

Psychiatric Re-evaluation

On Wednesday, John joined Peter at their bench. "Ya know, Petey, I hate that fuckin' shrink. Psychiatrist, shit. Calls himself a doctor. Witch doctor if ya ask me. Man, I shoulda stayed here yesterday and talked to ya. What a waste of my fuckin' time goin' for that fuckin' re-e-val-u-a-tion. Ya know, they really piss me off. Think they know fuckin' everything.

"Brown starts lecturing me 'bout goin' off my meds. Ya know, he never stops to ask me what I think. Just calls me a fool for goin' off my meds. Tells me I had a breakdown 'cause I went off my meds. Shit, I didn't have no fuckin' breakdown. I got me some head. I only went off meds a couple a days on the bus, and found me a mental health center soon as I got there. I decided to go with Hanna fully medicated. Don't he get that? I made up my mind on meds, not off 'em. Don't he listen to me? I asked him when was the last time he had a hot girl wantin' to give him head on a bus to California. She gave me $300. What would he do?

"Well, he tells me he wouldn't give up everythin' he had for $300 and a blow job. Shit, that's when I stop talkin'. He don't understand. What does he mean, he wouldn't give up everythin'? He's already made his $300 this morning. And he'll probably get head from his wife tonight. How can he say that he wouldn't give up what he had for $300 and a blow job? Don't he see that it's me sittin' 'cross the desk? Don't he understand that I decided to go with Hanna with a clear head? Don't he understand that I ain't no child? I wanted to do it, and I did it."

As John pauses, Peter pictured himself walking up to his apartment. He knocks on the door in 2-1-2 sequence. The door slowly opens. Shirley appears and in a sultry voice says, "I'm glad you're home." After they kiss, Peter hands over his paycheck. "$300!" she exclaims. Peter unzips his pants. Watching from his bedroom door, Peter sees Shirley on her knees, by the kitchen table, her head in Sammy's crotch as he finishes his milk and cookies.

"Ya know, Petey, sometimes I just wish I had fuckin' cancer. My uncle had that shit, and man, did they fuck him up with drugs. He went bald, looked somethin' terrible, couldn't do nothin' for days after chemo, zapped him with radiation. Sometimes he wanted to give up. He finally did. Refused the fuckin' treatment and died. But nobody never looked down on him. It was always his choice. No one told him he couldn't choose. That's what I call respect. That's livin' and dyin' with dignity. But there ain't no dignity for us psychos. We make a few fuckin' mistakes… Okay, we make a whole lotta fuckin' mistakes. But that still ain't no reason to tell us what to do."

Stopping to take a drag on his cigarette, out of the right corner of his mouth, John turns toward Peter, saying, "Talking 'bout dignity, here's one for the books. Last spring Brown tells us 'bout Mellaril. It's a medicine I've taken for years; it keeps ya from comin' when ya come. It's fuckin' embarrassin'. Can ya imagine? You're at a peep show watchin' some hot whore dancin', and nothin' comes out. You're so 'fraid she's gonna laugh her head off – not that they never do, they're so fuckin' stoned – ya put toilet paper over your dick so she don't see nothin's comin' out."

Peter suddenly thought he was at the peep show, John in the booth next door. As John's dancer moans, "Ooo, I want to see you come," Peter looks over at John, his penis looking like a large fountain, spurting semen in all directions. Peter looks at the dancer in front of him, smoking a cigarette, her hand on her hip cocked to the side, a scowl on her face. Turning to John's girl she says, "Look at this character." With no bulge in his pants, wearing a blindfold, fully clothed, a plastic bag with toilet paper inside covering his penis, secured by a rubber band, wrapped in air conditioning filtration material, Peter moves slightly as he comes.

"So ya think he'd change my meds? Not this asshole. He tells me I need the medicine and it ain't really a problem I don't come. 'It is a fuckin' problem,' I scream, 'so change my goddamn meds!' Before ya know it, he calls the cops, and sends me back to the hospital. Guess what? They change my meds there.

"Ya see what I mean? He's a fuckin' asshole. Thinks I'm stupid. But he don't understand that I hear what he says. I know I need the medication but hell, I'm lonely and I'm horny, and I want to fuck, and I want to come the way you're supposed to. I took off with Hanna Banana 'cause I'm horny, but I ain't stupid. I went straight to mental health as soon as I got to Nebraska.

"Now, can ya imagine if I were still on the Mellaril with Hanna? Can you imagine how I woulda felt if that crazy girl sucked me off and nothin' came out? Bad 'nough she screamed 'Rape!' Hell, I'd rather go to jail than have her laugh at me for not comin' the way you're supposed to. Tell ya, that Hanna's a crazy girl. I'm just lucky they're so fuckin' prejudiced in Nebraska. Probably woulda locked me up if she'd been a Christian girl."

Peter felt a strong desire to touch his own crotch. Holding his hands steady by his side, at 50° angles, turned inward $1/16$ of an inch away from his legs, suspended $1/8$ of an inch above the bench, Peter continued picturing himself in the peep show with John. As they gawk at the girls, the fat man taps Peter on the shoulder. *Closing time?* asks Peter. LOCK UP TIME. With bars all around, Peter's led to his cell. YOUR TOILET, the guard says, pointing to the metal commode in Peter's cell. BUT WE NEED YOUR PANTS FIRST. Wearing one of Peter's suits, briefcase in hand, John enters Peter's cell. *It's a tough case,* he says. *Ya didn't come like you're supposed to.*

"By the way, talking 'bout fuckin' Hanna Banana again, did I tell ya, I saw her yesterday? Yep, the fuckin' whore's back in the program. I'll tell ya, I was shit-faced when I saw her. Thought she'd call the cops for sure. But no, she's in outer space, acts like she don't know me at all. But ya know it's July again, and guess what, she's off meds, smilin', laughin', wearin' lots of makeup. And guess who she's comin' onto now: a fuckin' dyke! God, last year she sucks my dick. Now, she wants cunt. Well, ya know what I say – Women, ya can't live with 'em, ya can't live without 'em."

John stops, thinking about what he had just said, proud of himself for coining this phrase.

"Well anyway, Petey, I gotta get back to the program. Crazy Hanna Banana, Dr. Brown or not, they got a good lunch today and I always like group therapy."

■ ■ ■

Peter returned to work thinking about John's stories: *I've got to take off my pants, too.* So like many other days after work, he went straight to the peep show. This time though, he wanted to masturbate openly: He wanted to take his organ out and emit semen under the proud eye of his exotic dancer.

He went straight to a private viewing booth and saw yet another anonymous, stoned dancer on the other side of the screen. With the usual request for money, the screen went down. Peter put his money in the slot and the screen went up again. As the woman danced, Peter reached down to open his fly. Realizing he did not have an erection, he stood there, immobilized.

Peter quickly left the booth, planning to go straight home and masturbate by himself. On his way out, however, he noticed a section of video booths featuring pornographic tapes instead of live dancers. He darted into a booth, placing several coins in the slot. He immediately started to have an erection watching a couple have sex on the screen. He pushed a button, the scene changed. Switching between ten channels, Peter watched men and women, men and men, women and women, and groups of people engage in various sexual activities. With great difficulty, he opened his zipper and took his organ out. Half erect, Peter masturbated to the visual images on the screen before him.

As he went on, Peter started feeling close to the figures on the screen and this scared him, so each time it felt too close, he pushed a button that switched the scene to a different channel. Watching different people copulate, he was able to continue his actions. As he approached orgasm, the people in the film seemed to stop their own activities to watch Peter, who felt he was the main attraction in a large amphitheater.

Afterwards, Peter walked to the bus, thinking to himself: *You did well.* Although disappointed that he could not expose himself to a live dancer, he was proud that he could climax while being watched.

Peter thought of himself like a young woman who had just given up her virginity: It didn't matter if it was good, it was only important that he had crossed a line.

■ ■ ■

That night, Peter dreamt he was in a clearing in a forest, thatched huts surrounding an open fire. Men in scant buckskin clothes, bare-breasted women like the ones he masturbated to in *National Geographic* magazine last week, Peter, a member of this aboriginal tribe, sits tied to a chair. The chief, a large man with gravy on his buckskin, starts the ritual. *Virgin, virgin, virgin,* he chants, pointing to Peter. Tom Carroll speaks, "So did you fuck her, man? She was really hot for you." The other children jeer, YOU'RE A JERK. NO ONE WANTS YOU. As everyone starts having sex, Peter opens his fly. Masturbating by himself, his penis exposed, Peter watches his semen slowly come out. Looking up, he sees that the others have stopped their own activities to watch him climax. With a loud round of applause, Peter wakes up. He reaches for his calculator, notepad, pen, and pencil and calculates the number of days he had lived, waiting to expose his penis.

19

Penny

As Peter walked to the park Thursday at noon, he spotted John pacing at the far end, near the children's playground, shouting and punching his fist in the air. Peter thought he should go over and help until he noticed a leaf on the bench where he planned to sit. Forgetting about John, he reached into his pocket, took out his plastic glove, slipped it on his hand, and carefully picked up the leaf. After placing the leaf in the refuse container, he walked back to the bench, where he noticed a minuscule stain where the leaf had been. Staring at the stain, he proceeded to calculate its Graduated Dirt Rating, certain it would qualify as minor dirt, when he was interrupted by loud footsteps from behind.

"Those fuckin' assholes. Can't just do their goddamn re-evaluation and let it be. Not enough to call me an idiot. Now, the whole fuckin' program's on my case. Fuck you, Brown!" John looks in the direction of his program calling out, "Ya listenin' to me, Brown?" extending the middle fingers of both hands in the air screaming, "FUCK YOU!"

John sits down next to Peter, pulls out a cigarette, and lights it with a match from his pocket. He blows out smoke furiously. "I give up, Petey. If they wanna get ya, they'll get ya. I go back to the program after I left yesterday and Jim, my counselor, pulls me aside. 'Ya can't come right back,' he says. 'Brown wants to know you're serious 'bout treatment and ya ain't gonna stop your meds again.'

"I just fuckin' blew up. Don't think I'm serious. I took my meds before I got on that bus. I joined a program as soon as I got there. Man, I'm screamin' my fuckin' head off, but it don't make no difference. They gotta meet with me again this afternoon before they let me back in. It's bullshit, Petey, pure bullshit."

Realizing he had rated the stain using the revised GDRS, Peter recalculated its score with the original GDRS. Comforted that the stain scored minor dirt with either calculation, he began scanning the ground to find other dirt samples he could rate with both procedures.

"Now let me tell ya what real treatment's like. That's what they got in Nebraska. The mornin' after I got there, I knew I was in trouble, gettin' paranoid, so I go to the mental health center. Soon as I get there, I know it's different. It's clean, the people are friendly. They really care. I ain't got no appointment but it don't matter. I just walk in. Not only do they see me, they apologize for makin' me wait. Man, nobody apologizes for shit in this town. Before ya know it, I'm on meds and in their day program. It was the best day program I ever saw. And the best part was Penny."

Then John leans over toward Peter, cupping his mouth with his left hand to make an exaggerated whisper, adding, "I think I'm in love." Sighing deeply before lapsing into the first sustained silence he spent with Peter, John says, "I've got half a mind to get on a bus and go right back to Nebraska."

Peter sat quietly eating his sandwich, not certain he heard John's words clearly, as John sat in deep thought, remembering the Anderson Mental Health Center, Day Treatment Program's annual Spring Picnic.

■ ■ ■

At 9:30 a.m. Penny, two mental health aides, John, and the other patients boarded a bus for Winding Creek State Park. Throughout the morning, John was edgy, arguing over his seat in the van and complaining about the Planned Activities. Finally, Penny separated John from the group when he began raging at another patient for taking two hamburgers before he had taken one for himself. They walked together until they found a fallen tree to sit on.

"Motherfuckin' asshole! I'll break his fuckin' face!" John raged all the way, periodically turning back to aggressively point his finger at the other patient. Once they were alone, Penny asked him, "What's wrong, John? What do you care if he took two hamburgers?"

"He's a pig," John railed. "A goddamn, motherfuckin' pig! Whadaya mean, what do I care? I hate pigs. He's a fuckin' goddamn pig and I'm gonna break his fuckin' goddamn face. Watch me, Penny. I'm gonna do it!"

Penny responded, "You're not going to hurt him: I know it; you know it. Why are you so upset?" But John still wanted to stomp around and threaten the other patient, for in his mind this would impress Penny, so John slowly looked her over, stared in her eyes, and calmly said, "What would ya do if I did hurt the fuckin' bastard?"

Penny thought for a moment before replying, "I'd feel real sad. It's been nice having you in the program; I'd hate to see you go. But you know the rules: no violence. We'd call the police and contain you the best we could until they arrived. Then you're out of the program. If you're really getting sick, we'd send you to the hospital and maybe let you back when you were better. But you're not, so we'd press charges. And you know how people feel about that 'crazy New Yorker' who blew into town. They'd have you out on a rail. So as I said before, I'd be sad but you'd still have to go."

John knew he was beaten. As Penny sat back thinking about what she had just said to John, saying to herself, *You're good, Penny, You're real good,* John took a deep breath and casually said, "Ya know. I really miss Petey."

Shocked back to the moment, Penny asked, "Who's Petey?"

"My best friend," John replied. "Well maybe not my best friend – I gotta lotta friends back home – but my… " John pauses, looking for the right word. "My normal friend."

"I'd really like to hear about Petey," Penny said softly, imagining herself speaking in the clear voice of Dr. Maggie Hillman, her instructor in Social Work Technique I.

"Petey's this guy I used to have lunch with. Ya know, most of the guys are nuts, I know 'em from the program. But not Petey. He's the president of a local bank. One day I went in as a goof and asked him for a loan. Would ya believe it? He takes me real serious. Now, I ain't dressed no better than I am here, and I've tried this before and gotten the royal brushoff. But Petey takes me real serious. So I fill out the whole fuckin' application and he asks me for my credit references. I don't know what the hell to do; I ain't got no credit. But

I remember the time Sparky lent me ten bucks; I paid him back most of it. So I tell him Sparky and he writes it down. I think the guy's gonna throw me the fuck outta his office, but he don't. Just tells me to come back tomorrow.

"Hell, I'm no fool. He's just fuckin' with me, or maybe he's gonna call the cops; I can't figure out if I'm comin' back. But I don't know; somethin' inside told me to go back. So the next day I'm in Petey's office again. Tells me I'm approved for a $100 loan to pay back when I can. Has me sign some fancy-lookin' contract and gives me $100 straight outta his wallet.

"Next day I see Petey on a park bench. He sees me and calls me over. I'm startin' to get it; he's fuckin' gay and thinks he's gonna get me. Well fuck him, I think, but I go over. Ya know, I used to let fags suck me off for money when I was a kid. So I'm tryin' to decide. Do I roll him? Do I fuck him? But it ain't like that; he really wants to be a friend. Shit, Petey and me been gettin' together for lunch, right out there in the park... for months. Can ya imagine a guy like Petey talkin' to me?"

Penny felt sad listening to John. And because they were alone in the park on a beautiful day, sitting on a fallen tree together, she felt a strong urge to tell John about herself. "You know, I have a friend, too, in California. I miss her a great deal. She's the kind of person you say something and she instantly gets it. Sometimes I call her and we talk for hours. We just laugh and laugh. I don't have to explain why I hate Anderson; she just gets it – the people, the attitudes, the false values. She gets it all. I don't have anybody else to talk to who does."

Touched by Penny's candor, John instinctively put his hand on her shoulder. She responded by putting her hand on his and looking him straight in the eye. She said, "Thanks." John slowly leaned over, and kissed her. Throughout the slow, sweet kiss, Penny sat motionless, not returning his kiss but not pushing him away either. Pulling back, John said, "I'm sorry." Penny smiled and replied, "It's OK."

After a moment, John hesitantly said, "I thought you wanted to." "No, I didn't," said Penny. "That's not what we're here for. But don't be ashamed. It's natural to want a woman, not just a prostitute here or there or even a blow job on a bus. Sure, those things have had their place in your life, but you need a lover, a partner. It's natural.

You're a good man, and I want you to believe you can have somebody who loves you."

John thought about Penny's words, unsure how to respond. Taking out a cigarette, he lights up and sucks in through the right side of his mouth. Blowing out the smoke, he turns to Penny, and says, "Ya know, it's a crock of shit, this shit 'bout smokin' bein' bad for ya. It ain't the smoke; it's how ya smoke the cigarette. Most people smoke with both lungs, like this." John demonstrates regular smoking. "It'll get ya fuckin' sick. But I smoke like this." He again draws the cigarette in through the right corner of his mouth. "All that nasty shit goes in my right lung, leavin' my left lung free and clear, able to breathe in only good air. Next week I change to my left lung and give my right lung a chance to heal. A lotta folks can't do it but I can, cause I'm ambi-lung-uous."

Looking for a response, John turns to Penny. At first, she tries to control herself but she ends up laughing so hard she can't even talk. And after a few minutes when she regains her composure enough to speak, she says, "That's the most ridiculous thing I've ever heard." As soon as she said it, Penny regretted her words, having never laughed like this at a patient before. And John didn't know if he should be offended or if he actually agreed with her. Not knowing what else to do, he went on.

"Really, man, it works. Here, I'll show you; try it yourself," he says, giving her the same cigarette he just smoked. Penny, who had quit smoking five years before and is hesitant to smoke again, decides to go along, hoping to undo the harm of laughing at him. So she takes the cigarette and draws the smoke through the right side of her mouth. An earnest teacher, John guides her through the nuances of right-lung smoking. After the fifth try, he congratulates her perfect performance. And although he tries to discourage her from smoking with the left lung on the same day, Penny, who by now is having too much fun, demands the chance. John immediately applauds her proficiency at left-lung smoking and pronounces her left lunged, without hesitation.

That night, Penny bought a pack of cigarettes on her way home, wanting to show her husband, Mark, what she had learned. Before she came home, she took one cigarette out, discarding the rest of the pack. "Guess what, Mark? Look at what I learned." She showed him the cigarette, quickly adding, "Now, don't worry. I'm not going to start smoking again, but watch." She lit the cigarette and smoked it out of the right side of her mouth. "Now, watch," she added, this time smoking from the left side. Putting the cigarette out, she proudly declared, "I'm ambi-lung-uous."

His face red with rage, Mark shouted, "Don't let me ever catch you smoking again, you idiot," and smacked her across the face. The argument mounted. Mark threw a chair across the room before going to bed. That night, Penny called her best friend in California.

The next day in their regular therapy session, John told Penny he thought he might go back to New York. Penny, distracted by her difficult night, responded by saying, "Yeah, my friend thinks I should leave, too." Immediately recognizing the terror in John's eyes, Penny tried to apologize and assure him that she was staying. But John simply said, "I tried to call Petey last night, too, but they said he's off in Paris workin' on some big bank deal. Ya know, Petey's a rich motherfucker, and he don't mind sharin' his money with me. Did I tell ya 'bout the time he took me fishin'?"

"No," Penny replied, still feeling off-kilter and distracted.

"The dude's got this big motherfucker of a boat. I tell ya, it's so big ya gotta take a cab to get from one end to the other. So we go out fishin'. Now Petey don't know I know how to fish, so he gives me a pole and asks if I wanna try. I play him on and say 'Guess so.' Shit, I'm pullin' in one fish after another. The guy tells me I'm a helluva fisherman, says he ain't never seen nobody fish so good the first time. So I just break out laughin' and tell him it ain't my first time. No, I fished lotsa times with my dad. He was some helluva guy. Used to take me everywhere. Went fishin', huntin', ball games, everywhere. John and Pop. Never seen him without me or me without him. A helluva guy."

Still hoping to re-establish her therapeutic stance, she said, "Tell me more about your dad."

"He was great, Penny. You'd never seen a better father. He worked real hard but always had time for me. Coached my baseball team, led the Cub Scouts, played catch. I tell ya, all the time. The guy was with me all the time. One day Dad came home with a giant smile, thought it would crack open his fuckin' face, smilin' from ear to ear. Ya know, it's the kinda smile that ev'ry kid knows means somethin' big. I couldn't figure out what the hell was goin' on but before long, I'm smilin' as much as he is. 'Tell me, Daddy, tell me, whatdidyaget me?' Well, my mom tells me to hush up, 'Your daddy ain't got nothin' for you, boy, we can't afford nothin'.' But I knew he got me somethin'. Shit would ya believe, he had the biggest, best, shiniest bike ya ever saw. I was fuckin' happy. I heard 'em fightin' later. Mom thought he shouldn't a done it but that's my dad. Some helluva guy."

John broke from his thoughts and looked up. It was 1:10 p.m. and Peter was gone.

20

The Candidate

By the time he got home, Peter was tense and filled with dismay, thinking about John's words over and over again: *I've got half a mind to get on a bus and go right back to Nebraska.*

For a moment he pictured himself falling into a deep, dark hole, a rope neatly coiled at the top, John standing there looking down. John looks away at an oncoming bus, a sign boldly declaring its destination: Nebraska. John turns back to Peter, disdainfully saying, "Keep your penis in your pants."

Peter shook the thoughts, remembering that John has always treated him kindly. He imagined himself calling John on the telephone, "Hey buddy, were you serious about going back to Nebraska?" and after a pause for the answer, saying "Phew, that takes a load off my mind. I'd hate to see you go." *Yeah, that's what I'll do,* he thought, before remembering. *I don't know where he lives. I don't know his number.*

Peter thought back to a card Dr. Johnson once handed him while Peter was in psychoanalysis. The card – part of a standard, projective personality test – showed a man walking away from a woman who was sitting with her head bent down, her face in her hands. Two children tugged at the man's coat, desperately trying to hold him back. Hoping to start a dialogue after months of silence, Dr. Johnson asked Peter to make up a story telling what was going on in the picture. Peter responded, "There are four people here." When the doctor inquired about their relationships, he answered, "They're together." In response to the next question, "Can you make up a story about these people?" Peter answered "Yes, they're all in the same room."

Frustrated and angry, Dr. Johnson demanded that Peter make up a story for the card. "Are they laughing, talking, dancing, arguing, fucking?" he snapped. Peter responded, "They're buying shoes."

That night, Peter dreamt there had been a thermonuclear explosion. Everyone suffered painful deaths except Peter, who emerged physically unscathed but doomed to suffer the pain of loneliness. He envied his dead compatriots and longed to atone for his survival. Walking through the devastated city, twisted bodies and rubble everywhere, he spotted a few other survivors who were sitting around a deep pit in which there was an enormous fire. As he approached, he saw that they were, one by one, jumping into the fire, committing suicide. Before each suicide, they warmly hugged and said good-bye to each other. But as Peter approached the group, one of its members turned toward him and coldly pointed to another burning pit, several blocks away. Dejected, Peter slowly walked off to jump into the fire, alone.

■ ■ ■

On Friday when Peter arrived, John was already sitting calmly on the bench. "I'm back in the program. Jim's OK, says they now wanna hear 'bout Nebraska, maybe they'll learn somethin' new. It's a crock. They don't wanna learn nothin'. But I'm back in so it ain't so bad. But I gotta tell ya, Petey, they could learn somethin' cause Penny ran a helluva program. Ya know when I first realized how good it was: in Current Events Group."

Peter looked at the bench, seeing John's rear end perched squarely between the center and left end of the bench. Drawing two imaginary lines trisecting the bench, he saw that one line cut through some new dirt starting just under John's left knee and splattered across most of the unoccupied parts of the center section, crossing slightly into Peter's seat. If Peter sat precisely in the middle of his seat, his thigh would brush against the dirt. So Peter positioned himself 3/4 of an inch off-center, protecting himself from any contact with the dirt.

"Yeah, they got Current Events here, too, but they don't do it right. Here, Greg runs the group. He turns on the midday news while everyone sleeps. If ya try to talk, he tells ya to shut up. If ya really try to talk, he shuts ya up by telling ya what he thinks. He won't let nobody else pick the station.

"Now Penny does it all different. We don't watch TV. We talk 'bout things in the news. And we don't just talk, we vote. No shit. Penny took the fuckin' group, all the psychos out to Town Hall and registered us to vote. Believe me, it ain't as easy as it sounds. A lotta those nuts are scared to vote, but she got us talking 'bout it until everyone had 'nough courage to go. Then, get this. After we signed up, she invites the candidates to talk to us, askin' for our votes.

"Petey, it's the most amazin' thing: Here, we're shit. There, we're a voting block, or that thing Penny called us: a constitution-ary? So here I am, in the middle of nowhere, and two candidates for judge… Can ya believe it? For judge… are tryin' to win my vote. I'll show you how it went."

With that John got up and walked around the park as if he were looking for something. While he was gone, Peter began eating his sandwich, thinking about the one time he tried to vote. It was 1976, the presidential election between Jimmy Carter and Gerald Ford. Walking through the park, Peter saw a middle-aged woman wearing a 2½-inch-diameter button pinned prominently to her enormous left breast, commanding in big red letters against a pale blue background: VOTE. Curved along the edge of the button were other words in black: League of Women Voters. As Peter stared at her breast, she asked, "Are you registered, sir?"

"I'm sorry," Peter said, turning away, expecting to be slapped. "Don't be sorry," the lady smiled. "Just vote." Directing him to a folding table, where a man and another woman sat, she asked for his name, address, and identification, and registered him to vote. "You'll receive your registration card and a sample ballot in four weeks. The election will be held on November 2, the first Tuesday of the month. If you can wait a second, I'll give you the location of your voting booth."

For the next two months, Peter masturbated nightly, picturing himself in the booth watching the registrar dance naked for him. Certain she had been aroused, assuming, like an engorged male organ, her large breasts meant she was close to climax, Peter was sure she was the one woman he would finally have.

On November 2, Peter got up early and rushed to PS 38, the

school at the corner of 87th Street and Columbus Avenue where Peter was to vote. Inside the school, the first voter in line, Peter walked up to the table, signed in, and entered the booth. There, Peter found a full-blown ballot like the sample mailed to him. Waiting for a screen to rise, his naked registrar behind, Peter soon realized that nothing would happen. As he heard the taunts, HA-HA-HA, HE WANTS A GIRL, NO ONE WANTS YOU, he inadvertently put his hand in his pocket and began rubbing his penis.

"Sir. Is there a problem?" a voice called from outside. Without speaking Peter rubbed himself quickly, climaxing in seconds. "Anything wrong, sir? Is the curtain stuck?"

"I'm not sure what to do," Peter answered.

"Look to your upper left. There's a lever. Turn it to the right, and you'll get out." Peter turned the lever and left, without ever casting his ballot.

■ ■ ■

"Listen, Petey. This is how it went." Looking up, Peter saw John carrying an old wooden crate. "I'll pretend I'm Harold Fairview giving you a campaign speech." John puts the crate on the ground, steps on it with his right foot, the crate cracking beneath his weight. Catching his balance, John shakes the crate off his foot, kicking it hard to the side. "Goddamn crate!" John shouts. "I'm gonna fuckin' sue the... " He stops, bends down, and reads the words printed on the side of the crate, "*Sunrise Fruit and Vegetable Company.* Ya gotta pen, Petey, I gotta write this name and address down." Peter hands John a pen. While John writes the information on the inside of his hand, Peter thought: *Wow, great kick.* He laughed to himself thinking about Simon.

"Now let me show you how it went. I'll stand on the bench and pretend it's the box, and that I'm running for judge." As John steps on the bench, Peter noted his position, on the far end, spoiling that seat for tomorrow's lunch.

"I'm Harold Fairview. I want your vote. Vote for me and I'll be a great judge. Then after ya vote for me, I'll fuck ya over. But I'm great 'cause blah, blah, blah. Blah, blah, blah. Blah, blah, blah, blah, blah, blah, blah. Blah, blah, blah. Blah, blah, blah. So in conclusion, blah,

blah, blah, blah, blah." John jumps off the bench and sits down again. Looking around, Peter saw three people watch them at about 25 feet SSE, snickering. "That's just what he said, I swear. And I fuckin' voted for him."

As John gets up to leave, he asks, "So, whaddaya think? Pretty good speech? Maybe I'll run for office, too. Well, have a good weekend; I'll see ya Monday." As John walks away, Peter saw him stop several people on the way, offering his hand, "Hi, I'm John Waller. I'm running for judge. Hope you'll vote for me."

21

Washington, D.C.

Peter woke up at 3:30 a.m. Saturday morning. He dreamt that as he gave him a blow job on a bus, John laughed and screamed rape. He dreamt of John and Penny – Penny in the form of a woman he passed on his way home from work – as loving parents, taking good care of him. He dreamt that he rode horseback with John through a tall field of Nebraska corn to have sex with both John and the horse. Then he had the same dream with Penny instead of John as his partner, the horse the same. He dreamt that he entered a voting booth with John and sees that they are the candidates for the Ambi-lung-uous Party; Peter running for president, John running for judge. But then Peter stands in front of Judge John, sentenced to castration for his peep show habit. Finally, it is Peter proudly marching down Pennsylvania Avenue for his inauguration. Standing before Chief Justice John, he holds up his right hand with his left hand placed on a Bible as John administers the "fuckin' oath."

Peter opens his eyes to look around the dark room. The room seems unfamiliar: nothing the way it should be. Now certain he has gone mad, Peter reaches over to the night table for his calculator, notepad, pen, and pencil to figure the number of days he has been sane; these items just where they belong, precisely placed to meet his arm's extension from the middle of the bed. Yet the table seemed different, higher than he recalled and with a telephone on it. *Why a telephone,* he puzzled. Frightened that someone planned to call him when they were ready to take him away, he lay frozen in the bed – afraid to turn on the light so he could make the required calculation, afraid to go back to sleep. Trembling with fear, Peter waited for the morning light, hoping it would take away the distortions of the night.

But when morning came, the glimmering light revealed an unfamiliar space: this was not Peter's room. Cautiously, he rose out of his bed. He saw his ruler on the night table; he must have used it to measure the placement of the calculator, notepad, pen, and pencil. On the other side of the bed was a second bed. Walking over to it slowly, he inspected the bed and found no signs of use. *Why another bed,* thought Peter. *Is that for John?*

Looking across the room, he saw a television, two chests of drawers, a desk and a table with Howdy Doody, Buffalo Bob, and Clarabelle Clown on top of the table. To the left, there was a small bathroom and on the toilet seat a paper wrapping announcing that the seat was "Sanitized for your Protection." Thinking back, he could vaguely recall removing the paper carefully to use the toilet and then replacing the wrapping the way he found it. He looked to the right and saw the door, and posted on it was a sign announcing the Rules and Regulations of the Washington, D.C., Hotel Commission with the maximum rates for the room. He was not at home but in a hotel. Somewhat relieved that he was not in his own room suffering from distorted perceptions, but also distressed that he was in a hotel miles from his home and clueless about how he got there, he walked back to the bed to sit down and think. But before he sat down, he realized that the second bed had not been used the night before and was cleaner and less contaminated than the bed he woke up in. He shuffled over to that bed and sat down.

Unable to recall coming to Washington, D.C., at all, he thought about the two other times he found himself in places without recalling how he got there. Shortly after his mother died, Peter woke up in a motel room in upstate New York, not far from the Beaver Christian Camp. He spent the weekend in the room, struggling to decide if he should call Aunt Maureen, but in the end returning home Sunday having done nothing but sit and fret the entire time. Also, after discontinuing psychoanalysis with Dr. Johnson, he found himself at a government office, applying for a passport, again with no recollection about how he got there. When he reached in his coat pocket, he found an airplane ticket to Vienna, Austria. Ashamed, he discarded the ticket without using it or asking for a refund.

Rising from the bed, Peter walked to the dresser, where he spied a piece of paper with an itinerary for today written on it: breakfast, get tickets for the White House, visit the Jefferson Memorial, Lincoln Memorial, the Washington Monument, and Smithsonian Museums, as time permits, depending on when the White House tour begins. To the right there was another paper with detailed plans for the following day. Peter sat and thought but could not remember planning this trip at all.

Although Peter never traveled, he spent many hours thinking about the many places he wanted to go. Now here was his friend John who acted on his feelings, unashamed of the strange things he thought and did. John acted on impulse, he was free. Peter wanted to be like John. He would follow the itinerary he had planned. After looking at his watch and seeing it was close to 6:45 a.m. – breakfast on his agenda – Peter began his Washington trip by eating a banana from the table.

By 7:30 a.m., Peter was in line at the White House information center, where he stood for forty minutes until he received a ticket for the 1:30 p.m. White House tour. He took off to the Jefferson Memorial. Once there, he counted the steps ahead of him – forty-four Type 2 steps – looked at his watch, and climbed at a pace 10 percent less than average, to reach the top at exactly 9:30 a.m., his scheduled time of arrival.

Indistinguishable from the other tourists, with camera in hand, Peter Branstill felt exhilarated knowing that he, too, could partake in this great American ritual. No longer a nerd but a regular tourist, Peter felt normal – and free. By 10:45 a.m., standing before the Lincoln Memorial, a towering white structure, like a vast cloud against the wide, blue sky, Peter felt calm, refreshed, and uncommonly guilt-free. But at 11:30 a.m., he approached the Washington Monument and began to feel afraid when he recognized the structure's phallic symbolism. Relieved that lunch was next and that he would be on a park bench – his favorite spot – at noon, Peter stopped to reflect on the successes of his day. So far he had spent half a day touring the city, and except for a few erotic thoughts about the Washington Monument, he had proceeded without a major problem. Peter questioned if he should go on any further, but with the schedule clear, and destined to follow routine, he persevered and went to the White House for the 1:30 p.m. tour. As he approached, and got closer to the President's home, he felt uneasy. The Memorials were open and informal, and Peter could plan his approach, but the White House was secure and heavily guarded, and once Peter spotted a secret service agent, he knew he could not join the line knowing that he was being watched. Peter stood there completely immobilized. He would not queue up with his fellow tourists to be watched, counted, and exterminated. He began dwelling on the thought that this gathering was staged specifically for him, that they would trick him into entering the White House and once he had passed through the facade, he would be trapped behind the barbed wire, led to the showers, disrobed, shaved, and sent to his death. Terrified, Peter quickly walked away.

Peter went back to the bench where he ate lunch to ponder this quagmire. As he looked at his itinerary and Washington, D.C., tourist brochure, he inadvertently reached in his pocket pulling out a small notebook with detailed records of this year's elevator rides to and from his office each day. Checking his watch, he suddenly remembered that today was the Saturday he studied the elevator's yearly performance while sitting in front of Mom's grave. Looking at the city map, with Arlington Cemetery nearby, Peter decided to spend the rest of his day there.

■ ■ ■

Exiting the subway with the other tourists, stunned by the majestic beauty of Arlington National Cemetery, Peter walked through the archway, picturing Mom buried deep at Woodcrest, all alone. Veering from the tourists, he looked for a solitary grave where he could sit and work out next year's elevator plan. After completing his calculations in front of the grave of Colonel Jenkins, a World War II hero born January 27, 1920, Peter looked to the north, realizing Dad's grave was 240 miles away. Quickly figuring the dimensions of a triangle proportional to the family's seating arrangement at Aunt Cindy's apartment, and the triangle formed by his chair, Colonel Jenkins' grave, and his parents' graves in Woodcrest Cemetery, Peter realized he would need to move his chair into the Atlantic Ocean to create the required proportional triangle.

Peter pictured himself riding by cab to the far end of Fred's yacht, looking out the window, watching the fish jump high out of the ocean, John and his dad sitting near each other in the back seat. *John and Pop. Never seen him without me or me without him. A helluva guy.* As they leave the cab, Peter looks back seeing his own dad at the other end of the boat, a pork chop in his mouth, grease all over his face. Tell your dad to join us, John says. *Aunt Cindy says he can't fish.* As Peter reels in one fish after the other, an awed John proclaims: I ain't never seen nobody fish so good the first time. As a shark jumps on board, Peter realizes he's in Arlington Cemetery, his penis erect. Turning away from some people standing at a nearby grave, he gets up and walks carefully back to the train to return to his hotel room.

■ ■ ■

That evening, back in his room, Peter lay in his bed, gazing around, when he noticed that the hotel left him a complimentary newspaper. Picking it up, he read the news, then progressed to the entertainment section, and noticed an advertisement for an adult theatre. It looked like there was a pornography district in town, and not wanting to masturbate, he put the paper down. For the next half hour he struggled with guilt but still got aroused picturing the shark biting off his penis. He finally got back up, left the room, went downstairs, and hailed a cab. After a brief ride, Peter came upon the familiar sights and sounds of any city X-rated zone. Among the prostitutes on the street and the several XXX theatres, he spotted a peep show and quickly entered. He spent little time there, quickly relieving his anxiety and returning by another cab to his room.

Sunday morning, Peter awoke in his room and reviewed the planned itinerary for the day. First, he ate breakfast, clearly labelled, Breakfast – Sunday. After showering and dressing, he proceeded out of his room, determined to follow the plan, but as soon he felt the warm summer air outside the hotel, he suddenly changed his mind, hailed a cab, and went back to the pornography district.

As he exited the cab in the bright daylight, the street seemed less sinister, so with an air of respectability, he looked around while walking down the street. No longer ready to dart into the first peep show, he carefully studied the various places before coming across a place with a large sign announcing *The Capital Girls*.

Sporting a cheap facade that looked like the White House, the establishment promised *A Peep Show of Historical Significance*. Once inside, Peter stood in awe seeing a large replica of the Washington Monument, accurate except that the point was redesigned to look like the head of a penis. He gazed at the walls decorated with American flags and red, white, and blue streamers. He listened to patriotic music blasting out over the sound system. Looking around, he saw the various stations of a full-service peep show.

To the right was the familiar selection of pornographic magazines and videotapes for sale, but here there was a sign displaying the Bill of Rights with Freedom of the Press highlighted from the rest of the words. There was a cabinet with sexually stimulating gadgets for sale. The cabinet had a sign exhorting, "Products of American technology. Made in the U.S.A." Below this was a sign saying, "Give me orgasm or give me death."

Peter turned left toward the familiar private peep booths. He saw two rows. On each side, there were six enclosed rooms with girls displaying their wares hoping to provide private sessions with the clientele. Each booth was designed to look like the memorials Peter had seen the day before. The girls in the booths on the left sat nude in their chairs wearing stovepipe hats. The girls to the right sat naked wearing wigs in Jeffersonian style.

And the booths sported signs intended to highlight the historical significance of the place. On the left, there was "Honest Babe," "Gettysburg Undress," and "Be my John, Booth." On the right, there was "Mount My Cello," and a marker indicating that two adjacent booths had "Louise and Anna Purchase." Peter spent the next several hours climaxing to the girls of D.C.

■ ■ ■

Late that afternoon, Peter took the train home, with spirits high, thinking about his trip to Washington, D.C. He could not remember having felt this good in many years. He thought about John and his trip. John goes out west with a girl he hardly knows, gets a blow job, and the girl cries rape. He spends months in a strange town, voting for the first time, making a big mistake voting for Judge Fairview.

Peter shows up in Washington, D.C., with absolutely no recall of how he got there, yet finds a carefully planned agenda that he tries to follow. Yet while the other tourists see the sights, he alters the itinerary and spends half of his trip with the Capital Girls. Peter, whose life has always involved peep shows, ends up enjoying a weekend visiting the peep shows of D.C.

Peter drifted into imaginary conversations with a travel agent. "My name is Peter Branstill. I'd like to take a trip to… " One time it was Europe, another the Orient, the rain forests of South America. The destination kept changing, but the story stayed the same. "Yes sir, we have a nice package for you. Let me show you the brochure." Peter examines the brochure carefully. "Yes this is perfect, just what I was looking for." Peter waits while the agent confirms the reservation. "Oh sir, there is one thing. Do you have any information on the peep shows there." The agent responds, "Oh, yes sir. I'm sorry. You wanted the peep show package. Hold on one moment. We have an excellent trip planned… "

Peter kept replaying this conversation for most of the trip until another thought crossed his mind. For years, he had frequented peep shows practically unaware that he belonged to a group. At every place there were other men, hesitant, anxious, and embarrassed as he. Peter never considered that they shared an interest. They all shunned recognition. They never thought of themselves as compatriots.

Like thousands of tourists before him. Peter had finally visited the nation's capital. But the crowds at the White House frightened him. The men at Capital Girls were cronies.

Peter created several imaginary conversations between himself and the other men there. He pictured them sharing their thoughts about the sights, the girls, the Washington Monument replica, the various patriotic sayings, the stirring music. Peter had never before considered that he could talk with the other men at the peep show.

Peter had never before thought that he and his fellow peepers shared an interest. Some men play ball. Some men bowl. Some just get together over beers. Peter liked to jerk off at peep shows. In all his years, he never introduced himself to any of these other men. He never talked to them and they never conversed with each other.

Peter thought about the many buttons, bumper stickers, and baseball caps he had noticed representing a wide variety of interests. "I'd Rather Be Fishing," sported one cap. "Bowlers Have Balls," he saw on a bumper sticker. Why is there no pride among peep show users? *I'd Rather Peep,* thought Peter.

■ ■ ■

Sunday evening, Peter endured a restless sleep, struggling with new ideas about himself. *I'm not the only peeper. What if Andrew goes there? He's not going to fire me. We might even peep together. Peep together, what a wonderful idea. Why do we slither around as if no one knows what we're doing. We're just like anyone else. You'd think we committed some terrible crime.*

Peter picked up his pencil and pad, placed carefully as ever. He began to write:

Methodical
Afraid
Accountant

The words all described Peter. He continued writing,

Peep shows
Afraid to go insane
Alone
Contamination
Dad died
George

Peter looked at his list. *That's me. But where do I belong? John belongs in his day program. Where do I belong?*

■ ■ ■

Monday morning, Peter woke up. He had an insatiable desire to return to the peep show. He wanted to meet the other men shuffling by the private booths, never making contact with their compatriots. He wanted to speak with the fat man behind the booth and ask him about his day. He wanted to talk with the private dancer, not down and dirty, but just to converse: *So whatdayado in your free time? Any vacation plans this year?* he thought of saying before beating off to her rhythmical bumps and grinds.

Peter had to go there. But he would wait until the end of the day. First and foremost, Peter was "Methodical."

22

The Commission

On Monday, Peter arrived at the bench, picturing himself at the peep show tonight, talking with the guys, when John buoyantly approached.

"Hey Petey. What's happening?"

John often asked this question, paused, and then went on with the story of his day. But now Peter had exciting new ideas of his own to share, and he almost did except that in his hesitancy he lost the chance. John quickly went on to ask, "Did I ever tell ya how I left Anderson? It's one of the wildest stories you'll ever hear." Of course, John thought all of his stories were wild, not recalling that he applied the same attribution to his other tales.

"I tell ya, Petey, I arrived with a blow job. I left getting screwed." John laughed out loud for several minutes at his joke but Peter did not respond, didn't even faintly smile; he was off thinking about his own evening's plan.

John looked at Peter. "Did ya get that, Petey, a blow job getting there, and a royal screwin' when I left." Slowly, John's laughter died down and he took a deep drag on his cigarette and settled in to tell Peter the story of his exit from Anderson.

"Let's see, I told ya 'bout Judge Fairview. I voted for him. I listened to him speak, I even shook his hand. I fuckin' voted for him. So what happens? He railroads me outta town. I tell ya. I should sue the bastard. Yeah, sue him. I tell ya, Petey. There ain't no justice." John inhales a bit more, throws his cigarette on the ground and crushes it.

"It all started when I got horny. Hanna Banana's blow job was the last sex I had. Frankly, she wasn't that good. But I was havin' fun. I loved the program, a lot better than the one here. I loved Penny. The other patients were OK but the babes were kinda burnt out. After a while, I'm gettin' horny as hell. Well, I gotta get off somehow. I realize, there ain't no porn in the whole fuckin' town. They ain't got no 42nd Street there. How could they? There ain't forty-two streets in the whole fuckin' town." John laughs again while Peter half-listens and half-thinks about this evening.

"There ain't no porn street, no porn shop, no fuckin' peep shows. There ain't no adult videos, and there ain't no hookers. They got nothin' 'cept a whole lotta churches, but no fuckin' porn. So I figures I gotta beat off without the stuff but that ain't easy when you're on these fuckin' medications. Even without Mellaril, it ain't so easy. Ya can't just do it in your mind. Ya gotta have somethin' to look at. Hell, I got me a Sears catalog just to beat off to the underwear ads."

Oh, you beat off to underwear ads, too. I used to do that, but now I've got something better. If you can't find a good, X-rated magazine, try American Horseman, *or* Horse and Saddle. *Those fillies are hot,* Peter thought, picturing John standing by Peter at the peep show, just two of the guys.

"Anyways, just when I figure it's hopeless, I see this headline in the newspaper:

PROSECUTOR SMITH FORMS
PORNOGRAPHY COMMISSION

"Well, my first thought is, 'It's about fuckin' time.' I figures somebody finally saw the need. But then I read the article. They ain't talkin' 'bout bringin' pornography to Anderson, they're tryin' to get rid of the shit.

"Petey, I ain't never laughed so hard in my life; I thought I'd croak. This guy's supposed to be smart, a lawyer, the prosecutor; he don't need no commission. I coulda told him there ain't no porn in this whole fuckin' town. But then my brain moves into gear. I starts thinkin': Hey, maybe they know somethin' I don't know. Why would they form this commission if the stuff ain't here?

"The first thing I do is go all over town. Maybe I missed it. Maybe there's a street, a shop, an alley, somethin' I didn't see. Well, that don't work. Go all over the fuckin' place. Nothin'. I tell ya. Nothin'. But it's gotta be here. They ain't gonna have no commission if there ain't no porn in town.

"So I ask around a little bit, actin' like I'm against the shit. It don't take me long before I learn that there's one video shop. Get this, one video shop that rents the stuff. They're forming a whole fuckin' commission to keep this guy from rentin' porn flicks. Al Jones. He owns the Video King. It's right on Main Street. I've passed it a thousand times. Al keeps the shit under the counter and there ain't one sign tellin' ya it's there. If ya want it, ya ask for 'The List.' He hands ya the list, ya pick what ya want without ever seein' the cover, and he hands it to ya in a plain, black box.

"Can ya imagine, Petey? Goin' down to 42nd Street. Ya quietly enter an adult video store. 'Psst, psst,' ya whisper, 'Can I see,' your voice gets softer, 'The List.' Well, that's what they got in Anderson, one store quietly rentin' porn, and the prosecutor forms a commission. I tell ya Petey, people are somethin'."

As John stopped for another drag on his cigarette, Peter pictured himself standing in front of Joe's Newsstand: *Psst, psst, can I see The List.* Danny McGraw turns around and hands Peter a plain black box: Inside, a copy of *Horse and Saddle* covered with snot.

"One day I go in and ask for The List. He takes it out. I make a selection. He's outta this, he's outta that. What's he got? *Boob Ruth*. She's a fuckin' whore with tits like an elephant. She wears a baseball uniform for fifteen seconds, fucks the whole team, and ends up ridin' the baseball bat. I mean really low-class shit."

Oh yeah, I saw that. It's sure low-class, but better than nothing. Did you notice that oval around the words: Louisville Slugger. I would've preferred a more circular shape, but what can you do, that's the logo they use. Peter pictured himself sharing a hearty laugh as John slaps him on the back: *You're a card, Petey, but when you're right, you're right.*

"So I ask Al what happened to the rest of his shit. He tells me, 'stag night.' Well, I ain't got no idea what stag night is but I figures I should go and get to know these stags: Maybe they can help me fight this commission shit. And anyway, I figures we should do it for Al. If they're gonna close him down, we should at least fight for him. So I ask Al for more info. He tells me, 'Stag night. Ya know, the firemen. Stag night.'

"Al goes on to tell me that each year, the fire company has a fundraising gig. It's all men. They rent out most of the porn tapes and have a good time. The firemen go, the police go. The mayor's there, too. A lotta important people go to stag night. Well, this gets me thinkin'. Ya know I'm smarter than most people think I am. They had a bunch of articles in the paper about obscenity after they formed this commission: I read 'em all. The Supreme Court says ya can ban shit if it don't fit the community standard.

"I start thinkin', the more shit out there, the more people usin' it. The less shit out there, the less usin' it. It's a fuckin' paradox. If everyone's usin' it, and ya got lots of peep shows and shit like we got here, then the porno freaks make up the community standard. Sure, ya gotta problem. Hell, look at New York. Ya bring your kid to the big city, vacation trip, Times Square, and there's all this shit. It's a problem but it's the fuckin' community standard so ya can't do nothin' 'bout it. But, in Anderson, it ain't a problem. Ya can't find the shit. Your kids don't see it on the street. So, the Supreme Court lets 'em ban it 'cause there ain't no *community standard.*

"And ya know, when they say community standard, they ain't talkin' 'bout the whole community. They're talkin' 'bout the upper class, them snoot dogs with their noses in the air. There's lotsa folks who use the shit, but no one counts 'em. I got a haircut one day, took a long look at the barber. He uses it. Looked at everyone else there. They use it, too. Hell, been to 'nough peep shows to know."

Gee, thought Peter. *You can never tell who uses porn: Firemen, policemen, barbers, just common folk like me and you. By the way, did I ever tell you, I use the stuff, too. No kidding. I can beat off with the best of them, just a regular guy.*

"So I decide I'm gonna fight this shit. I go to Video King and talk to Al. Thought he'd 'preciate my help. No way. Tries to shut me up. Says I'm too loud. Well, thanks a lot, Al. So, I tell Penny. She brings it up in Currents Events. That's cool, but no one wants to do nothin'. But Penny tells me 'bout the First Amendment: I can say what I want.

"Petey, listen to this. That's what finally got me kicked outta Anderson. No, it ain't my rentin' movies from The List. It ain't my bein' a weirdo from New York. Here it is: the First Amendment.

It's the fuckin' First Amendment that got me kicked out. I tell ya Petey, they don't mind ya as long as you're weird. But if you're right, I tell ya, they'll fuckin' nail ya to the cross."

With that, John reached in his shirt pocket, took out a folded piece of paper, and handed it to Peter, who read:

> Dear Editor:
> While the Prosecutor's Commission works hard to define obscenity in Anderson, Nebraska, there are many of us who regularly or occasionally use pornographic materials. Social pressure has caused us to remain silent, even though there is great danger that the commission will overlook our tastes in defining obscenity according to the United States Supreme Court's community standards rule. I, for one, wish to stand out as a representative of the pornography-using community. I encourage other unknown users to speak out as well. Finally, I invite our town's upstanding citizens, the Chief of Police, Mayor Thompson, Travis Sanders (whose wife Mae Sanders leads the anti-obscenity movement), and our many dedicated civil servants, to speak out against this movement. I take the liberty of representing their views, which I believe were tacitly expressed when they attended the recent Fireman's Annual Stag Dinner. It is only through such public statements that the Prosecutor's Commission will be able to honestly and objectively evaluate the standards that now operate in Anderson, Nebraska.
> Sincerely,
> John Waller

When he finished reading, Peter handed the letter back to John. With a broad smile on his face, John said, "I wrote it myself." After a pause, he said, "Well, Penny helped me with it." Another pause and then, "Shit! Who am I kiddin'. She wrote the whole fuckin' thing. But it was just what I wanted to say. I held onto that letter for a week. I was fuckin' scared, man. I was afraid to send it but I did. They didn't print it.

"But once I sent it, there was no turnin' back. After a week, I sent it again. They still don't print it. By now, I'm gettin' real mad. So I call the editor. He don't talk to me. And it ain't like this is the *New York Times*. They just got ordinary folks, sayin' somethin' 'bout nothin'. They publish it all. All but my letter. No one wants to hear 'bout pornography. No one wants to accept that all sorts of people watch it. They ain't got crime there. They ain't got nothin'. It don't hurt nobody; it's just there. And Al does a great job keepin' it away from the kids. So what's the problem? There ain't no problem, and I can prove that it's in the community standard. If the mayor, police, and firemen watch it once a year, why can't the rest of us see it any day we want?

"I was mad. I felt like a motherfuckin' volcano. I had to explode. Hell, I've exploded a million times over nothin'. Now, I really got somethin' to say. First Amendment. Free speech. There ain't no free speech. So one day I figure I'll go real nice to the newspaper and ask them why they don't print my letter. They don't let me see the editor but take me into a room with a slick, young assistant editor. He gives me shit 'bout 'newsworthiness.' I don't know what the fuck he means 'cept that I sent my letter when this whole fuckin' commission's goin' on. Penny told me that makes it newsworthy. Well, I get real mad, and I feel like hittin' the motherfucker, but I know I can't, so I give him some shit and act like I ain't gonna go, but ya know I ain't gonna do nothin' so I talk shit a couple a minutes and then walk away. I'm halfway down the street and ya know what? There's Barney Fife, arrests me for disorderly conduct. He takes me to Judge Fairview. I starts to argue, and bam! contempt of court. They got me in jail. Then there's more charges. Assault. They claim I fuckin' assaulted the editor. Terroristic threats. I ain't threatened nobody. But in the cell, it's another story. Cops are real friendly. They're gettin' a kick outta the whole thing. They all been to Stag Night. I can tell that ain't the only time they rent Al's movies.

"Besides the police, I get visited by Penny and a lawyer they gave me, Mel Winslow. Mel tells me he's on my side but that ain't so. Sure, he wants to get me outta jail. But he don't want to take on the holy rollers in town. Says he can get me a deal. They'll drop the charges but I gotta leave town. Now, I ain't sure. I got a cause to fight. I got Penny. I got friends in the day program. But I took the deal and here I am."

John stands up, saying to Peter before he leaves, "I'm glad we're together again, Petey. No one in the program visited me. No one sent a card. It ain't my home, Petey. I belong to the city. It's sad, Petey. It's fuckin' sad." As he walks away, Peter stands up, and calls out to John, "Wait a minute, you're not the only one," too softly to be heard.

23

The Bold Move

By the time he returned to work, Peter had forgotten John's story, thinking only about tonight, the night he would finally "talk with the guys." At 5:00 p.m., he quickly left the office, walking briskly toward the porn district and into his favorite peep show. As usual, the fat man was perched behind the counter with its locked display case of erotic devices. The familiar VISA/MASTERCARD logo sat on the counter even though Peter never saw anyone use a charge card.

Almost as soon as he entered, Peter felt overwhelmed by the enormity of what he was about to do. He caught his own pale, but intent image reflected back from the cheap glass of one girl's booth: Peter Branstill, the boy with no friends. It was Peter Branstill, the man who never talked with anyone, Peter Branstill, who was now planning to strike up a conversation with his fellow peep show patrons. His chest constricting with stress, his palms sweaty, Peter almost left but, thinking about John, he stepped forward, noticing a slight-looking man with wire-rimmed glasses, his tie partly undone over an open collar. Peter thought he was probably a minor white-collar worker, like him, here after work. The man was fidgeting nervously, scratching his cheek, and brushing back his hair. On his small hands, on the fourth finger of his left hand, he wore a ring. Peter spotted the ring, realizing that this man must be married, wondering why a married man would go to a peep show, having always assumed married people lived blissful lives free of any sexual frustrations.

As he drifted in thought, Peter's concerns dissipated and, approaching the man, he felt a sudden surge of confidence. But just as he was ready to speak, the man walked to the back of a private viewing booth and disappeared.

Peter fretted over his own hesitation, silently berating himself as he tried to decide whether to leave now or find another person to approach. Maybe he should just get himself a booth and masturbate as he usually did. Feeling dejected, he chose the latter option. He picked a girl quickly and as he walked toward the back of the booth, he saw the slight-looking man coming out. They made unavoidable face-to-face contact. Normally, Peter would have glanced away, walking purposefully toward his destination. Instead, when they were about six feet away from each other, Peter looked directly at the man and said, "Hi, I'm Peter." Startled, the man scurried past Peter and quickly out the door.

Now, Peter felt even more humiliated, more dejected, more weird, realizing it was foolish for him to think they would want to know him. As Peter stood, stuck in his tracks, another man tapped him on the shoulder and said, "Hi, I'm Ralph."

Stunned, Peter could barely speak. "Uh, I'm Peter."

"I know. I overheard you. I know a place we can go."

Peter was shocked by this bold offer to go somewhere else. John was his best friend but they never left the bench. Peter simply wanted to talk with his compatriots, not leave the peep show.

Sensing that something was wrong, Ralph quickly became angry. "Hey! What the hell's wrong with you. Let's go."

When Peter still made no move to leave, Ralph screamed "Fuckin' queer!" and stomped out.

A few moments later, the fat man came up to Peter. "Hey, buddy, no soliciting allowed. Now get the fuck outta here before I throw you out."

Completely shaken and frightened, Peter left. He wandered down the street looking back over his shoulder. He did not understand what had happened. After checking to see that no one was following him, he darted into the next peep show and quickly masturbated to the dancer in the first booth he could enter.

Walking home, Peter pondered what had gone wrong. He had sincerely wanted to know his partners in porn and they had rejected him with their responses. Peter had wanted to bring John his own interesting story to tell at the bench. *Who am I kidding?* thought

Peter. John knows nothing about me: He thinks I'm home with my wife and kids. And I'm going to tell him I talked with some guys at the peep show?

As Peter walked home, he noticed other people. He saw a couple walking hand in hand, seeming to be in separate worlds, not saying a word to each other. He saw a homeless derelict sitting on the street, getting ready to sleep. Peter wondered if he had once been an accountant or a lawyer, a workman or a mental patient.

■ ■ ■

Peter came to an all-night bowling alley. A young man quietly exited carrying a fancy bowling bag in one hand, his bowling shoes slung over his shoulder. At the same time, two young men and women, undoubtedly on a double date, were walking into the building, laughing as they entered. Peter wondered what went on in this place. Did the bowlers know each other? Apparently this foursome did. Were they friendly with the other patrons? Were they friendly with the owner? Were they "proud to bowl"?

Peter's only experience with bowling was at the third grade birthday party. It was one of the rare times a child had invited him to a party and to this day Peter still did not understood why. Grossly uncoordinated, he had difficulty holding the ball in his hands, let alone rolling it straight down the alley. At that age, most of the other youngsters were just learning to bowl, so many of the balls ended up in the gutter.

Watching the other children, Peter thought that the goal was to get the ball down the alley without knocking down any pins. He heard one child scream out when all of the pins went down and misread it as a cry of distress. Hoping to get the best score, Peter put the ball directly in the gutter each time. Throughout the party, the other children laughed and snickered at him, making him feel more and more of an outcast. He knew he did not belong.

Peter continued home, observing people along the way. He had never been a good "people watcher," but now intent on having friends, he carefully watched several people enter and leave the all-night bowling alley. The foursome were gleeful and gay while the solo bowler seemed staid, serious, and confident. None carried the shameful air of a slithering peep-show patron.

Finally home and in bed, Peter pictured an imaginary sign at the entrance of the bowling alley: NO PETER BRANSTILLS ALLOWED. Restless and agitated by the night's events, Peter tried to sleep but couldn't. At three o'clock, he got up, dressed, and went back to the alley.

There were only a few bowlers left when Peter got there and most of them seemed tired and unenthusiastic. The foursome had left and in their place was a new group of young bowlers. They were rowdy and boisterous, obviously enjoying themselves. There were several lone bowlers at different lanes. There was little or no interaction between the different parties and as Peter looked toward the front desk, he saw an obese man behind the counter: The alley reminded him of the peep show.

Peter noticed a large banner advertising special midnight rates. Nearby, there were signs promoting family night, pizza night, and disco night. There were also posters with league standings. The alley sponsored men's, women's, mixed, and children's leagues. He saw a plaque for the "300" Club with several names on it, and next to the plaque a sign suggesting that your child's next birthday could be a bowling party. Video games, a pool table, and a snack bar completed the scene. Peter looked back at the bowlers who seemed mesmerized by the late hour. People here seemed no different from the men at the peep show. Except for the sound of falling pins, the place was still. Peter again thought back to the bowling party he had attended as a child. Then, the place had been crowded and loud and except for Peter, they all seemed to be laughing and having fun.

■ ■ ■

Peter returned home where he fell asleep and had a dream: He had entered his favorite peep show only to notice that the building now matched the interior of the bowling alley. At the end of each lane, there was a private viewing booth. The place bustled with activity and families – children, mothers, fathers, husbands, and wives – joined the other men for an enjoyable, wholesome night of family peeping.

When Peter woke up, he immediately thought about the man he had approached the previous night, not Travis Sanders at an annual fundraising event, but an ordinary guy with loved ones at home, excluded from this part of his life. *I wonder how he feels? Does he miss his wife while jerking off?*

It fascinated Peter how the bowling alley at night had differed from what he remembered as a child. He thought about the signs that foretold a different experience at different times. Peter wondered if a peep show could ever serve the whole family's needs, just like the bowling alley did. Soon he began to believe that his thought about a comprehensive, family entertainment peep center could be transformed into a vivid reality. Peter pictured the place: There would be children's activities like pinball machines and video games and the center could sponsor birthday parties. There could be organized peep leagues, ladies' night, pizza parties, and peeping for the kids. The peep show could become a new center for social interaction.

Excited, Peter stayed up all night. He couldn't wait to share his idea with John.

■ ■ ■

Finally, it was Peter's turn to talk. No longer willing to remain silent, he would tell John the truth about himself now that he, too, had a great idea. With no way to share his family peep show dream without divulging his true nature, Peter would bare it all. Hopefully, John would accept him the way he truly was. And if not, Peter was prepared to live with the consequences. Sure, John had been his only friend, but true friends can be real with each other: It was time for Peter to be real.

Throughout the morning, Peter's stomach churned; his heart raced; his palms sweat. In the past Peter would have worked hard to disguise these reactions. Today, he would openly be scared, but still tell John the thoughts that were on his mind. As the minutes and hours moved slowly toward noon, Peter felt proud that he was unswerving in his resolve.

At noon, feeling shaky but firmly committed to his plan, he left his office for the park. And with no more than fleeting thoughts to change his plan, Peter knew he would now be able to start the conversation. As he approached the bench, he saw John sitting there, smoking a cigarette, propped on the back as he typically did. Deep in thought, John did not seem to notice Peter's approach until just seconds before he reached the bench. And when he did, Peter stuck his hand out, inviting a handshake, and said, "Joh… " But John quickly interrupted Peter by saying, "Ya know Petey, there ain't nothin' wrong with cigarettes, it's only how ya smoke 'em. Here, let me show ya." And much to Peter's chagrin, John proceeded to smoke out of the left side of his mouth while telling the same smoking story – practically word for word – that he had shared with him during their very first meeting together.

But John laughed with delight as he bellowed out loudly the self-attribution, "Ambi-lung-uous," openly proud of his way with words. "Well, listen, Petey, I gotta get back to the program. Now remember: When ya smoke, one lung for an entire week and you'll feel great."

As he watched John leave, Peter felt angry at him. But after a few moments, he settled down as he ate his lunch and gradually felt sad realizing that John could not do any better. And before he got up to return to work, Peter chuckled to himself, feeling quite inexplicably pleased that he had finally seen left-lung smoking.

■ ■ ■

Peter returned to work disappointed in John but undeterred in his commitment to end his isolation. At first, he felt a strong desire to return to the peep show, to introduce himself to the fat man and explain his intentions: He was not soliciting sex, he was soliciting friends. He wanted to make him understand that he wanted to contribute to the ambience of peep shows, not detract from it. But by the end of the day, Peter had again changed his mind. He felt he needed to learn more about the social networks he wanted to have, to study people and their interactions. So after work, instead of going to the peep show, Peter went to the bowling alley.

■ ■ ■

In the evening, the bowling alley was filled with life. Men and women laughed, talked, ate and drank, while they bowled game after game. After sitting and watching for a half-hour, he noticed that something was missing. Something was bothering him. He felt grossly uncomfortable but could not put his finger on the problem.

Suddenly, Peter realized that he was watching while everyone else was bowling. The thought entered his mind that he, too, could bowl.

Peter approached the counter where a tough-looking, middle-aged woman stood waiting. As soon as she spotted Peter, she asked, "How many?"

As he rearranged the letters for *bowl* to spell *blow* – John had a blow job, I'm going to bowl – Peter looked at her blankly.

"How many in your party?" she asked.

"Oh, I'm here by myself," Peter responded.

"Shoe size?"

Uncomfortable with her question, Peter began thinking about the time an exotic dancer behind the glass partition begged him to expose himself. "Let me see that big old thing," she said as she danced seductively. And when he didn't display his organ, she simply went on and said, "You shy little cowboy. Ya gonna tease me and make me beg, and wonder what big surprise ya got in there for me. Well, ya can't fool me. Ya know what they say 'bout guys with big feet, and yours are so big. Ohhh, they really turn me on."

Now aroused by his own thoughts, Peter answered, "10½."

The woman put a pair of strange-looking shoes on the counter and asked Peter for one of his. Handing over his right shoe, Peter wondered why she wanted it: The ritual made no sense to him. But he was here to learn, so he stood there trying to figure out the reason they exchanged shoes, staring blankly waiting for something to happen, not knowing what he should do next. Finally, the woman – who by now was annoyed with him – pushed a sheet of paper toward him and motioned to the left, saying, "Alley 3." Noticing that Peter hadn't brought a bowling ball, she pointed again and added, "You can get a ball from one of those racks over there. Now put your shoes on and have fun." She looked at him, slightly shaking her head and smiling imperceptibly.

Peter chose an odd-looking orange ball that reminded him of the one he had used as a child. This ball was much lighter than he remembered, and the holes were too small for his fingers: He could only get his smallest finger into one of the holes.

Peter started to feel queasy as he looked down at the shoes: He needed a shoe, having given the woman his right shoe, but did not want to wear the shoes someone else had worn. After sitting for several minutes, he painstakingly slipped the right shoe on. At first, Peter could not understand why she had given him two shoes when he only needed one. But after looking around, it slowly dawned on him that others were wearing two matched bowling shoes, many with a number on the back like the ones she gave him, and realized that he was supposed to put both shoes on. But feeling contaminated enough with just the one shoe, he could not bring himself to put the other one on, too.

Looking at his alley and then at the other bowlers, Peter saw many pins falling, finally realizing that the object was to knock the pins down, not avoid them as he thought as a child. Peter suddenly felt very ashamed over his childhood bowling gaffe.

Because only his pinkie finger actually fit into one of the holes, Peter found bowling to be an awkward process. Nevertheless, determined to persevere, he strode to the foul line, still in his suit and tie, and with one street shoe and one bowling shoe on, Peter dropped the ball on the alley. He watched transfixed as the ball went into the gutter several feet away. On his next turn, Peter managed to send the ball more toward the middle of the alley, knocking three pins down in the process. But as soon they fell, Peter panicked. He could not tolerate having disturbed the symmetry of the pins. Flooded by guilt and feeling dirty wearing a shoe that someone else had worn, Peter proceeded to purposefully place the rest of his balls directly in the gutter – just as he had done as a child.

Now completely consumed with the feeling that he was dirty, Peter forgot the reason he was there – to study other people's behavior – and instead became an object of curiosity for the other bowlers, who were starting to watch him. By the sixth frame, a tall man tapped Peter on the shoulder and asked, "What the hell are you doing?"

When Peter gave no response, the man said, "Okay, weirdo, it's time to leave." Grabbing Peter, the man forcibly led him out the back door. Just as he was ready to slam the door behind Peter, he noticed that he still had on the rented shoe and said, "Gimme that fuckin' shoe before I call the cops, ya damn pervert!"

Peter quickly removed the shoe and, too embarrassed to call a cab, started walking home wearing only one shoe. Fortunately, he passed a peep show on his way and quickly went inside. No one would laugh at him here.

■ ■ ■

Sleeping soundly that night, Peter had an unexpectedly peaceful dream about nuclear holocaust. In the beginning of the dream, Peter and his fellow peepers were exiled to a tropical island where they were forced into a concentration camp. But before they could be annihilated, worldwide nuclear war broke out, destroying everyone except Peter and his doomed island compatriots. In the flames, Peter saw and heard a screaming inferno of terrified people, spread over a landscape littered with bowling balls, shoes, pins, and trophies. Only the exiles survived.

Later on in the dream, the island girls approach Peter and his friends, freeing them from captivity and telling them it was their duty to repropagate the world. The men gladly went about fulfilling their responsibilities, impregnating the girls, never once talking to each other. What a wonderful dream: The peepers of the world had taken over. He would never need acceptance from bowlers again.

24

Curly

On Wednesday at lunchtime, refreshed and relaxed, no longer wanting to be like the bowlers, speak with the peepers, or even have John listen to him, Peter walked to the park, his thoughts disrupted by a loud, plaintive sound. He had often heard people laugh and play and argue and shout in the park. The children sometimes fell on the playground, loudly crying for their mom. This sound, though, communicated great pain. It was a wail, not a cry, and it sounded out of control.

Peter arrived at the bench to find that John was the one wailing loudly. Passersby had stopped to help, and one man stood close to John, trying to provide assistance to the pained man. When Peter approached, he asked, "John? What's wrong?"

With that, the good samaritan left, satisfied that a friend was there. The small crowd slowly dispersed.

"John, what's wrong?" Peter asked again.

"CURLY!!!!!" John wailed loudly. Through deep racking sobs, John cried, "Curly, I killed Curly."

The tears continued until Peter sat down next to him. John composed himself and began to tell the story of Curly. "Did I ever tell ya 'bout Curly?" John asked, running his hands through his hair.

"Curly was fat. Bet he weighed 300 pounds or more. Ate everythin' he could get his fuckin' hands on. I'll bet if ya gave him a bowl of dog food, he'd skip the hands." As John laughed loudly, momentarily forgetting how badly he felt, Peter factored 300 into $2 \times 2 \times 3 \times 5 \times 5$.

"Well, Curly was a lifer. Curly was in institutions as a kid, and went to nuthouses as an adult. Curly had two things in his life: Food, and doin' what he was told. That was Curly.

"One day, at State, they decide the patients are gonna have a say in their treatment – called it em-power-ment. Ask me, it was a bunch of bullshit. No one was gonna empower nobody but they threw out a lotta fancy words. They were gonna have a 'therapeutic community.' Sometimes they called it a 'therapeutic milieu.' They wanted 'patient government.' All that meant was that they appointed someone President and told him what to do. And of course, there was 'deinstitutionalization.' That's how the day programs started. They sent people outta the hospital and into the community – where no one fuckin' wanted us. So they put us in programs to keep us offa the streets. But Curly, he's a lifer. Curly ain't gettin' out nohow. How could he? He wouldn't fit through the fuckin' door." While John again heartily laughed at this joke, Peter thought about Curly's waist. An average door has a 35" opening. If Curly can't fit through the door, his waist forms the circumference of a circle: $C = \pi D$ where D is greater than 35". Since π is approximately 3.14, Curly's waist must be greater than 3.14 x 35 or 110 inches. Wow! Curly really was fat.

"Somebody decided they would meet with each of the patients and have 'em help figure out their own treatment plan. Bullshit. I went to my meetin'. They just told me I was fucked up. Hell, I already knew that. Then they told me that the plan was for me to behave and take my medication. Anyway, it was Curly's turn. So he goes to his treatment meeting. Well, ya know me. I feel like bustin' on the guy. He comes out. He's got some paper in his hand. It's his copy of the treatment plan. I call out, 'Yo, Curly. Whatchagot?' 'My treatment plan,' Curly says. 'Lemme see,' I says to Curly.

"It's got eight goals and some other shit they call objectives. It looks like they're real serious 'bout Curly leavin' the hospital. He's gonna have psychotherapy and medication and art therapy, and activities of daily living, and they think they're sendin' him to a boardin' home. I know it ain't gonna work. They probably know that, too. Curly ain't goin' nowhere. Then I spot this one goal. It says Henry Davis, that's Curly's real name, will lose 5 pounds a month until he reaches a goal weight of 180 pounds. That's 120 pounds.

It would take the fucker two years to lose it if he wanted to. And Curly don't care."

Two years? thought Peter. *Twenty-four months times 5 pounds a month is 120 pounds. Wow, John's right, exactly two years to lose the weight.*

"Then I spot the objective: reduce caloric intake. I look at the bottom, and I see that Curly signed the fuckin' thing. So I says to Curly, 'Hey Curly, they're gonna put ya on a diet.'

"Curly don't say nothin'. I tell him again, 'They're puttin' ya on a fuckin' diet, Curly. Ya see this, ya agreed to go on a fuckin' diet.' Now, Curly looks upset. He says he ain't goin' on no diet.

"I point it out to him in black and white. 'They're gonna starve ya, Curly. They're gonna fuckin' starve ya. Make ya real skinny, dress ya up real nice, and send ya out to some fuckin' boardin' home where they'll take ya only 'cause they think ya don't eat nothin'.' Well, Curly gets real upset and starts lookin' for the shrink. The fuckin' shrink won't come outta his office and talk to him, so Curly gets real mad and goes right up to the nursin' station.

"'Hey, lady,' he says, 'You ain't takin' my food away.' Well, the nurse is one of them snooty-ass types. She says to him, 'OK, young man,' – by the way, Curly's forty – 'OK, young man, let's just see what's in your treatment plan. She thumbs through some papers. Yes, here it is, 1,000-calorie diet.' She looks up at him over her old spinster lady glasses, 'Sorry, son, it looks like a diet's been ordered starting this evening.'

"Well, enough for patient participation in the plan. Curly's on a diet. He gets real upset and starts to make a fuss. He screams. He cries. Now the doctor comes out. Remember that: the doctor won't come out to talk with Curly about the diet but he comes out 'cause Curly's screamin'. With the doctor comes an aide and a counselor. Well, Curly thinks he's gonna talk with 'em 'bout the diet but nobody wants to talk to Curly. They're just waitin' for the nurse who comes up from behind with a big needle ready to stick it in his ass.

"Curly gets more and more upset. Ya can see the staff talkin' to each other tryin' to figure out what to do. Nobody thinks to talk with him or just let him eat. Nobody thinks that a forty-year-old man has a right to make up his own mind. Nobody notices that their plan to involve the patients in the treatment is just a bunch of shit. As they're all talkin', Curly turns and looks behind and sees the nurse and an aide. The nurse gots the needle and the aide is holdin' restraints. Curly can't think of nothin' but his food so he bolts down the hall.

"Well I tell ya; I had no idea Curly could run so fast. I starts cheerin', 'Go Curly go, go Curly go.' Before ya know it, the whole fuckin' ward is screamin', 'Go Curly go.'

"The shrink yells down the hall, 'Stop him!' There's a big orderly near the door. He looks at Curly, he looks at the doctor, he looks again at Curly. Well, I've dealt with this man before. He's big and mean. He's restrained a lotta people in his day, and he'll do what he has to do to get ya down. But he's no fool. He looks at Curly barrelin' down the hall and steps aside.

"The doctor is still screamin' for someone to stop Curly. Then I see this skinny, student nurse run to close the door. Ya know they once locked all these wards but now we got deinstitutionalization, milieu therapy, and patient empowerment so all the doors are wide open. The nurse manages to shut this heavy metal door just before Curly gets there and then she jumps to the side. Now it's just the door that's in Curly's way. Knowing Curly, he probably woulda stopped if the nurse just stood there; he wouldn't hurt no one. But she jumped aside so now it's Curly and the door.

"We're all quiet. Curly could still stop if he wanted to. Nobody knew what he would do. Curly got closer and closer. Then, at the last moment, I saw Curly bend his head down. Like a charging bull, Curly crashed head-first into the door. I tell ya, I never saw nothin' like that before. Ya could hear the bones in his head crack. There was blood all over the place.

"It was fuckin' amazin'. Curly started his run as a fat slob, a child beggin' for food. When he hit the door, he was a big man. Well, I was impressed. They tried to take his food away. He took a stand. 'Give me food or give me death.'

"The staff was stunned. They tried to blame the patients. They did it in a real bullshit way. They called us together for a meeting. They wanted us to 'process' Curly's death. Process, my ass. They blamed us for Curly's death 'cause they couldn't just say they fucked up. They told us not to feel too guilty. Did ya get that, too guilty. They really wanted to make sure we felt guilty enough not to see what they did. It was our fault for cheerin' him on. It was never their fault for puttin' him on a fuckin' diet."

As John stops to take a drag on his cigarette, Peter returns to his thoughts about John's great calculation, two years to lose 120 pounds. I wonder if John also calculated the number of calories Curly would consume in those two years. If neither was a leap year, then he'd have 1,000 calories a day for two 365-day years or 1,000 x 2 x 365 or 730,000 calories consumed while 120 pounds were lost. Now if either was a leap year, that would add another 1,000 calories for the extra day, or 731,000 calories. If he knew the year this happened, he could complete his calculation. Peter turned toward John and started to ask, "When did... "

"Now, ya wanna hear how stupid they really are? After Curly died, they held a big meetin'. I know 'cause I read somethin' in my counselor's office – I don't think I was supposed to see it. They called it a Critical Incident Meeting and they talked 'bout Curly's death. They didn't invite any of us patients to the meetin', just staff and the jerks that run the hospital. Who knows, maybe the governor came. What do they come up with? Policies and Procedures. Policies and Procedures to prevent suicide by bludgeoning – I had to ask what the fuck that meant – one's head into a wall.

"They decide to pad the walls, which they never actually did 'cause it cost too fuckin' much. They decide to remove shoes on patients in danger of bludgeoning themselves to death against the walls. They wanted to keep 'em from buildin' up too much speed. And they made up this Bludgeon-to-Death Assessment Form to figure out which psycho was gonna run into the wall next.

"Now Petey, this place has been lockin' folks up longer than you and I have been alive together. They never had a death like this before. And this is what they come up with. No one thought that they could have kept Curly alive by lettin' him make up his own mind if he wanted to be on a diet."

Confused by John's story, which started with him wailing in pain because he killed Curly and ended placing the blame on the hospital staff, Peter said, "I thought you said you killed Curly." John screamed, "I killed Curly! I fuckin' killed Curly. It's my fault, Petey. I did it. Ya know, I never told no one this before but it's my fuckin' fault. I killed him. Died with dignity; what a crock. Curly didn't die with dignity, he had no dignity. He woulda died for a pork chop. Curly didn't care 'bout the meetin'. He didn't care 'bout the treatment plan. Curly knew he would get the food he wanted. I guarantee ya, Curly would not starve. He woulda eaten off someone else's plate. He woulda raided the garbage. He woulda gotten it from a staff member. They think they got a team. It ain't no team at all. Don't matter what the shrink says. At night, it's different. Some nurse or aide woulda fed Curly at night. He mighta taken it up the ass but Curly would have eaten.

"Curly's place in this world was to eat. He let others run his life as long as he could eat. That's all he ever wanted. Curly had no desire to be great, he wasn't a prophet or a politician. He just wanted to eat. And eatin' was what Curly did best; he didn't get to be 300 pounds by not eatin'. He had a flair for eatin'. And hell, this wasn't his first diet, either. This was just the first time some fool, like me, turned the diet into a crisis. I made Curly upset. It was my battle with the system, not Curly's. Believe me, Petey, I killed Curly."

John sat and smoked with both lungs for a minute before leaving.

■ ■ ■

After stepping off the bus, before walking to his apartment four blocks away, Peter stopped at Lou's Grocery to pick up a pint of 2 percent milk. Standing in line, he pictured the "Got Milk" ad in this month's issue of *American Horseman* magazine, the horse, owner, and jockey all sporting white milk mustaches. Remembering school, watching the others drip ketchup on their clothes, with chocolate covering their hands and milk on their lips, laughing, Peter sat by himself, eating his lunch carefully and methodically, never once making a mess.

"Is that all, sir?" Lou asked. Breaking from his thoughts, Peter looked up at Lou and noticed a book display out of the corner of his left – his better – eye. "I'll also take that," Peter said, pointing to a Pocket Size Calorie Counter.

After dinner, Peter retrieved the notebook he used to record his annual meal plan on the first Saturday of November each year. With the help of his new book, he calculated the number of calories he had consumed over the past thirty years. He then created a chart cross-referencing his caloric intake with his daily weights before returning his notebooks neatly where they belonged, for review this coming November.

25

Help

On Thursday, John was already at the bench when Peter arrived. He looked sad but today there were no tears, no uncontrollable wailing. Peter sat down, quietly opened his lunch bag, and placed the contents on his lap in familiar fashion. John was halfway through his cigarette. After a few drags, he handed Peter his pack, offering him one. As always, Peter refused. This time, though, John insisted.

"Here, Peter, take one. No, take the whole pack."

Peter did not know what to do. He also wondered why John was now using his true first name. "I don't smoke," he replied.

"I know," said John. "Maybe ya know someone who does." John's gift was profound. Peter knew that cigarettes were his lifeblood. John was the Marlboro man, an innovator in medical philosophy, a truly ambi-lung-uous man, a free spirit, an out-of-the-closet mental patient. John was his best friend. Now, John came with gifts. It didn't matter that the gift did not fit because Peter did not smoke. Peter took this gift of the Marlboro Magi and placed it in his pocket.

Peter thought back to his childhood, remembering himself watching others, from afar, smoke. Wanting to smoke himself, afraid he'd be taunted for trying to look cool, Peter pictured himself, a world-renowned surgeon, performing a complicated fifteen-hour operation. He saves two lives, operating simultaneously with his left and right hands between two tables. Peter walks out with blood-stained surgical greens and sits down. At last, the unbelievable Dr. Branstill can take a well-deserved break. The virtuous doctor is permitted a minor vice, a cigarette. Peter takes long drags on his cigarette following the innovative double-life-saving surgery. The grateful relatives stand by in deep admiration watching him. "Isn't he marvelous," they say. "He's only using his right lung."

Peter pats the pack of cigarettes in his pocket, deeply appreciating John's thoughtfulness.

"Peter, ya ever get tired?" John asks. John deeply sighs to highlight the feeling. In fact, Peter often felt tired, tired of thinking about horses, of counting days, of rating dirt. But he was not tired now. His interest was piqued.

"I'm tired," John said, "I'm tired of fightin'. I'm tired of fightin' for somethin' to live for. I'm tired of fightin' the shit in my head. I get excited over shit that don't mean nothin'. It's all a drama. I go to Anderson and fall in love, then they kick me outta town for tellin' the truth.

"They raise money for charity watchin' porn and form a commission to take the shit from us. They want us jerkin' off here in this porn ghetto. They don't wanna know their husbands do it, too. Shit, the only time I'm ever OK is in the peep show. It's honest. She gets paid, I get off. I don't know her. I don't have to touch her. The money keeps us apart. Hell, them bitches in Anderson don't know their own husbands. It's a cash deal, they just don't know it.

"Somethin's wrong, Peter. The medications don't work no more. They got me on Prozac. I used to think the world sucks. Now that I'm takin' this shit, I know the world sucks. Brown wants to see me today and I know he's gonna tell me to go in the hospital. I ain't goin'.

"By the way, I hope ya never believed that shit I told ya 'bout my dad. Fishin', shit. He never fished with nobody but Jack Daniels. No, he died a drunken bastard. His heart gave out, but not real easy. Shit, he had two bypass operations; his heart failed three times. They just kept bringin' him back. A fuckin' waste of public money. They shoulda let him die.

"The last time, he asked for me. Called me a sonofabitch and a failure. Said he hated me. Blamed me for killin' Mom. Told me he wouldn't have hit her so hard if it weren't for me. It was my fault 'cause I took drugs. He spent fifteen, twenty minutes tellin' me how rotten I was. Then he sobbed. He sobbed and sobbed. He asked me to forgive him. I wouldn't. He told me to get the fuck outta the room. Peter, I didn't know what I would do. I wanted to smother him with the pillow. I started out.

"Just then, I heard him gasp. I looked at him and knew he was gonna die. I didn't call no one. He said 'Get the fuck out,' so I did. When I came back, he was dead.

"So whaddaya think Brown's gonna do: lock me up or let me go? Promise ya one thing for sure. I won't do nothin' without lettin' ya know first." With that, John got up and walked away.

■ ■ ■

Sitting on the bench, haunted by John's words, "I heard him gasp. I looked at him and knew he was gonna die," Peter pictured himself a small boy with Mom and Dad, eating dinner, studying the stew for its geometric patterns. Right before his eyes, Dad scoops a large portion, with the piece of meat Peter planned to take, from the serving plate to his mouth with his hands. With his head fixed forward, Peter's eyes slowly drift to the left, following Dad's hands, watching him shovel the meat into his mouth forming a circular ring around his lips. Gravy dripping down his chin onto his red flannel shirt, spreading to the right side of his trunk, the left side well covered from previous servings, Peter counted three pieces of meat, none the prized portion he had just picked, fall down, two on the table, one on the floor landing 3¾ inches to the right of Dad.

Seeing Dad's face turn blue, Peter turned his eyes right until he was looking directly at the serving bowl. As Sally chattered on and Peter began searching the plate for his next selection, George struggled up from his chair. Neither Sally nor Peter realized that George was in trouble when he fell backwards in his chair, dead by the time he hit the floor.

"It's 5:30," Sally said, excusing Peter from the table. While Peter sat in his room drawing perfect equilateral triangles, Sally cleared the table, washed the dishes, wiped the counter, and carefully mopped the floor around George, trying not to disturb his sleep.

At 7 o'clock, Sally came into Peter's bedroom. Already having changed into his pajamas, washed up, and brushed his teeth, he was sitting in bed waiting for Sally to read him the story of Jack and the Beanstalk.

"Once upon a time, there was a boy named Jack.

> I wonder how he got the name Jack. They could've named him Bill, or Ted or Tom, but I guess they decided on Jack because Jack's a nice name and that's the name they use in Jack and the Beanstalk. My sister was really upset when I named you George. She always thought I should've called you Peter, but I didn't even know it was my choice. I would've called you Peter or Joe, or even Jack, but I wouldn't have wanted you climbing up beanstalks. I never knew how those beanstalks kept people up. I guess they're stronger than a vine, or a rose bush. I know they're not as strong as a tree. You can climb a tree. Of course you can get hurt if you fall out of a tree. Cindy always says your dad musta fallen out of a tree, but that's not what happened. He was just born the way he was... "

At 7:30, Sally stopped the story, pulled up the covers, and tucked Peter in with a goodnight kiss.

Later, at 9:30, Peter heard a scream. Frozen to his bed, he waited fifteen minutes until Aunt Cindy came in and told him to dress. As he left, he saw the gravy-stained shape of Dad's body where he fell on the kitchen floor. The next day, Peter went to the police station, where he described to the police artist in intricate detail the fatal plate of food. By comparing her autopsy findings with the artist's rendition, the medical examiner was able to pinpoint the exact piece of lethal food. Peter shuddered, realizing that his father had choked on a piece of meat with excellent geometric properties. But even worse than losing his dad, Peter recalled, was spending the next month with Aunt Cindy while his mom was away in a psychiatric hospital.

Looking at his watch, seeing it was 12:55 p.m., Peter returned to work.

That night, Peter woke up from a terrifying dream. Among a crowd of gaunt inmates, Peter and John march along a dusty road, herded by their Nazi masters toward the Porn Ghetto. Chilled by the haunting, vacant stares of naked, masturbating men, Peter takes his place in line. As the others hold their organs erect, Peter reaches through a small hole in the right pocket of his prison fatigues, slipping a wad of toilet paper in a plastic bag over his penis, securing it with tape and a rubber band. John leans over and whispers to Peter: I know a place we can go. Hearing a click, Peter looks up to see a German soldier standing behind a machine gun aimed directly at Peter.

■ ■ ■

When Peter arrived at the bench Friday, John was already there, agitated, circling the bench.

"GODDAMN WHORE! FUCKIN' BITCH! SLUT, TRAMP, CUNT. FUCK HER! I told 'em I'd fuck the bitch and I fuckin' will. Here! Eat this, I told her. Who the hell does she think she is? A fuckin' dyke, that's what she is. I shoulda jammed my prick up her ass, the goddamn whore. And whadda they do. Nothin'. Goddamn nothin'. Let her dance 'round like that, the fuckin' bitch. And they wanna send me away. Shit, I'll blow the fuckin' place up before they do that."

John sits down on the cleanest section of the bench, telling Peter to sit next to him, right on a piece of dirt. Quickly estimating its Graduated Dirt Rating Score, Peter knew it was probably major dirt. Yet John's demand was so compelling, he sat down anyway, surprised at how little it bothered him.

"I tell ya. I shoulda taken my prick out and come all over her face, the fuckin' bitch. Can ya believe? Last year she takes me away and sucks me off. Now, she's off with a fuckin' dyke. But I got her. Told her to eat some pussy for me, too, as she left."

John stops, takes the last drag on his cigarette before dropping it on the ground and crushing it out. Then he wails, "Aaaaaah!" His eyes fill with tears. Face in his hands, sobbing, he leans toward Peter and places his head on Peter's left shoulder as Peter sat there, stiff, trying to calculate the number of days since the day Uncle Charlie hugged him at Aunt Maureen's house.

"I can't take it," John cries between the sobs. "I'm so alone. I've got nobody. I've never had a woman. I ain't even got a daughter. Well, I do and I don't. I lived with her mom; we were both on crack.

Her mom was some psycho I met in the hospital. When she got busted, I told everyone the girl was mine, but it's just a lie."

"Aaaaaah!" John continues to sob, leaving tears on the shoulder of Peter's suit No. 4.

"Brown says I gotta go in the hospital. He thinks he's sendin' me this afternoon. He'll commit me if I don't sign myself in. But I ain't goin' back there. And I ain't goin' home neither. They'll fuckin' call the cops and pick me up. I gotta just chill 'til Monday, then I'll be OK and go back. Listen, just have a good weekend. I'll see ya Monday... "

As John gets up to leave, Peter said, "John." Not sure what he wanted to say, he blurted out, "John, I'm working Saturday. If you're around, I'll be here for lunch."

26

The Lost Weekend

Perhaps the only accountant in New York to work a strict 9-to-5 schedule, even through tax season, Peter never worked on the weekends. Today, twenty-five years after starting with the firm, he would finally go toward the office on Saturday.

Sitting in the kitchen, watching the clock move slowly toward 10:31 a.m., the time he'd need to leave for the bus with an extra ten-minute margin of error, Peter stared at his bag of unwashed laundry, thinking as he had all morning long: *I should have gone to the laundromat.* Peter had decided to skip this chore even though there was plenty of time to do his wash even if his machines were in use. Peter figured he could wash, dry, and fold his laundry in the allotted time as long as the machines were at least ¼ of the way through their cycles when he got there. But Peter worried about the personal variable, knowing that not everyone could be counted on to remove their items promptly when the cycles were done. Throughout the morning, regretting his decision, Peter considered alternate plans: *I could wash my clothes in the afternoon or on Sunday morning. I could buy new clothes.* Peter kept thinking about possibilities until interrupted by a loud sound, BRRRRNG! his alarm clock signalling it was time to leave for the park.

Walking toward the bus stop, Peter planned his arrival at the park, facing a seemingly unsolvable dilemma: *I can either go straight to the bench after exiting the bus or I can first walk to the office building before going to the bench.* If he went straight to the bench, John might see him arrive from a different direction, spotting his ruse. If he first went to the office building, he might be seen by someone from Lerner and

Schwartz. When he arrived at the bus stop, Peter took out his pencil and notebook, scribbled a few calculations, and realized there was only a four-minute difference in walking time between the two routes. While he pondered his decision, Peter felt uneasy, sensing something was wrong, failing to recognize a more serious problem with his plan. Finally, Peter put the pencil and notebook away, deciding to take a risk and walk past his office building before going to the bench: John had become much more important to him than his job at Lerner and Schwartz. It would be worse to lose John than to be exposed by his colleagues. For a moment, Peter felt comfortable as he stood at the corner, waiting for his bus.

Peter stood alongside a lone elderly woman, wondering why there were no other people waiting for the bus. And although at first he enjoyed the sparse crowd, his calm feeling began to dissipate as he realized that no bus had come when it should have. Peter looked nervously at his watch; according to his calculations, the bus was already two minutes late. After five more minutes had elapsed, Peter began to panic. *Why isn't the bus here?*

Peter looked at the old woman standing by him. He wanted to ask her what was wrong, he wanted to scream as the precious minutes ticked away, "WHERE'S MY BUS?!" Peter again looked at the old woman, who had become noticeably unnerved by Peter's stares. He desperately wanted to ask her what was wrong but knew he could never do that. She probably had the information he needed but he was too afraid to ask. The woman quietly added some distance between herself and Peter.

The bus was now ten minutes late and Peter anxiously realized he had now lost his margin of error. He again looked down the avenue but there was still no bus in sight. *Something's wrong,* Peter thought. *I don't get it.*

Trying to relax and reassure himself, Peter thought back to his copious, detailed records. In twenty-five years at Lerner and Schwartz, he had been late only sixteen times, or one-quarter of one percent of his entire employment. Today he had added an extra ten minutes, but the time kept ticking away. By now, Peter had waited fifteen minutes. With no further delays, he would just make it on time. Again reviewing his calculations, Peter realized his choice had been made for him by circumstance: Even if the bus arrived now, he would have to go directly to the bench.

Still wondering what could be wrong, Peter again looked at the old woman. Now, however, he saw there was a second woman waiting for the bus. It still seemed strange: fifteen minutes of waiting and only two people at the stop. During the week, there were usually crowds waiting. Today, however, only two in fifteen minutes. That's it, he thought as the words, "during the week," resounded in his head. *During the week, during the week,* he thought again. That was it! The bus schedule. Peter suddenly realized he was travelling midday on the weekend. Of course, there were fewer busses.

Peter immediately started walking toward the office. Less than a minute later, he broke into a run. It was 11:30. No matter how fast he ran, there was no way he could get to the park bench on time. Even at top speed, Peter pictured himself arriving no earlier than 12:15. John might be gone by then, might be gone forever. John might be dead.

Peter began sprinting as hard as he could but found he was out of shape and needed to alternately walk and run. Looking back for the bus, which was nowhere in sight, he spotted a cab. Desperate, anxious, heaving, Peter hailed the cab. His head spinning as he arrived at the park, Peter threw the driver a $10 bill and exited, not waiting for change.

It was 12:10. He had surely missed John. He sprinted over to the bench, sat down on some recent bird droppings, and reached for his lunch bag; it wasn't there. In his haste he had left his lunch in the cab. He saw the cab pulling away and thought of grabbing another cab to follow the first cab and retrieve his lunch. But what if John came? He was already ten minutes late. He could not afford to leave the bench.

Peter touched his face and realized he was sweating and dirty. His tie had come undone and his shirt was partly out of his pants. With no lunch, and grungier than he had ever been before, he knew the ruse was over. A small tear, too small to drop on his cheek, formed in the left corner of his right eye. Surely John would reject him for lying about Saturday work, for being unkempt, for presuming they were really friends, for thinking he could help. It's all nonsense anyway. It's 12:20 and John's not here. He came and went. I let him down.

Absorbed in his thoughts, Peter failed to notice an approaching presence until the familiar words rang out. "Hey there, Petey. Gotta smoke?"

■ ■ ■

John had no idea how Peter had arrived, and did not comment on Peter's disheveled appearance. And if, as he suspected, Peter had staged this meeting for his benefit, he was grateful. But almost as soon as they met, John's usual cheerful greeting gives way to a more somber mood.

"Hey man, ya saved my life. I'm grateful ya had to work today. Don't know what I woulda done without ya. Don't think I'd have made it through the night. Thinkin' 'bout ya kept me alive."

John briefly glances at Peter. He sees something different about his friend, but he isn't sure what. "Somethin's wrong. I haven't felt right; I can't breathe. You've heard me cough lately, ain't ya?" John coughs a bit, as if to demonstrate the problem.

"I bet ya think that's a smoker's cough but it ain't. Here's what a smoker's cough sounds like." John demonstrates a smoker's cough. "This is a clear-your-throat cough." Peter listened, puzzled about the difference, as John coughs again. "Here, let me show you what it sounds like when ya just got a tickle in your throat." After demonstrating six coughs in all, John continues, saying, "Brown thinks I got TB. I never had ya over to my place, but ya don't wanna go there. Some fuckin' sick people there. He's thinkin' TB 'cause he's fuckin' scared for himself. They all gotta get them tests to work there. I'm sure he's afraid he'll get sick himself. Hell, he don't shake nobody's hand in the program. Petey, I ain't worried 'bout TB, they got meds for that. I wouldn't tell no one but you, I think I got cancer."

John pauses while Peter tried to think of something to say. He wanted to suggest that John see a doctor to check it out, thinking he could take John to a doctor himself, until Peter heard shouts from the children: JOHN'S GOT COOTIES. PETER'S GOT COOTIES. JOHN AND PETER COOTIES. "I ain't afraid to die, Petey. I'm gonna die someday. I don't care if it's now or later. No man, I ain't afraid to die. I'm just afraid to die after livin' a miserable, useless life.

Even if you're fucked up, ya gotta have some reason to live, but I ain't got shit for reason.

"I never told ya 'bout my dad. What a fuckin' piece of shit. Used to make up stories, tell everyone how great he was, takin' me fishin' and huntin', golfin', and Cub Scouts, and shiny bikes. I even believed the shit. No, he was just a drunken bastard, beat me all the time, beat my mom, and worst of all, fucked my sister. He'd call Mom a frigid bitch, and then fuck my sister. Then he'd call Sue a whore and beat my mom. Said it was Mom's fault, then it was my fault. Once he made me sit in a chair and watch him fuck Sue. Sick shit, Petey, real sick.

"So guess what? He was still my Pop. I still loved him. I remember one day, when I was big 'nough to get him back, he's callin' me a fuckin' pussy and tries to take me on. I musta been twenty by then. Comes up to me. 'Hey, boy, think you're tough. I'll show ya what a piece a shit ya are.' Petey, it's my old man, and he's fuckin' old and drunk as shit. I coulda killed him, and he's fuckin' pickin' a fight. So whadaya think I do? I fake a swing, stick out my face, and let him fuckin' break my nose. He walks away, a big smile, 'Ya ain't shit,' he says."

"I know that ain't true for ev'rybody. I've met some dudes in the hospital that knocked their own parents off. Remember that big trial out west? Those kids that got off for self-defense 'cause they were abused. I give it to 'em. I couldn't do it. He was still my old man. All I could do was let him die by himself. So ya take drugs. Ain't nothin' else to do.

"Petey, remember when I told ya I was ambi-lung-uous? There's a crock a shit. Let me tell ya what happened. When I was a kid, I wanted to be real cool. Ya know how it is: ya smoke, ya drink, ya drug, ya talk shit. I started smokin' cigarettes at nine.

"I remember one kid sayin' he was gonna smoke Raleigh cigarettes and save the coupons for his cancer operation. Everyone laughed but me. I was fuckin' scared. I figured I'd just smoke outta my right lung – ya know that stuff I show ya – so if I lose a lung, I'll have the other ready to take over. Well, I got a good laugh so I kept sayin' it. After a while, I began to believe it. Smoke with your right lung, protect the left lung. Then one day, I try the left side; it worked. I told everyone I was ambi-lung-uous." Coughing again, John added,

"What a crock a shit."

John looks at his watch, and notices it's 2:15. He smiles at Peter, "Long lunch today, huh." Peter thought of making some excuse that Saturdays were only half days at work but he didn't.

"Thanks," John says. "Thanks for takin' a – thanks for takin' a long lunch today."

■ ■ ■

After John left, Peter took the No. 7 subway line from Times Square to Woodcrest Cemetery. Sitting by his mother's grave, too distracted to review his plan for cleaning his apartment, Peter sat silently daydreaming about work.

Come to my office! Andrew shouts as he hurriedly walks past Peter's desk, vanishing behind a slamming door: ANDREW LERNER, PRESIDENT, LERNER AND SCHWARTZ, PUBLIC ACCOUNTANTS.

I saw you Saturday, smoking in the park. Ambi-lung-uous? What a crock. You ain't shit, Peter. You've got no friends. You can't smoke. You can't add. Ha, he laughs. *You'll always be a 72.*

Picking him up, Andrew throws Peter against the wall before charging head first. Peter digs in swinging, his kick missing Andrew's balls. Andrew grabs him by the chest, pulling out his cancerous lung.

A whiff of smoke jars Peter from his thoughts. Looking up, he sees an older man, around sixty, walking by, smoking a cigarette. The man stops in front of Peter, talking as he points back toward a crowd of mourners at a funeral about 500 feet southwest. "What a bunch of hypocrites. Not one of them gives a damn about JC one bit, but they're all there paying their respects. Respects, my ass. They don't respect nobody, just a bunch of freeloaders who don't care about no one but themselves. Here, get up. I'll show you."

Tugging at Peter's arm, the man leads Peter from Sally's grave toward the group, averting Peter's efforts to stay where he was. "Come on, don't be afraid. They're harmless, just damn hypocrites." Peter arrives just as the priest ends the prayers and the mourners turn to each other to talk.

"Jean, you remember Stanley," the man says, introducing Peter to a strange woman. The woman bursts into tears and throws her arms around Peter, muttering the name, Stanley. "It's okay, Jean. Stanley missed you, too. Why don't you guys talk for a moment, there's something I want to say to Uncle Bob." Peter and this strange woman stand speechless in front of each other for four minutes, when the woman finally says in a halting voice, "I'll see you at Mom's house later," and walks away.

The man comes back, puts his arm around Peter, and leads him back to Sally's grave, "You see what I mean. She don't know you, but then, she don't know nobody. She's so into herself, she don't know for sure that she don't know who you are. Well, thanks for playing along, you've been a big help." As Peter returned to his chair, the man asked, "So who's that?" pointing to Sally's grave. "My mom," Peter responded. "May she rest in peace, Mr. O'Brien," the man said, offering a handshake before returning to his group.

■ ■ ■

Peter looked at his watch. Seeing it was 5:00 p.m., he packed up his things and walked to the subway. Riding home, he kept replaying in his mind what happened at the cemetery until, after returning to his chair the 23rd time, he looked up and saw the tombstone, now engraved Peter Branstill, with the name O'Brien scrawled into the stone, the "O" one quarter of an inch above the "B," ascending at a 30° angle. As Peter lay in his casket, a crowd of mourners standing around, he hears John say, "Hey man, ya saved my life. Don't know what I woulda done without ya." The old man he met today adds, "Thanks for playing along, you've been a big help." Joining the group, Andrew Lerner adds, "He did a helluva job at the Sterling and Warner audit." As the three men continue to laud Peter's virtues, Shirley and Bernie approach the casket. Shirley places her glove on Peter's right hand. Bernie puts a yarmulke on Peter's head. Tom Carroll says: "You should have fucked her, man. She really wanted you." The Reverend John Waller leads the service, "It's a crock of shit this shit that smokin's bad for ya." No one watches Peter as he's lowered into the ground, the crowd intently listening to Reverend John, everyone smoking with one lung.

■ ■ ■

That night, Peter dreamt he was a child having Sunday dinner with the family in a graveyard laid out like Aunt Cindy's apartment. On the table sits a huge birthday cake for Aunt Cindy. The family gathers around as Cindy makes a wish and blows out the candles. Wanting to see, but unable to break through the circle, Peter waits until they finish singing Happy Birthday to reach his aunt, now that the group has dispersed, to say: Happy Birthday, Aunt Cindy. Tapping him on the shoulder from behind, John says, "She's so into herself, she don't know for sure that she don't know who you are."

■ ■ ■

Sunday morning, Peter woke up, put on outfit No. 43162, and looked at his laundry bag sitting by the door. *Maybe I should do my wash today,* he thought. *But today's Sunday, the day I sit for two hours pretending I'm in church.* Pondering his words, *pretending I'm in church,* Peter thought, why pretend, I could go to church. Thinking about the scene he witnessed yesterday, a crowd of mourners listening to the priest, he got up and went to the door where, again, he spied the laundry bag on the floor. *If I can leave the house, why not do the laundry? So what if it's Sunday, I can do what I want.* As Peter picked up the laundry bag, he again thought about church and put the bag down. For the next two hours Peter alternately picked up the bag and put it down as he tried to decide if he should go to church or do his laundry.

■ ■ ■

At noon, Peter realized it was time to go to Aunt Cindy's, so he put the bag of laundry down and walked to her apartment. Taking the key from his pocket, he opened the door and went in. Sitting on the only chair in the apartment he rented the week after she died, Peter took a sandwich out of his lunch bag. As he sat and ate, he thought about John, worried how John would handle the rest of the weekend. Peter could not believe he had actually helped him hold on. He never recalled feeling important to anyone before. The concept that his presence could be soothing was mind-boggling. He always thought he was a cancer, a pariah, destroying goodwill, not preserving it. *Limitless friendship, limitless friendship. John and Peter, best buddies.*

Then Peter thought, *I've got it. John needs a place to stay to hide from Dr. Brown if he has to.* He thought about John's words: "I never had ya over to my place, but ya don't wanna go there. Some fuckin' sick people there." *That's it, John needs to live here. I'll give him this place.* For the rest of the afternoon, Peter pictured John living with Aunt Cindy, and each Sunday, Peter and John having dinner with her. As Peter slept soundly in the spare bedroom, he could picture Aunt Cindy and John getting it on, Otto's voice in the background, "Everyone knew she always whored around, but at her age. Must have been some strange dude."

■ ■ ■

That evening, Peter's moments of pleasure vanished when he realized today was Sunday and John was alone. Peter regretted that he hadn't claimed he needed to work today: John did not seem to care whether Peter told the truth or not, as long as he was there. John was out there on his own. Sunday became a day of treachery and impending doom, the day that John might leave Peter forever.

An expert at tolerating pain, Peter thought about John's pain. Meaninglessness. Peter feared the insanity that John lived. He had failed at life, at picking out safe pieces of meat, at camp, at therapy, at hundreds of other big and small things throughout his lonely life. He had no relationships. And while others might see him as a successful accountant, for Peter this meant little. His life had always lacked a purpose, until now, for a moment, he offered a soothing presence to the ailing John. No longer afraid he would go insane, Peter feared the loss of his insane friend.

■ ■ ■

Peter awoke Monday with night sweats and knots in his stomach. He dreamt about John all night but could not remember what John looked like. It felt like John was quickly fading from his life – just like the woman on the bus who had danced for him one night. John's image was dispersing into oblivion while Peter frantically dwelled on John's life-threatening depression.

Now Peter was feeling so bad that he didn't want to go to work. With the exception of one occasion when he had a high fever, Peter had not missed a full day in twenty-five years. That day, afraid of recriminations for varying his routine, Peter had purchased several thermometers. Without shaking them down, he labeled each one carefully, and kept a record of how his fever had progressed throughout the illness. Armed with his thermometers, he returned to work the next day. He had panicked that Mr. Lerner might not accept the authenticity of the recordings. But instead of doubts, Peter was met mostly with concern for his well-being. They had only questioned why he had come back so soon. One co-worker feared contagion for herself, causing Peter to believe it was his very essence that was malignant and infectious, instead of the microorganism that may have entered his body.

But today, Peter made no excuses. He simply called in sick. When asked what was wrong, he replied, "I just don't feel well." He made no effort to document his malady.

Peter stayed home all morning. Unable to read, watch TV, or even masturbate, he lay in bed for hours wondering what had happened to John. At 11 o'clock he thought about the park bench, his now lonely park bench without Peter or John. Peter wondered whether he would ever return to the bench now that John was gone.

Peter thought about John's death, imagining the funeral, which would be a large affair. Penny would fly in from Nebraska to bid John farewell, quietly revealing her previously unspoken love for him. She would turn to Peter and tell him about how often John spoke about him in her program. Because Peter had been special to John, she would want to preserve her memory of John by knowing him better. After the funeral, Penny would ask Peter to take her back to her hotel room in New York, where she would ask Peter to make love to her as she had often fantasized making love with John. Peter would feel awkward, having never known a woman before. But he would do it for John knowing Penny would be grateful for his kindness.

He replayed this scene several times before Peter noticed the clock read 11:15. Peter started thinking back to his last meeting with John at the bench. He had been alive when he left Peter. It suddenly dawned on Peter that he did not know if John was really dead.

My God! thought Peter. *John's alive and looking for me.*

Fortunately, Peter was fully dressed and ready to go. Following a well-rehearsed procedure, he assembled his lunch in ninety seconds and rushed out the door. The bus came right away. Again, he faced the possibility of running into his co-workers. He knew the consequences would be far worse on a sick day than a Saturday, yet he was far less worried about being fired than that he might miss John. So after the bus arrived on time, Peter got off and walked directly to the bench, where he knew John would already be there waiting for him.

27

Taking a Stand

John thanked Peter for his help and told him he was feeling better, that he thought he was over the hump. Peter quickly decided he would not offer John Aunt Cindy's apartment.

They met every day that week, with John continuing to arrive before Peter. John seemed glad to see Peter, but on Friday, they nevertheless parted company without making any weekend plans. On Monday, Peter went to work, slightly concerned about John's weekend alone until he saw that John, again, was there. And each day that week and through the beginning of the next week, Peter and John met daily, without fail, at noon on the bench. But on Thursday of that third week, John didn't show.

By now, Peter had come to believe that the new John was regular, reliable, kept his appointments, didn't act out on impulse. On thirteen consecutive occasions, he had been punctual for their meetings, but now he was gone. In the past, Peter had tolerated a lengthy absence without much question. Today, fifteen minutes seemed like an eternity. After thirty minutes, Peter became alarmed; he could not contain his fear once lunch was over. He returned to work hoping to convince himself that this was just the old John, nothing new, nothing odd, nothing to worry about. John was erratic by nature; still, Peter could not get rid of the thought that John had somehow changed.

Maybe he's just busy or had an appointment with his psychiatrist. Maybe there was a special function at the day program. At worst, he was in the hospital. Maybe John decided that it was time to go in. Or maybe they committed him against his will.

He was already missing his friend. He wanted to visit him in the hospital but where would he be? Peter remembered John's story about the man who castrated himself before going to Pilgrim State Hospital. Maybe John was there. Peter thought about how he might visit him. The hospital was on Long Island so it would take several buses to get there.

Out of the blue, Peter thought that John might be off getting head. He laughed to himself: *That John. What a card. Crazy John. Off with Hanna Banana in Nebraska, getting head.* Either way, he knew John would be safe. Safe at Pilgrim State or safe in Nebraska. But Peter, unsure why, wanted John here in New York, locked up and under control.

■ ■ ■

For the rest of the evening, Peter sat and thought about John, worried that he was gone forever. He couldn't sleep as he lay in his bed, nervously replaying the events of the past three weeks. At any moment, he expected John to knock at his door, call him on the phone, or float through the window with his usual greeting, "Hey Petey, gotta smoke?" But instead, Peter tossed and turned all night thinking about his friend until the alarm woke him at 6:00 a.m. The morning light brought renewed hope. *So what if John had missed a day? It had happened before; John missed many days.* It had never mattered before that John came and went. Unpredictable John, passionately pained, he would return.

As Peter readied himself for work, he began to feel angry. He stifled the feeling, not wanting to admit that John had violated a covenant. In the past, John came when he wanted to. Now, things were different. Peter demanded fidelity. John was no longer free to come and go, to follow his star, to follow a blow job if it took him away from the bench. Like a jilted wife, Peter wanted an explanation. *Where were you? You couldn't have called? I worried myself sick. You think you can do what you want! I hate you!*

At work the next day, Peter sat at his desk having an unusually hard time maintaining a steady work pace as he watched the clock, each minute an eternity, move slowly toward noon. *What if John isn't there?* Another night, perhaps a weekend, days or weeks at a time, without knowing if John would ever return: a lover's lament – waiting and wondering – with only one place to look and one time to search.

What if John is there? How should I act? thought Peter, rehearsing his response over and over again. *Where the hell were you? Who do you think you are? Thank God you're here.* He alternated between bracing himself that his friend would not be there and imagining how he would feel when he saw him. For a moment, he thought he might even give John the silent treatment, but even Peter himself laughed out loud at the very notion. *The silent treatment. Now there's a novel idea. Maybe the noisy treatment instead,* Peter thought. In the end, he decided to greet John first and then not say anything else. Otherwise, John would not know he was being shunned.

As noon approached, desperate to see his friend, Peter became even more restless, wondering if John would be there. So at exactly noon, with great trepidation, Peter rushed out of his office and went directly to the bench. John was not there when Peter reached the bench, so he sat down, after carefully evaluating the available places to sit, opened his lunch bag, and began to eat. He looked at his watch and saw it was 12:10 exactly. Nervously looking around, he checked his watch again at 12:10.50. Less than a minute later, Peter again checked his watch. *This is nuts,* thought Peter as he tried to settle himself. *That's John, good old late, unreliable John.* Peter again looked at his watch: 12:12.10.

Vowing to enjoy his lunch, he tried not to look at the watch again. Peter began eating, working hard to seem calm, but at 12:14, panic-struck, he again looked around. *I can't keep doing this,* thought Peter, so he decided he would only look at his watch every five minutes from now on. Since it was 12:15, he set the alarm on the watch for 12:20. Peter could sit, relax, enjoy his lunch, and wait for John. At 12:18, Peter looked again. *Only two more minutes until the alarm rings,* he thought, two more minutes before he would start worrying about John.

Peter tried to wait until the alarm rang but glanced again at 12:19. He watched it until the number changed to 12:20 and the alarm rang. He looked around before he looked back at the watch and set the alarm again for 12:25. Throughout lunch, Peter kept playing games with himself, trying to calm down, but nothing worked. He just kept looking around and glancing at the watch. 1:00 p.m. arrived and still no sign of John.

Too distraught to move, Peter stayed glued to the bench for the next half-hour, and feeling dejected he finally walked back to work. "What's up, Peter? You're quite a bit late," Andrew Lerner asked shortly after Peter entered the office. Andrew would not normally care except that Peter had been working on some important figures and the client had called during lunchtime with a question. Andrew had confidently proclaimed he would have the answer shortly after one. In Peter's absence, he had adeptly fielded the question but still felt compelled to note Peter's tardiness.

Peter, however, was too upset to care about the repercussions. He did not even feel guilty. He quickly dumped his problem on Andrew.

"Andrew, something's wrong. There's this friend of mine. I went to meet him for lunch. He wasn't there."

"Well, Peter, these things happen. Not everyone is as reliable as you."

"No, something's wrong. Something's terribly wrong! He wasn't feeling well, I know something happened."

"OK Peter, just calm down. Let's see what we can do. Now, what's this fellow's name?"

"John."

"John what."

"John Waller. He used to be President and CEO of Waller Enterprises, Inc."

"Okay," Andrew says, pressing a button on his telephone.

"Yes, Mr. Lerner," a voice asks through the speakerphone.

"Get me the number of Waller Enterprises."

"There is no Waller Enterprises!" Peter protests.

"I thought you said he was President and Chief Executive Officer."

"Yes, but it doesn't exist. It's just in his mind."

Strange, thought Andrew. "OK, where does he live?"

"I don't know. Don't you get it? I don't know. I don't know his address. I don't know his telephone number. I'm not even sure John Waller's his name. I just don't know!"

"Okay, calm down. Let's think this out. You were going to meet your friend, John Waller, for lunch. He's a bigwig with Waller Enterprises, but it doesn't really exist. You're not sure his name is John Waller, where he lives, or how to call him. Okay, let's try the restaurant. Did you leave your number there? Did you ask if anyone came in looking for you?"

"It's not a restaurant. The park, we meet in the park."

"The park's large. Are you sure you went to the right part of it? Maybe he thought you meant a different place."

"No, it's always the same. We meet at the same bench every day. I have lunch; he joins me for a smoke. He wasn't feeling well and now he's suddenly gone. Something's wrong."

"So this is some acquaintance you met in the park. I thought you said he's your friend."

"He is!" At this point, Peter didn't care anymore what anybody knew or thought. "He is. He's a mental patient who's spent his whole life in institutions, but now goes to a day treatment program nearby."

"Oh, you mean Midtown Mental Health Center. They're right across the street from Jeff Calhoun's office. A few weeks ago I saw it when I went over to audit Jeff's books. We even talked a bit about the center. I asked Jeff if they got in the way of his business. He said they're not a problem, that he would have moved out a long time ago if they were. Jeff says they run a very quiet program... "

Peter heard very little beyond *Midtown Mental Health Center... across the street from Jeff Calhoun's office.* Quickly composing himself, he thanked Andrew and picked up the phone, called information, and after getting the center's telephone number, he called. The telephone answered after a few rings. *Hello, you have reached Midtown Mental Health Center. If you have a touchtone phone, and know the extension of the party you want, please dial that number now. If you are interested in having an intake appointment, please press 1, if you are...* Knowing that there would be no message that said "If you want to learn the whereabouts of John,... " Peter impatiently slammed down the phone.

Then, realizing he should have waited for the entire tape, he dialed again, but the line was busy. He tried again: busy. Finally, on the third try, the phone rang and the message began again: *Hello, you have reached Midtown Mental Health Center. If you have a touchtone phone, and know the extension of the party you want, please dial that number now. If you are interested in having an intake appointment, please press 1; if you are inquiring about location or hours of operation, press 2; if you have a billing question, press 3; if you wish to talk with our personnel office, press 4; for the outpatient department, press 5; for the day program, press 6 ...*

Peter pressed 6, and after a few rings, he heard another message: *You have reached the day treatment program. No one is free to take your call now. If this is a true clinical emergency, press the star key; otherwise, please leave your message after the tone. Beep.*

For Peter, this was an extraordinary emergency, so he pressed *. A few rings later, Peter heard: *Hello, you have reached Midtown Mental Health Center. If you have a touchtone phone and know the extension of the party you want, ...*

Frustrated, angry, and wanting to forcefully slam the phone down, Peter remembered that there was a selection for the location of the center. He listened on and again heard, *... please dial that number now. If you are interested in having an intake appointment, please press 1; if you are inquiring about location or hours of operation, press 2...* Peter pressed 2 and heard *Midtown Community Mental Health Center is open each weekday from 8:30 a.m. to 4:30 p.m. We have evening hours on Tuesday and Thursday until 8:30. We offer a full range of outpatient services during those hours. Our psychiatric day treatment program is open from 9 a.m. through 3 p.m. Monday through Friday. You can walk in for an initial evaluation any morning between 9 and 10 or schedule an intake appointment during our regular working hours. The Midtown Community Mental Health Center is located at 56 West 40th Street ...*

Peter looked at his watch. It was 2:10 already. 40th Street was about ten minutes from the front of his office. Including the elevator ride down, and walking at a normal pace, he could be there by 2:25. Peter rushed out, and when the down elevator didn't show after ten seconds, Peter ran to the stairwell and raced down four flights of stairs, two stairs at a time, to street level. On the street, Peter checked his bearings and realized he needed to cut across the park to get to the center. Racing at full speed, he reached 40th Street, turned left, and found the Midtown Mental Health Center, aided by a large sign across the street, *Jeff Calhoun, Appraisals.* Entering the front door, Peter saw a second, locked door with a buzzer. He pressed the button and without delay or a request to identify himself, Peter was let in.

The building was a poorly maintained, dreary setting. The furniture was old and the carpet worn through to the linoleum in spots. There were a few people waiting for appointments. He went to the reception desk and asked about the day program. The receptionist asked if he had an appointment and he said, "No, I just want to see the day program."

"Were you referred here? Are you a patient in any other part of the mental health center?"

"No," Peter said impatiently. "I just want to see the program."

"We're not allowed to just show you the program. If you have some interest in joining, I can schedule a general intake appointment. When you meet with the intake worker, she'll discuss day treatment with you. Now, I can offer you a scheduled appointment in a week and a half. If you can't wait that long, we have walk-in hours each morning from 9 to 10."

Noting the distress in Peter's eyes, the receptionist suggested that he come back on Monday morning during walk-in hours.

"I can't wait until Monday. I have to see the day program now. Don't you see, it can't wait."

The receptionist understood that many patients cannot make it through the weekend. She explained the procedure for after-hours emergencies. "If it's a real crisis, you can go to Memorial Hospital Emergency Room. They can see you over the weekend."

"NO!" shouted Peter, "I'm not waiting until the weekend. I want to see the day program now."

"OK sir, take a seat and I'll have someone come to talk with you now."

The receptionist dialed a number and minutes later a young man came to meet Peter. "Hello, I'm Mr. Greene, the clinic director. I understand you're looking for some treatment services but can't wait until Monday."

"No, I don't need any treatment. I need to go to the day treatment program. I have a friend, John. He goes there and something's happened. I'm afraid something terrible happened and I need to see if he's OK."

A knowing look came over Mr. Greene's face. He asked Peter to wait while he called down to the day program. About ten minutes later, a large, casually dressed man introduced himself as Lou, the head of the Day Treatment Program. He shook Peter's hand. He and Mr. Greene asked Peter to come into Mr. Greene's office. "Mr. Branstill, you say you have a friend, John, in our program. What is your relationship with this John?"

"He's my friend. I've met with him often for lunch in the park. I'm afraid something's happened. I want to help him. I need to know."

Lou looked over to Greene. Then he turned to Peter, "Are you a relative of this John?"

"No, I said I was his friend." By this point, Peter was noticeably calmer. He knew that they knew something and would be able to help him.

"Do you have some identification?"

This seemed to be a reasonable request, so Peter took out his New York State ID card.

Lou looked at the card and then passed it over to Greene. Greene looked at it too, jotted down Peter's name, and then handed it back to Peter. Lou and Greene glanced once more at each other and then they both again looked at Peter. Greene said, "Would you excuse us a moment."

When Mr. Greene and Lou left the room, Peter noticed it was close to 3:00 p.m. and began worrying that the program would close before he could see John. Perhaps they had gone downstairs to tell John that Peter was here. It was a confidential program. They probably could not bring Peter to John until he authorized the visit. Peter felt more confident than ever that John was there, safe and sound. Peter started feeling foolish for having intruded on John's space. He only knew John from the park bench. John had never come to his office: What right did Peter have coming to John's program?

Peter wanted to quietly slip away but there was no escape now. They had taken his identification. Perhaps they were calling the police. No matter what he did now, John would know that Peter had violated his private space. When Greene and Lou returned to the office, Greene spoke first. "Mr. Branstill, we are governed by the laws of confidentiality. We are prohibited from giving you information about this John. We are not even allowed to acknowledge whether or not we know this person."

"BULLSHIT!" screamed Peter. "No, this is not confidentiality. You could have told me that from the beginning. You know something. What happened?! If he's there, you could have brought him up. He could have decided to meet me. He wouldn't just stay down there with me up here." Peter was not completely sure that was true. "You know something. Tell me."

Now Lou spoke. "Sir, our hands are tied. The law is very clear."

"Oh no you don't. You tell me right now. What happened to John?" Peter's voice was cracking.

Greene became more stern. "Listen, we have to insist that you leave now. If you don't, we'll call the police."

"Call the police, I'll show you what I think about calling the police." Peter hesitated. He had no idea what he would show them. He had never been this angry before, at least not in public. He never took a stand, had never had an argument or a fight. He did not even know how to fight. All he knew was to do as he was told, follow directions, and stew inside. "I'll show you what I think about calling the police."

Peter looked around the room searching for something to display his feelings. Spying a chair, he feebly pushed it over. Shocked by his own brazen behavior, he was ready to apologize. But when Peter looked at Greene and Lou, he saw in their faces the response of seasoned professionals dealing with a madman. They began to speak calmly with him.

My God, he thought, *they really think I'm crazy. They think I'm a threat.* Peter liked the fact that he had this effect. They did not call him a wimp, or laugh at him. They responded to him as if he was a serious threat. So Peter knocked another chair over. As soon as he tried to turn Greene's desk over, several men entered the room and wrestled him to the ground. They did not hit him, though. This was nothing like the abuse he took at school. The men were determined to control him but they did not want to hurt him. As Peter lay passively on the floor, he felt an unfamiliar, warm glow, and wanted to hug Lou.

Several minutes later, two policemen came. They were considerably rougher than the staff at the mental health center. For a moment, he even thought they were Tom Carroll and King George. They cuffed him and called for an ambulance, which took Peter straight to the hospital emergency room. By the time they arrived, he had calmed down enough to notice that the sign indicated he was at the same place they had told him to go if he could not make it through the weekend.

The EMTs rolled Peter's stretcher past the main waiting area into a special section marked Mental Health Crisis Unit. Passing the main, medical reception desk, Peter pictured a different sign in his mind: Psychos Need Not Apply.

Peter was interviewed by a young, friendly woman. Her nametag said Stacy Davidson, BA, Crisis Worker. Stacy asked Peter several questions; he did not answer them. Peter wanted to ask about John but he was tired, ashamed, and afraid to rekindle the rage he had felt less than an hour before. After several futile efforts to elicit information, Stacy gently patted Peter on the arm and said that she would get the psychiatrist. Several hours later, Dr. Wang came to meet with Peter. Despite his poor English skills, Dr. Wang was a very gentle man. Peter chuckled to himself; this was his kind of doctor. *He can communicate no better than I,* thought Peter.

Dr. Wang asked if Peter wished to enter the hospital. When Peter failed to respond, he indicated that he would have no other choice but to involuntarily commit Peter. He asked him again to sign a paper so that he would not have to send him to the State Hospital. Peter signed the forms and agreed to go in. He noticed the part that required seventy-two hours' notice if he wished to leave. The notice went on to say that the doctors could choose to commit him during that waiting period. Peter knew he was signing away the freedom he no longer had anyway.

After a further wait, Peter was taken upstairs. By now it was evening and he would spend his weekend in the hospital, waiting for the treatment team to arrive on Monday. To his surprise, Peter found the hospital relaxing. The house doctor conducted a physical examination and ordered medications that were calming and sedating. At night, he took a sleeping pill that worked very well. Except when medications were given, there was little to do. A chaplain visited Peter and prayed for his recovery.

28

Home at Last

On Monday morning, the ward came alive. Shortly after breakfast, Janet Pearson called Peter to her office. She had Stacy's notes before her and introduced herself as Peter's counselor. She asked Peter why he was here. "I was looking for my friend, John. They wouldn't tell me where he was. I got mad. I lost control. I'm sorry."

Janet quickly glanced through the chart. "It says you're a first-time admission without prior psychiatric history. Were you going to Midtown for outpatient therapy?"

"No, but John was. He went to the day program. He was missing. I thought they might know where he was."

"So, did you find your friend?"

"No, they wouldn't tell me. He was supposed to meet me for lunch in the park. He seemed real sad. They wanted him to go to the hospital but he didn't want to. Who knows what he did? Last year he took off to Nebraska for many months for… " Peter stopped and thought. "He went to Nebraska with another friend."

Janet seemed pensive. She asked, "What's John's last name?"

"Waller. He used to be President of Waller Enterprises." Peter hesitated before going on. "In my mind, I called him John Marlboro. He had some strange ideas about how to smoke cigarettes. I thought of him as the Marlboro man."

"John Waller?" Janet repeated blankly.

"Yes, that's him. Do you know where he is?"

"I don't know how to tell you this," Janet said. "They brought him in Friday morning. He was in a coma. He died last night."

Peter wept. He had never cried at his mother or father's funerals but he cried now.

"Carbon monoxide. He sat in his room with a lawnmower running. He apparently had just purchased it the other day. The windows were shut tight and he had rigged up a blanket to create a small chamber for him to breathe the fumes. The neighbors heard the engine running and called the police. By the time they arrived, he was unconscious. He never woke up before he died. It was suicide."

When Peter composed himself, he asked if he would be able to attend the funeral.

"I'll ask," said Janet. She then asked Peter what would help him now. Peter did not know. Janet showed him a schedule of groups and activities on the ward. "It's up to you. You're welcome to attend anything that goes on here. I'll meet with you three times each week while you are here."

Janet never adhered to her offer for regular meetings because there was always one crisis or another to consume her time. Peter thought back to his crisis on Friday night, which may have interfered with someone else's session time. The contrast to his private therapy was striking: The sane get regular sessions, the insane have to wait until they explode. Still, Peter did not mind. He preferred to meet John's friends over talking with Janet.

Peter looked at the schedule and saw group therapy coming up. John talked favorably of groups so Peter decided to go. The group took place in the dining room, where the tables had been pushed aside. The chairs were arranged in a reasonable approximation of a circle. Several patients were already seated, but far fewer than occupied the ward. A strange-looking man sat at one of the tables pushed along the wall. He drank tea and seemed disconnected from the forming group.

The leader announced that group was about to start. She described the rules: Listen to Others When They Speak. Stay in Your Seat. Do Not Curse. Do Not Leave the Room or if you absolutely have to leave, Don't Come Back. No Violence Allowed. Everything said is held in confidence.

Shortly after establishing the rules, the co-therapist entered the room without explaining his lateness. The leader herself left to field an urgent call, returning a few minutes later, after which the co-therapist got up to get a cup of coffee. The dining room door had been left open and several people looked in, listening to what was being said. Privately, Peter questioned why the leaders were not following their own rules.

The leader announced that two new members had joined the group. She invited both to explain why they were here. The first man mumbled inaudibly in response to her question so she turned to Peter for his reply. "I'm here because my best friend died," Peter stated. Peter felt pleased with the ease of his disclosure. This group did not intimidate him. When none of the other group members responded to his statement, the leader invited Peter to go on.

"He used to join me for lunch in the park: I ate, he smoked. They tell me he killed himself, went into a coma on Friday, and died here Sunday."

Herb, a member of the group, spoke up. "John was my friend, too. You must be Petey."

"How did you know it was John? And my name?" Peter asked, a little disarmed by this man's access to information.

"John talked about you a lot. To John, you were the greatest. Man, I never expected to see you here. Why didn't you go to a fancy private hospital, or just hire nurses and doctors to take care of you on your yacht?"

Peter looked down. He could picture John boasting about his wealthy friend. Peter sat silently, letting the ruse stand. He pictured himself, a small person, in a tiny tunnel, walking slowly back as the light dims and his access to the outside is lost. By himself, in the dark recesses of the tunnel, he feels the presence of Aunt Cindy. A faceless, hostile Aunt Cindy, inhabiting every pore of his being, demands perfect obedience: YOU'RE WORTHLESS. NO ONE LOVES YOU. YOU'LL DIE ALONE.

Peter broke from his trance, realizing there was an argument going on between Herb and a very high-strung man in the group.

"He ain't gotta be rich, man," Herb shouted. "It don't matter. John loved him. That was John. John was himself and Petey is himself. The man's dead. What difference does it make what the real Petey's like? If John loved him, I wanna know this guy. I know the Petey John told us about, and I wanna know the real Petey, too."

"Don't gimme that shit! John was a fuckin' liar! That's all there is to it. The guy was full of horseshit when he was here. I bet he crapped it all out when he died. I never trusted a word he said. I'm fuckin' glad he's dead." With that, the other man left.

About half the members sat silently, as if in another world. But the other half quickly came to Herb's defense, loudly condemning the bully. Peter never recalled any group that would have protected him from a bully.

Herb then looked at Peter and said, "No one really believed John when he first told us about you. He said you were a big movie producer who stopped him on the street and offered him a part in a new movie. Like lots of John's stories, I knew it was bullshit. But you kept showing up in his stories, and that never happened before. I never quite knew what to make of you except that you musta mattered to him, and that you were out there working, and not in this nuthouse. I figured you were pretty special. Except for losing John, I don't know if you're here for any other reason, or if there's something you'd like to tell us, but I'd sure like to know."

Peter held his breath for a minute, debating. Then the leaders announced the end of the group session. Peter got up and started toward the ward, but Janet intercepted him before he got halfway there. "You can't go to the funeral," she said. "The psychiatrist doesn't think you're ready to go out on pass. And anyway, the family wants to keep his funeral small and private, no patients, just family."

Peter did not respond; he just continued walking down the hall to his room. That's OK, he thought later as he lay in his bed thinking about Janet's words, "No patients, just family." It was strange: Before he actually became a patient, he would not have known about John's death. But now that he had become a member of the club, he was excluded because of his illness.

Peter found the hospital bed peaceful, and in fact felt tempted to sleep away his stay. He usually only slept in his own bed, but the hospital bed was much more comfortable, more inviting, safer than the other foreign mattresses he had come in contact with. He felt safe inside. Yet, he wanted to meet the other patients, the other members of the club.

Peter ambled up and down the ward, carefully observing his

environs. He noticed a smoky day room where many of the patients sat, smoked, and watched TV. Disliking the noisy smoke-filled atmosphere, Peter continued looking for another place to go. He walked back to the dining room and saw that the door was open. There were a few patients quietly sitting there, but outside of meal times, the room was stark and uninviting. The day room was the hub of activity.

Walking back, Peter pictured the smoky air and thought how it reminded him of John. Maybe not smoking was why he felt different from others. But now, tobacco's out and being healthy was in. The ward, it seemed, was a symbol of times past, when smokers ruled. And hospital social life seemed to revolve around access to cigarettes, as Peter noticed several interactions evolving out of the pursuit of smokes, the trade of tobacco. No one, though, had John's pizzazz or novel ideas when it came to the fine art of smoking or scouting for smokes.

Peter ventured into the day room and found the air reminiscent of his friend's smell. Comforted, he walked in to see several people staring ahead at Oprah. Peter had never liked TV but he sat down anyway. Herb, who was sitting across the room, immediately spotted Peter and nodded toward him. Peter saw the gesture but questioned whether his reading of it was accurate. The nod seemed to constitute a greeting but he wasn't sure. He thought back to Shirley's romantic overture in study hall when he thought she was looking for her glove.

As Peter dwelled on his social ineptitude, Herb walked across the room and sat down next to him. "So, you're Petey," he said. "I never bought the whole story but the essence made sense. You meant an awful lot to him. Quite a wild guy. Burnt himself out with drugs. Arrested a couple of times. But he wasn't no criminal. They'd've killed him in jail. Don't think he ever knew what he wanted, not till he got back. It was too late then. Couldn't get there, couldn't go back, so he just quit."

Peter looked at Herb with a painful, plaintive look: "I want to go to his funeral but they say that I can't."

I want to go to his funeral, thought Peter. *I want to sit with everyone else. I want a friend. I want a girl. I want ...*

"No one can," Herb responded. "His family's too ashamed of him. They always stayed involved but they couldn't stand who he was. John's got real friends here. We should go to his funeral. Sure, some of us are too spaced out, too afraid, or too bizarre to go, but there's several who would. Without the label, they'd let us go. I could be his neighbor, or work with him at the plant, or belong to his church. It's like we didn't exist. Call them yourself. Tell them you're Petey, they've heard about you."

"How would I get the number?" Peter asked, afraid to get his hopes up.

"Who's your therapist?" Herb asked.

"Janet."

"She's cool. She'll get it for you. Wait a minute. I'll get her. She's cool, and I know she don't agree that they exclude us."

Less than fifteen minutes later, Herb came back with Janet. "You want to go, Peter. Here's the number," she said, handing him her card with a telephone number written on the back.

"I'm not going," Peter said, as he abruptly got up and walked back to his room. Peter lay in his bed, feeling like he was now the King of the Hill. It was he, Peter Branstill, and he alone who could go to the ball. He was a star; someone to reckon with. Of all John's friends, only Peter could attend his funeral.

Peter yawned and stretched and thought some more. Wow, I've finally gone mad and it's not so bad. He closed his eyes and instead of masturbating, he laughed himself to sleep.

■ ■ ■

"How are you doing, Mr. Branstill?" asked Dr. Palmer Tuesday morning.

"OK," Peter replied.

"You seem pretty good to us. It appears that you had a brief psychotic reaction. I mean a depressive reaction with psychotic features," quickly correcting himself, remembering the recent changes in the Diagnostic Manual. "It's sort of like mourning but a little worse. You ever lose anyone dear to you?"

"My mother and father both died."

"Exactly," Dr. Palmer said. "Let's see. I didn't see anything in your record about a prior history. Did you get out of control then, too?"

"No," Peter replied.

"That's what I mean. You had a similar reaction to losing your parents, only a bit worse. When you lost your parents, it was normal mourning. With this loss, you suffered a major depression with psychotic features. Sort of the same, sort of different, wouldn't you say, Mr. Branstill?"

I kept looking at the meat as Dad died. Then they changed my name. Peter pictured Mom's room in his mind, perfectly clean with new sheets each week long after she died, before he looked up and nodded slightly.

"Well, we think you're ready to go, Mr. Branstill. Is there someone at home who can pick you up tomorrow?"

That's it, Peter thought. *The long-awaited breakdown has finally come and I'm ready for discharge tomorrow.*

"Mr. Branstill? Is there someone who can pick you up tomorrow?" Dr. Palmer repeated.

"No, I live alone."

"What about a friend?"

"John was my friend."

"I know," Dr. Palmer said, feeling slightly sad himself. "What about another friend?"

"John was my only friend."

There was a brief pause. Peter broke the silence: "I'll be all right. You can send me home."

"Now I did want to talk with you about treatment after you're discharged. You'll need to see a psychiatrist to continue your medications. I can't say right now how long you'll be on them but generally we think you should be medicated for no less than six months to a year after the first episode. You'll need something to do while you get readjusted to the outside. Maybe a brief stay at the day program would help."

Peter liked the idea of day treatment. It was John's world. But Peter had a job, an apartment. He had the peep shows and the bench, and Howdy was waiting home for him. He needed to go back, back to his world, and start there before making his next plan. "No, I don't think so," answered Peter. "I'd rather just go home. I have to call my boss and get ready for work next week. I think I'll just leave."

"But you've got to have someone follow the meds. The clinic that sent you has some fine doctors."

"I know a doctor. Dr. Johnson. Can I just see him?" Peter asked.

"Sure, where is Dr. Johnson's office? Or do you have his number?"

"He's with the Psychoanalytic Institute. They'll have his number there."

Dr. Palmer paused. "I'm sure he's a fine doctor but I don't think you need a psychoanalyst. This is a biochemical problem, that's why you need medication."

A biochemical problem? No, a mathematical problem. Peter looked at Dr. Palmer, noticing his asymmetrical nose, the left nostril wider than the right, his neatly trimmed mustache accentuating the flaw. A horizontal plane bisecting the mass of his nose would form a 93° angle with a straight vertical from the center of his head to the floor. Dr. Palmer could solve his problem by trimming his mustache along a plane formed midway between the nose horizontal and his upper lip line.

"OK. I'll go to the clinic," Peter said, knowing even as he said it that he would never keep the appointment. Leaving Dr. Palmer's office, Peter did not even feel the least bit guilty.

■ ■ ■

Peter spent the rest of that day and evening in the day room. He talked with Herb and some of the other patients. That night, he slept well. After a brief discharge meeting with Janet and Dr. Palmer, Peter left the hospital by cab, arriving home with plenty of time to call the office. He assured Andrew that he was fine, and would be back to work on Monday.

29

One Day the Following Spring

Peter was sitting by himself on the bench eating lunch. It had been a long, pensive winter, spent alone counting days, scoring dirt, gawking at naked women through a glass partition, tormented except for a few rare moments of peace thinking about John. Peter knew there was another way, he just didn't know how to get there.

With no effort, Peter met John. A once-in-a-lifetime chance encounter. Peter knew that if he wanted other friends, he would have to pursue them. *Do I deserve friends? I tried to come through but it wasn't enough. Perhaps that's the best I can do, being there with a fraction of what they need.*

"Hey there," a voiced called out, jarring Peter back to his present reality. Peter looked to his left and saw Herb coming his way, accompanied by a man and a woman.

"Hi! It's such a beautiful day," Herb said as he approached the bench, "we thought we'd take a walk in the park. Fancy that, meeting you here."

Peter was genuinely pleased to see Herb. He knew that Herb would never be his next friend but he appreciated the warmth in Herb's voice, as well as the sheer fact that he had recognized Peter.

"This is where I always have lunch," Peter responded. "It's a tradition."

"Of course. You used to meet John here. Hey guys," Herb said as he turned toward his friends, "This is Petey. You know, John's friend. I met him in the… " Herb stopped short. Placing his finger on his lips, he whispered, "Privacy. My lips are sealed."

Herb asked Peter how he was doing since they last met and then he and his male friend engaged in an active exchange of small talk, which Peter thoroughly enjoyed. Peter noticed that while Herb and his friend chatted with him, the woman – slight, plain-looking, almost pretty, in a black dress with unseasonably long sleeves – who accompanied them was extremely quiet. Peter wondered what she was thinking as the three of them conversed.

Peter had casually glanced her way several times before he realized that she was looking at him, actually staring, almost imperceptibly. If he were less sensitive to the condemnation of others, he might not have even noticed her glances. But Peter, acutely aware that she was observing him, found her look totally unfamiliar and difficult to read.

Peter rejoined the conversation, while periodically catching glimpses of the woman out of the corner of his eye. Peter felt as if she was studying him just as intently as he had studied the dirt on the bench only minutes before. *What is she doing? Why is she looking at me?*

"Petey, it was great to see you again. We've got to get back to our meeting," Herb said carefully, disguising the words, as he shook Peter's hand and prepared to leave. Then, as he started to take off with his friends, he turned back around.

"How rude of me, Petey; I didn't even introduce my friends. This is Dave. And this is Anna."

■ ■ ■